# Bad Seed

By

## Heleyne Hammersley

## Also By Heleyne Hammersley

Forgotten
Fracture

*DI Kate Fletcher Series*
Closer To Home (Book1)
Merciless (Book 2)

…in memory of Maggie Godwin.

# Chapter 1

DI Kate Fletcher unbuttoned her jacket, breathing heavily in the humid air as she studied the scene in front of her. The body of a woman was lying on its back amid the lush vegetation which bounded much of Doncaster's Town Fields like the hair around a monk's tonsure. The body was surrounded by crime scene technicians who continued their work as Kate approached. She kept back beyond the blue and white crime scene tape and followed the step plates with her eyes, knowing that she wouldn't be welcome to approach until she'd donned protective clothing.

She could make out dark hair and pale limbs but little else from where she was standing. As the body had been dumped amongst nettles and cow parsley that were as high as Kate's waist in full June growth.

'What have we got?' she asked the nearest overall-clad figure. He turned to face her and she recognised her colleague, DC Barratt. He took a couple of steps towards her and lowered the hood of his overalls, messing up his hair and revealing patches of pink scalp through the thinning strands.

'Body of a woman. Looks like she's about thirty or so. Undressed from the waist down so possible sexual assault, but obviously we won't know until the test results are back.'

'Cause of death?' Kate asked.

Barratt glanced round at the other people attending and then lowered his voice. 'They haven't been able to establish that yet but there's a whacking great wound in her abdomen. They were just debating whether it was pre or post-mortem when you arrived. There's also bruising round her neck and throat so strangulation's another possibility.'

Kate nodded and glanced again at the body. She was tempted to find a set of overalls and get a closer look but she didn't want to undermine Barratt. She knew that there would be photographs and notes and she also knew that Barratt's report would be fastidiously detailed.

'Who found her?'

Barratt gestured to a support van parked on the running track that went around the top section of the field. A man in sports clothes was sitting on the back step, nursing a cardboard cup of something that Kate hoped was hot and sweet. Another of her DCs, Hollis, was standing next to the van but he didn't appear to be talking to the man.

'Bloke over there with Hollis. He was setting up a football training session for a team of pre-teens. Does it at weekends and in the school holidays. Thankfully he found the body before the kids arrived.'

Kate thanked Barratt and crossed the grass to the van where the man had stopped studying his drink and was looking up at her expectantly.

'DI Fletcher,' Kate introduced herself. 'I understand that you found the body?'

He nodded and stood up, holding out his hand, which Kate ignored. 'Duncan Cawthorne.'

'Okay, Duncan. I want you to tell me what happened this morning. My colleague, DC Hollis, will make notes if that's all right with you?'

Cawthorne watched as Hollis took a notebook and pencil from the inside breast pocket of his suit jacket. 'I get down here early on a Sunday,' he began. 'Have a bit of a run and then set up for the kids.'

Kate appraised him as she listened to his account of arriving at the car park, jogging for half an hour and then retrieving the cones and balls from his car so he could set up a course for 'the kids'. He was probably in his early thirties, well built and tall. He was wearing baggy grey tracksuit bottoms and a zip-up red hoody with a Doncaster Rovers badge below the left shoulder. His hair was hidden under a tight-fitting grey beanie hat with DRFC emblazoned across the front. He'd obviously dressed for his role as a football coach. His broad face was clean-shaven and tanned – Kate suspected a sunbed or a spray considering the grey cloud that seemed to have enveloped Doncaster for much of the spring and early summer.

'And then I saw her,' Cawthorne was saying. 'Just lying on her back in the bushes.'

Kate glanced across to the police tape. It was a few hundred yards away from the neat row of miniature traffic cones that had been set up next to the running track. She looked at Hollis. He'd stopped making notes and was looking at where the body lay. He'd also spotted the anomaly.

'Duncan,' Kate said. 'I don't understand. You can't see the body from where you've set up the cones and the running track is easily two hundred yards from the bushes. So why did you go over there?'

This could be it. It wasn't uncommon for the perpetrators of crimes to want to be involved in the investigation and Kate's mind was wide open as far as Duncan Cawthorne was concerned.

'I… er… I thought I could see something strange so I went over to check.'

Hollis walked over to the furthest of the cones, his long legs covering the distance in a handful of strides. He made a show of shading his eyes with a hand peaked above his eyebrows while he looked in the direction of the forensics team.

'I doubt I'd be able to see anything lying flat over there,' he said. 'And it's not like her clothing was brightly coloured. You must have cracking eyesight.'

Kate watched as Cawthorne coloured and looked down at his empty cup. Hollis loped back across the grass and shook his head at Kate to indicate that he wasn't convinced by the man's story but he didn't want to challenge him until Kate had had a crack.

'Duncan?'

The man continued to stare at his cup.

'Duncan. I'm fairly convinced that you couldn't have seen the body from where you were. DC Hollis has almost perfect eyesight.' Kate was improvising now, she had no idea about the quality of Hollis's vision. 'And he says that he wouldn't have been able to see it. So shall we try again? You went over there for some reason, didn't you?'

Cawthorne looked up at her, his eyes narrowed with embarrassment. 'I needed a pee. It's quite a walk back to the loos in the car park and I wasn't sure whether they'd be open anyway, so I thought I'd just go in the bushes. I saw the body after I'd finished. I was just, you know,' he gestured to his lap, 'making myself decent, when I saw one of her legs. I didn't get very close – I swear. I just stepped back and rang 999. Then I waited by the track.'

Hollis gave the other man one of his disarming grins. 'We've all been there, mate. Got caught short. But if anybody had seen you, you'd be done for indecent exposure.'

'I know. It was stupid,' Cawthorne said.

He looked back down at his cup. Kate raised her eyebrows questioningly to Hollis who wrinkled his nose and shook his head. Obviously, his gut was telling him that Cawthorne's story was probably true but they would need to get a formal statement from him and a DNA sample, just in case his story wasn't quite accurate and he had actually urinated much closer to the body than he'd admitted.

Kate explained this to him carefully and he nodded his understanding, still red with embarrassment.

'I didn't kill her,' he said, finally looking Kate in the eye. 'I know you have to look at whoever found the body but this has nothing to do with me. I've never been in any trouble with the police before. I'll do whatever you want.'

He was in a tricky position. Anybody who has contact with kids has to be cleaner than clean these days. It would potentially cost Cawthorne his coaching job if he got into any trouble with the police.

'As long as you co-operate,' Kate said, 'I can't see any need for the details to become public knowledge. Get yourself over to Doncaster Central and sort out your statement. And leave DC Hollis your contact details before you go. Just in case.'

She sighed as Hollis noted down Cawthorne's details before the coach walked off in the direction of the car park. 'How fantastic it must be to be a man. The whole bloody world's your toilet.'

Hollis tucked his notebook back into his pocket and smiled at her. 'Penis envy? Should I buy you one of them Shewees? You know, so you can pee standing up.'

'Don't you dare! Some of us have some decorum.'

'And some of us can pee anywhere.'

Kate laughed. 'I suppose it could have been worse. You don't think he had anything to do with this?'

Hollis shook his head. 'Nope. He was far too shaken up and I'm fairly certain that his embarrassment was genuine. I think he's just a bit of an idiot who was in the wrong place at the wrong time. What did Barratt tell you?'

Kate looked across to the main crime scene. There were fewer people there than there had been when she'd arrived, which she assumed meant that they were ready to remove the body.

'Not much. Female. Half-naked. Large wound to the abdomen and bruising round her neck. No ID so far.'

Hollis followed the direction of her eyes. 'Could be a prostitute,' he said. 'The area around Town Fields is well known for it. It's been quite mild the last few nights, maybe she'd decided to try her luck away from home.'

'Could be,' Kate agreed. 'But I'm not sure her clothes looked right. She was quite well dressed and well nourished. I only caught a quick glimpse though. Barratt might be able to tell us more when they're done.'

As she spoke she saw two figures moving towards the crime-scene tape carrying a stretcher which bore a folded black body bag. A third lifted the blue and white barrier high above his head so that his colleagues could get under it without having to duck or bend.

'Looks like they're moving the body. Let's see if we can grab Barratt.'

She led the way back to the area of undergrowth where Barratt was removing his overalls, wriggling his shoulders as he lowered them to his waist. He looked up at her, his face grim. 'Did you get anything from the football coach?'

'Not much,' Hollis said. 'He came over to take a leak and spotted the body as he was finishing. He says he was well clear while he was peeing and only saw her afterwards.'

Barratt nodded, running a hand through his hair in an attempt to smooth it down, but it was a hopeless task after it had been confined in the sweaty hood of his overalls. His hooked nose and deeply set eyes gave him a hawk-like appearance as he stooped to remove his shoe covers. 'He's probably telling the truth. The body wasn't wet. Maybe a bit damp from the vegetation.'

'So they think she'd been there all night?' Kate asked.

'Looks like it. According to her body temp she's been dead between eight and fifteen hours. Hard to tell though. The PM will give a more exact time.'

Kate laughed. 'Ah, that's why Kailisa isn't here,' she said, referring to the pathologist with whom she'd locked horns on two previous occasions. 'He's deputised you.'

Barratt gave her a faint grin, obviously embarrassed by her joke. 'Sorry. I just realised that I sounded exactly like him. Just repeating what I was told. I'm hardly an expert.'

'I know,' Kate said with a smile. Barratt was like a sponge; he soaked up details of cases and seemed to be able to remember everything that he heard. It was what made him such a valued member of her team. 'So what did the SOCOs find?'

'Not much. She'd been undressed from the waist down, but her clothes were left next to her. She was wearing decent gear. Not designer but not cheap. No handbag. No phone. No purse. Her hair looked recently styled – dark with reddish highlights. Her teeth were in good condition.'

Kate read between the lines. This woman didn't fit the usual profile of a prostitute or an addict in need of a fix. It sounded like she was somebody who would be missed. 'What about the injuries?' she asked. 'You said there was a wound and some bruising?'

'The bruising was consistent with manual strangulation,' Barratt said, sounding as if he was on a witness stand in court. 'Suspected hyoid fracture.'

'What about the wound to the abdomen?'

Barratt frowned, obviously trying to make sense of what he'd seen.

'That was the weirdest thing,' he said, shaking his head. 'It looked like whoever killed her had performed a caesarean section after she died.'

# Chapter 2

Kate rolled over and slapped at the alarm clock, desperate to stop the annoying bleep before it woke her up properly. She knocked it onto the floor, a plastic clatter and a mumbled curse, before realising that it wasn't a cruel joke; it really was time to get up. The light seeping round the blackout blind told her that it was morning and the heavy arm across her midriff told her that she'd be better off if she stayed in bed.

Shifting position, Kate eased herself up until she was sitting with her back against the headboard. The arm moved slightly and then tightened around her, its owner mumbling an incomprehensible syllable of complaint.

'Nick?'

Another mumble.

'Nick. It's time to get up.'

The arm was removed as Nick Tsappis turned onto his back, his dark hair sticking out at odd angles and pillow marks carving tram lines down one olive-skinned cheek. 'Remind me again why you have to get up at this ridiculous hour?' he grumbled.

'Because it takes me at least three hours to look fabulous in the morning.'

'Only three,' Nick teased.

Kate gave him a light slap on the shoulder and reluctantly threw back the duvet. 'I wish I could stay, you know that, but I've got to get to work.'

Nick threw his arm around her and pulled the duvet back up to her waist. His other hand moved to her upper thigh. 'Surely we've got time for a quickie?'

Kate laughed. She'd been seeing Nick for nearly three months and still hadn't quite accepted his seemingly insatiable appetite for her body. He was an oncologist at the Doncaster Royal Infirmary and she'd met him earlier in the year whilst investigating a case involving a cancer patient. It had taken four weeks for them to finally have dinner together and a further two weeks for them to fall into bed but, Kate had to admit, the wait had been worth it.

'I'm sorry. I really have to get ready for work. I've got a tricky case to work on and it's the PM today.'

Nick's hands stayed on her body. 'Tricky how?'

Kate sighed. She really wanted to tell him but she knew that to discuss details of an active case was totally unethical – even if Nick was a doctor.

'I know,' he said. 'You can't tell me.'

Kate's brain stumbled over her last thought. *Nick was a doctor.* 'I can't tell you,' Kate said. 'But I can ask you a couple of questions that would help me.'

His fingers tickled her thigh. 'It'll cost you.'

'Okay. But you'll have to submit an invoice and I'll pay you later.'

'Is that a promise?'

'Absolutely.'

'Done,' Nick said. 'So what did you want to ask?'

Kate took a deep breath. Her question wouldn't compromise the investigation in any way and she could ask any other doctor but it seemed silly to squander an opportunity when she had one in her bed. 'Do you know how to perform a caesarean section?'

Nick's hands moved quickly as he hoisted himself up into a sitting position. 'Why do you ask? Please tell me you're not pregnant.'

Kate glanced at his face. He was half smiling but she could see that she'd unsettled him. 'No. Of course not. Christ I'm practically menopausal.' She stopped, suddenly aware of how unsexy that sounded. 'Well… nearly… maybe. It's not about me. I just need to ask a doctor. Any doctor.'

'So I'm just convenient?' Nick's smile became more genuine, forming lines around his dark brown eyes.

'Yes. Exactly. I need to keep a tame doctor on hand so I've been inviting you back to my flat on a regular basis in case you came in handy. And now you have.'

'Very "handy",' he said, running a finger across her stomach.

Kate pulled away trying not to allow herself to be distracted by the arousing contrast between Nick's darker skin and her own paleness. She loved how they juxtaposed each other – not just in personality but physically. Where she was blonde, Nick was dark; where Kate was slim, Nick was sturdy and where she wasn't especially short, Nick towered above most people he met.

'Seriously. Would you know how to perform a C-section if you needed to?'

Nick went quiet for a few seconds, frowning as though he was trying to remember something. 'Probably. In an emergency. I learnt the theory in my second year of medicine and I've seen a couple done. I assisted on one when I was a junior doctor, but I've never made the cut myself.'

'Would any doctor know how to do it?'

'Probably. Obviously some would be specialists.'

'What about nurses?'

'A bit unlikely. It's a surgical procedure. But everything's changing in medicine at the moment so I can't say for sure. It's not my field.'

'Is it difficult?'

'It's major surgery. You have to cut through the abdominal wall, avoid the colon and the bladder then into the uterus.'

Kate felt her insides tightening in response to his description.

'And the woman would be anaesthetised? Normally?'

'Either under general anaesthetic or an epidural could be administered.'

She tried to imagine the scene. The victim dragged into the bushes, subdued, strangled and then…? Did he cut her before she'd died? If so, how did he stop her from screaming? If Barratt's account was correct it seemed more likely that the procedure had been carried out after she'd lost consciousness. Or after she'd died.

'Does that help?' Nick asked.

'It might.'

'But you can't talk about it.'

'I can't but you've given me something to think about,' Kate said, swinging her legs from under the duvet. 'I'll pay you back tonight.'

Nick linked his hands behind his head and grinned at her lewdly. 'Oh, you will indeed.'

\*\*\*

Kate had just poured herself a coffee when her phone rang. She tucked it between her ear and her shoulder leaving her hands free to add milk to her drink. It was Raymond, her DCI at Doncaster Central.

'Sir?'

'Kate. We might have an ID for the body on Town Fields. A misper report came in in the early hours. Bloke from Rossington hasn't seen his wife in over twenty-four hours. Your team's body fits her description. I've sent a uniform round to accompany the husband down here and I want you and Hollis to do the interview. Half an hour.'

He hung up. Kate checked the time on her phone. Just gone seven. She'd been planning an early start anyway to get her team up to speed before she had to attend the post-mortem, but not quite this early. Pouring her coffee into an insulated mug, she grabbed the slice of toast that she'd buttered but not even managed a bite from, shouted a loud goodbye to the beautiful man in her bed and headed for her Mini.

\*\*\*

Ryan Buckley was waiting in an interview room when Kate arrived at Doncaster Central. She met Raymond and Hollis in the observation suite where they were discussing strategy. Hollis grinned at her as she entered the room but there was something a bit off about his smile – it didn't quite reach his eyes. His jacket sleeves were wrinkled as if he'd been rolling them up and he had a scruffy growth of stubble across his chin and neck. Kate frowned at him, puzzled by the deterioration in his habitually tidy appearance.

'You okay?' she asked. 'You look like you've been up all night, and not in a good way.'

'I'm fine,' he responded, turning back to the DCI who had been watching their exchange with irritation. Raymond *did* look immaculate. His charcoal suit was sharply pressed and his white shirt was almost dazzlingly bright. The cut of both accentuated his recent weight loss as did his short haircut and his closely shaven face. Kate had noted the transition in her boss over the past few months and wondered if he was having an affair but, having met his wife, Diana, that seemed a little unlikely if he wanted to keep his testicles.

'Done with the pleasantries?' Raymond snapped. 'We have a suspect to interview.'

'Suspect?' Kate asked. 'You're convinced that it was his wife's body that we found yesterday?'

Raymond nodded gravely. 'Fits the description. And the time frame. He hasn't seen her since he left for work on Saturday morning. He rung everybody he could think of before reporting her missing. He gave a statement to the attending officer who flagged it up because of the body we recovered yesterday. Obviously, if it is the same woman, we need to tread carefully; wouldn't be the first time a murderer reported his victim missing.'

Kate turned to the glass between the observation suite and the interview room.

'He looks pretty upset. Why aren't we interviewing him in his home?'

The man was sitting with one ankle crossed over the opposite knee, his foot jiggling frantically. His hands alternated between drumming on the table top and picking at an invisible thread on the sleeve of his fleece jacket.

'He offered to come down here to add to his initial statement, to save time,' Raymond said.

'Which gives us a chance to observe and assess,' Kate added.

'Fletcher, you lead. Hollis make notes. He might be completely legit and we need to be sensitive to that. And don't mention the body – especially the injuries.'

Hollis led the way to the interview room in silence. Kate would have expected him to ask her about her strategy but he kept his back to her until they entered the room, obviously lost in his own thoughts, or trying to avoid any more questions about his appearance. They both took seats opposite Ryan Buckley and Hollis left Kate to introduce them.

Buckley listened attentively as he was given their names, his eyes fixed on Kate expectantly. His hands had stopped fidgeting and he leaned forwards slightly in his seat. He was solidly built; big hands and a broad face. His hair was shaved quite close to his scalp leaving a thin covering of dark bristles, which matched the stubble around his mouth and on his chin. He was huddled in a dark blue fleece jacket and he stuffed his hands into the pockets as he leaned in to talk to the two detectives.

'Have you found her?' he asked.

'Mr Buckley,' Kate said, ignoring the question. 'We need to establish the facts around your wife's disappearance. I need to ask you some questions and your answers may help us to find Melissa as speedily as possible.'

His shoulders sagged and he lowered his head. 'So you've not found her.'

'Not yet. But, with your help, we hope to do so soon.'

He snorted; half laugh, half grunt of disgust. '*With my help*. I know how this works. Now you've got me here you want to know if I've done away with my wife. That's it isn't it? Always look at the husband or the boyfriend because they're the most likely murderer or kidnapper or whatever. Well go on then, ask me your questions. I've got nothing to hide.'

He pushed his chair back from the table, spread his legs and folded his arms across his chest in a challenge.

'But make it quick will you? *I* need to try to find my wife.'

'That's not what's happening here, Mr Buckley,' Kate lied. 'We want to help you. I've looked at your statement and I want to get more detail, establish times and places as clearly as possible. Is that okay?'

A curt nod from Buckley.

'Right,' Kate opened the folder containing Buckley's initial statement and scanned the first page. She'd already read it but she wanted to convince him that he was being taken seriously. The description he'd given matched the body that had been found the previous day but the woman wasn't especially unusual. Average height, average build, dark hair. Buckley said that his wife had still been in her dressing gown when he'd left home which didn't help with using clothing to identify her.

'Is there anything you can add to your description of your wife? Any scars, tattoos, birthmarks?'

Buckley's eyes flicked backwards and forwards as though he were reading an image of his wife's body, looking for clues. 'She has a small scar on her left knee, came off her bike when she was little. It's a crescent shape. She's also got three moles on her left shoulder blade – like a triangle. No tattoos. Her ears are pierced a few times though, but she let some of the holes heal up.'

Hollis noted down the details while Buckley started to look even more agitated. He obviously realised that such details could be used to identify a body.

'Have you found her? Or somebody who looks like her?'

Kate shook her head. 'We're just trying to gather as much information as possible, Mr Buckley. The more help you can give us the more chance we have of locating Melissa.'

He seemed to accept this, his shoulders dropping slightly as some of the tension was released from his body.

'So you last saw your wife the day before yesterday when you left for work at 7.45am. Is that correct?'

'I usually leave before her,' Buckley confirmed. 'She does shifts and she's been on late morning starts for the last few weeks. I work alternate Saturday mornings and she works one weekend a month.'

'Where does she work?'

'She works for LNER – on the trains.'

'So she travels?'

Another nod.

'And did you think she was away for her work on Saturday night? Is that why you didn't report her missing sooner?'

Buckley sighed and dropped his eyes, scanning the table top, unable to look at Kate. She was prepared for a lie or, at least, an excuse but when Buckley raised his head again she felt convinced that he was about to share a difficult truth.

'I wasn't sure where she was,' he said. 'I rang some of her friends on Saturday night but nobody would admit to having seen her.'

'Admit to? That's an unusual way to put it. What do you mean by that?' Kate asked, alarm bells ringing.

Buckley uncrossed his arms and wiped a hand across his mouth and chin, inhaling sharply through his nose. 'We'd been arguing a lot recently. I know how that's going to look but I might as well tell you now in case you find out later. We'd not been getting on and Mel had spent a couple of nights away from me – to get some headspace, she said.'

Kate felt Hollis tense beside her, his writing hand stilled as he regarded the man opposite them.

'What sort of mood was Melissa in when you left for work on Saturday?'

Buckley flushed as he admitted that his wife had been in a 'foul' mood.

'And what had caused her to be in a bad mood?' Kate could see where this might be going and thanked the forces of the universe that Buckley was here voluntarily. He might keep talking with a bit of encouragement.

'We'd been arguing the night before. I slept in the spare room. When I heard her getting up I went down to the kitchen, to make peace, like. But she was having none of it. Called me a selfish bastard, went back up to our bedroom and slammed the door. You can see why I wasn't surprised when she didn't come home. I thought she might be with one of her friends – that's what she did before but, like I said, nobody seems to have heard from her. Her car's missing so she must have gone out somewhere.'

'What does she drive?' Hollis asked.

Buckley described a red Ford Fiesta and gave Hollis the registration number. Kate knew what her colleague was thinking. Trace the car and they might trace the woman. And, if she *was* the body on Town Fields then the car might prove very informative.

'Tell me about the argument,' Kate said. 'What was it about?'

'Buckley gave her a regretful smile. 'Same as ever. Money.'

'But you work?'

'I work at Selby's. I'm a mechanic.'

Kate was aware of Hollis writing down every word. They'd visit Selby's Garage at some point during the day and get a picture of this man from his workmates.

'Pay not good?'

'It's fine,' Buckley said. 'But it's never enough. Bills to pay, mortgage, that kind of thing. You know how it is for everybody these days.'

Kate smiled in agreement but her mind was busy calculating what the couple might earn between them. Enough to cover a modest mortgage at least. She'd seen from Buckley's statement that they had no children and the area where they lived wasn't known for being expensive. Perhaps there were debts?

'Okay. What about Melissa's friends? You rang a few people?'

Buckley dug in the pocket of his jacket and pulled out a crumpled piece of paper. 'Tamsin, Lucy, Ellie. Their names and phone numbers are on there.' He slid the paper across to Kate. 'My mobile's at the bottom. I suppose you'll want to check that I made the calls and what time.'

*He's well prepared*, Kate thought. Either he really did want them to find his wife or he'd done a very thorough job of covering his tracks.

'I'll need Melissa's mobile number as well,' Kate said, passing him the piece of paper back with a pen. 'And any other friends that you haven't managed to contact.'

Buckley scribbled down more information and then passed pen and paper back across the table. He'd added two more female names and his wife's mobile number. Kate put the paper in her folder, closed it and stood up. 'I think we have everything we need for now, Mr Buckley,' she said, extending her hand for him to shake. 'My colleague will walk you out and I'll be in touch as soon as we make progress on your wife's case.'

Buckley looked down at her hand then up at Hollis as though he wasn't quite sure what he was supposed to do next. He got to his feet, shook hands and allowed Hollis to lead him out into the corridor while Kate went to join Raymond in the observation suite.

'Well?' she asked her boss who was still staring through the glass.

Raymond turned and smiled. 'He's lying.'

Kate grinned back. 'You got that as well? Whatever he and his wife argued about, it was more complicated than just money. I'm not sure what they did fight about, but when we find out, we might find out what happened to her.'

# Chapter 3

'Right folks, listen up,' Kate addressed her team, each of them staring at her expectantly. She'd organised the use of one of the incident rooms so that she could gather them together and explain her concerns about Melissa Buckley. Now, seated around the conference table, all eyes moved from Kate's to the whiteboard behind her as she tapped the remote for the projector.

'We've got a missing woman who matches the description of the body found on Town Fields yesterday,' Kate said as an image of Melissa Buckley filled the screen. It was obviously taken at a party as Melissa had a champagne glass in her hand and her cheeks were flushed with either alcohol or excitement. She was wearing an ivory-coloured dress which highlighted her dark hair and eyes and her subtle make-up added to the effect. She was stunning.

Barratt narrowed his eyes as he took in every detail of the photograph. He was the only member of the team to have seen the body close up and Kate was relying on him to confirm the ID; or not. She waited until he looked away and raised her eyebrows at him. 'Well?'

'It's her,' he said.

'How sure are you?'

He stood up and pointed to where Melissa had tucked her hair behind one ear. 'See there. There's an earring and three other holes. A bit unusual, like she might have been a Goth or a punk in a previous life. The woman we found yesterday had four piercing holes in each ear. No earrings but the marks were obvious. Her hair is shorter in the photograph but I'm convinced that the body is that of this woman.'

He sat back down, his eyes flicking around the faces of his colleagues as though he was expecting a barrage of questions but they all remained silent, waiting to hear what Kate had to say.

'Okay, good,' she began. 'Her husband reported her missing at just after one o'clock this morning. He claims she'd left for work on Saturday morning and hadn't come home. He'd rung a few of her friends but nobody admitted to having seen her. He gave it another twelve hours or so and then rang it in as a misper.'

'Did she go to work on Saturday?' Cooper asked. The youngest member of the team, Sam Cooper was still feeling her way into her role and had only recently discovered the confidence to express her ideas in briefings. 'If she didn't, then that raises questions.'

Kate smiled at her. 'Early days, Sam. That's something that we need to find out. She worked for LNER out of Doncaster Station.'

'So she would have been in uniform. They used to wear long red coats and smart dresses. It might have changed though.'

'Nothing like that at the scene,' Barratt said. 'She'd been wearing jeans and a scoop-neck top. Not even red.'

Kate noticed O'Connor's moustache twitch upwards as Barratt stumbled over 'scoop-neck', obviously enjoying his colleague's discomfort when describing women's clothing.

'So we need to check if she was expected at work – it might be that employees have changing facilities at the station,' Kate suggested. 'There's also the question of her car. Red Fiesta. We need to see if it's in staff parking at Doncaster Station and, if it's not there, get all the streets around Town Fields checked as well. Dan, any thoughts?'

Hollis glanced at the photograph and then back at his boss looking exactly as if he'd been asked a tricky question at school and hadn't been listening properly. 'CCTV around Town Fields?'

Another twitch of O'Connor's moustache. Hollis obviously hadn't been listening very carefully. CCTV was a given in this type of case.

'Follow up with the friends that the husband spoke to?' O'Connor suggested. 'Work colleagues as well. Get an idea of who she was, what the relationship was like.'

Kate nodded.

'And the bottom end of Town Fields is well known for "nocturnal activities". I could ask some of the girls if they saw anything on Saturday night.'

Typical O'Connor; straight to the seedier side of the community.

'Right. Good. Jobs then. Sam – follow up on CCTV. Try to get bank details as well, the husband said that they had money worries but I wasn't convinced. Steve – see if you can use your contacts to round up anybody who might have been working round Town Fields that night. Matt – organise the search for the car and get down to the railway station, see if you can find any of her colleagues to talk to.'

Barratt stood up, raring to go as usual.

'Dan, with me.'

She waited until the others had left and then studied her colleague. His blond hair was unusually scruffy-looking, suggesting that he hadn't had time to gel it and the stubble on his face was a couple of shades darker than his fair hair making him look like an out-of-work George Michael impersonator. He'd pushed the sleeves of his suit jacket up over his elbows, adding to the creases she'd noticed earlier and his bloodshot eyes refused to focus on her face.

'Are you okay?' she asked. 'You're really not yourself today.'

He blushed and looked down at the desk. 'Is there a problem with my work?'

'No. But you're not on the ball. CCTV? Is that really the best suggestion that you could come up with?'

Silence.

'Dan. I can see something's wrong. You look like you slept in a ditch last night, if you slept at all and you're not your usual stylish self.' She waited for him to smile. Teasing him about his clothes and hair had become part of their routine and he never refused to rise to the bait when she commented on his spotless appearance. This time though his face remained grave.

'I'm fine,' he said. 'Just a bit tired. I've not been sleeping well, that's all. You know how it is, pressure of the job and all that.'

Even if Kate hadn't known the DC very well she would have been able to tell that he was lying, but there was nothing that she could do if he refused to tell her what was wrong.

'Okay, fine. I want you to follow up on the friends that Ryan Buckley rang about his wife. Check that he called and find out what they think of him. There's a secret in that relationship and women usually tell secrets to their girlfriends. Find out what Buckley's not telling us.'

Hollis got up from his seat and left the incident room without another word.

***

Kate sat in the morgue's viewing gallery checking her email on her phone. Hollis had managed to speak to two of Melissa Buckley's friends and both confirmed her husband's story. Buckley had rung them on Saturday night and had seemed genuinely concerned about his wife's whereabouts. Tamsin had said that he'd been fairly polite, but Lucy had insinuated that he was belligerent and that this wasn't the first time. Both had been worried about their friend but reluctant to speculate about her relationship with Ryan. The third friend, Ellie, had her mobile turned off. Kate emailed Hollis back and urged him to keep trying. Normally she wouldn't have bothered, as usually he could be trusted to do the right thing, but, after his earlier attitude, she was worried that he'd lost focus or that he'd miss something important. She suddenly wished that she'd sent Barratt with him, but the Dan Hollis that she knew would have resented the implication of being teamed up with another DC on such a simple assignment.

'We're about to start, if you're ready,' Kailisa's voice crackled through the intercom like that of a Dalek and with approximately the same amount of emotion. Since her return to South Yorkshire, Kate had encountered the pathologist on numerous occasions and was still sometimes surprised by his brusque manner when dealing with the police. She had learnt to put up with his snapping and barbed comments because his professionalism was exceptional and his respect for the dead almost reverential.

'Of course. Sorry.' She waved her phone at him and pantomimed putting it back in her pocket. Kailisa's assistant, a young woman with close-cropped bleached blonde hair that stood out against her dark skin, risked a flicker of a smile but Kailisa's face remained stony and his brown eyes showed no spark of humour.

Kate listened as the pathologist recited a preliminary description of the body which confirmed what Barratt had already told her; the woman was in her late twenties or early thirties, white and well nourished. Bruising on her upper arms and around her neck stood out starkly against her pale flesh and the wound in her abdomen was a gory smile a couple of inches below her naval. Looking at it made Kate nauseous. Not because of the dark blood and tissue but because of the implications of such a wound. Had someone deliberately targeted this woman because she was pregnant? Had her husband found out that she was carrying another man's child and decided to get rid of them both? Or was this random? The latter seemed the least likely explanation but, until Kailisa had finished his work, Kate could only speculate.

The pathologist was examining the bruises on the woman's throat, angling a high-intensity light towards the left-hand side and measuring his findings with a ruler.

'There are bruises to the throat and neck consistent with pressure from fingers, suggesting manual strangulation, and bruising to the upper arms which suggests that she was knelt on as he strangled her, presumably to subdue her arms and prevent her from fighting back or scratching him.'

He manipulated the throat.

'The hyoid bone appears to be fractured. X-ray will confirm. Or dissection if necessary.'

Kate knew that he'd be reluctant to cut into the throat as there would need to be a viewing at some point to confirm the identity of the dead woman. The bruising would be relatively easy to cover with make-up but a throat wound would make the process even more difficult for the loved ones.

His assistant noted down the findings while Kailisa checked the eyes of the victim.

'Petechial haemorrhages in both eyes, also suggestive of strangulation.'

He moved the light down the body.

'There is an obvious wound to the abdomen, approximately fifteen centimetres in length and one centimetre wide, curving slightly upwards. Lack of vital response in the tissue suggests that this was carried out post-mortem.'

Kate let out a breath that she hadn't realised that she was holding, thankful that the horrific wound wouldn't have caused any pain. It looked like the cause of death was probably strangulation then, but she knew better than to ask Kailisa for cause and time until he'd finished the PM. His opinion of pushy police officers had been made abundantly clear to her on more than one occasion and she'd learnt to bide her time and allow him to work through his findings in his characteristically methodical manner. He continued to scan the body with the light and a magnifying lens, occasionally using tweezers to remove items invisible to Kate, which he placed on pre-prepared slides.

'Sorry to interrupt,' Kate said, remembering Ryan Buckley's description and feeling faintly ridiculous for apologising to the metal box on the wall next to her. 'But we have a potential ID on the victim. Could you possibly look for identifying marks?'

She dug out her phone and scrolled through to the photograph of a paragraph of Buckley's statement. 'She might have a scar on her left knee. Small, crescent shaped.'

The pathologist glanced up at her then leaned in to the body as though he was about to inhale her aroma. He grasped the left knee in a gloved hand and tilted it backwards and forwards to catch the light in different ways. 'There's something there. Small. Curved. Looks like a very old scar.'

Kate felt her pulse begin to race. 'Okay, thanks. She might also have three moles on her left shoulder blade. Like a triangle.'

Kailisa gestured to his assistant who helped him to gently roll the body over so he could see the shoulders. He muttered something and the blonde woman grabbed a camera and took three quick pictures.

'I'll display the images on the screen up there,' Kailisa said. He lowered the body carefully, took the camera and fired off a few quick shots of the knee. Three or four keystrokes on his PC and, moments later, the blank monitor in the observation gallery flickered into life.

'That's the knee,' he said, stating the obvious as Kate stared at the image. Just below the knee cap was a small mark which could have been the scar that Ryan Buckley had been describing. 'And here's the shoulder.'

The display filled with a blown-up image of the dead woman's skin with a triangular pattern of moles clearly visible. Kate was in no doubt that she was looking at the body of Melissa Buckley.

'Shit,' she whispered, trying to work out her next move. She'd need to tell Raymond and she knew that he'd want the husband brought in for further questioning, but would that do any good? There was no evidence that Buckley had harmed his wife in any way and they might need his co-operation if they were going to be able to trace her movements.

All she could do for the moment was watch the PM. She knew that Kailisa would be less than impressed if she walked out halfway through, and it would allow her some time to think. She observed as the pathologist performed the Y-incision and eased back the skin and layers of flesh of the woman's chest and stomach. She knew what he was looking for – the reason for the abdominal wound and, if what she suspected were true, she needed to be here to listen to his conclusions.

Kailisa stopped working for a few seconds, his hands completely still as he tilted his head on one side and looked down at the body. She heard him say something to himself but couldn't make out the words.

'DI Fletcher,' his voice crackled over the intercom. 'Please come down here. There's something that I'd like you to see. And please, remember a gown and gloves.'

Two minutes later, and appropriately attired, Kate was staring at the dead woman trying to work out what Kailisa had seen.

'Here,' he said, indicating the abdominal wound with a gloved finger. 'It looks like somebody tried to perform a C-section, yes?'

Kate leaned closer.

'But here,' he peeled back layers of skin and fat to expose the abdominal cavity. 'There is no wound. The incision doesn't go through to the abdominal cavity. It's broken through the skin and the first layers of fat but it doesn't breach the fascia.'

Kate stared at the wound, baffled.

'What does that mean? Is this a C-section or not?'

'Not,' Kailisa said with a quick shake of his head. 'This isn't an attempt to deliver a foetus and, judging by the size and shape of the uterus there was no foetus to deliver.'

Kate looked away as he leaned in, scalpel grasped firmly in a steady hand, to confirm his suspicion.

'This woman was not pregnant, DI Fletcher, and this wound is not a caesarean section.'

'So what is it?'

'I have no idea. It wouldn't be fatal as it hasn't penetrated to the colon or any of the major organs. It serves no purpose in subduing the victim as, despite its appearance, it's really rather superficial and it appears to have been inflicted post-mortem. If I were to hazard a guess, and I'm not known for my guesswork, as you are aware, I'd suggest that this was ritualistic in some way. It meant something to the person who did it, but that meaning may be obscure to us.'

Kate nearly snapped at him to tell him that she was well aware of what ritualistic meant but she needed information and biting off the pathologist's head wasn't the best way forwards.

'But it looks like a C-section? The size and the curve?'

'It does,' Kailisa confirmed. 'There are a number of ways to perform this particular operation but only two ways to make the initial incision; a straight line or a slight upward curve. They may vary in length but the shape will always follow one of these two patterns.'

Kate remembered the conversation that she'd had with Nick earlier.

'Is it likely that whoever did this had medical training?'

Kailisa angled the lamp so that they could both get a closer look at the wound.

'Look here,' he said, pointing to the upper edge. 'The cut is one single line; there are no overlaps.'

'So he knew what he was doing?'

'Or he was in a position to be able to take his time. He wasn't concerned about being disturbed.'

Kate stepped back trying to picture the scene. The woman was already dead, strangled, and her attacker wanted, needed, to make some sort of statement. So he undressed her and cut her open in a way which suggested a surgical procedure.

'Did he use a scalpel?' she asked.

Kailisa frowned and pulled an angled magnifying lens down from the array of lights and tools which hung over the dissecting table like the legs of a giant spider.

'He used a fine, sharp blade consistent with a scalpel.'

Kate took that as a *yes*.

'So he might have access to medical equipment? Again that might suggest he's a doctor or a surgeon.'

Kailisa's face was impassive as moved the lens down the body. He stopped at the woman's pubic hair, which looked recently waxed with only a thin strip remaining, and asked his assistant for a fine comb.

'She was raped?'

Kailisa sighed heavily, his patience with her questions obviously running out.

'That is what I'm trying to ascertain,' he said, running the comb through the delicate curls. He tapped the comb on a piece of white paper and pulled the magnifying lens back.

'No obvious sign of contaminant pubic hair but I'll take a sample and test for skin cells or lice.'

Kate shuddered and then looked away as Kailisa gently parted the woman's legs.

'I'll swab for semen,' he was saying. 'If he used a condom we might find traces of lubricant but that obviously won't give us DNA. Otherwise…'

Kate sensed that he'd stopped moving as he stopped talking and turned to see what he'd found. He was staring at something between the woman's legs, a swab held between his fingers, his top lip slightly curled up in either disgust or horror.

'What have you found?'

Kailisa shook his head as if he was trying to clear the image from his mind.

'As you know, DI Fletcher, even with the evidence of semen or lubricant, rape can be difficult to prove. The vaginal tissues are extremely elastic and any swelling or bruising tends to subside within a few hours. However, our victim didn't have a few hours. There are two scratches on her upper left thigh and her vulva is swollen and contused. I would suggest that her attacker penetrated her with some force.'

'Bastard,' Kate hissed. She tried to imagine what had happened. Had the attacker lured the woman into the undergrowth and then killed and raped her or had the attack occurred somewhere else and Town Fields was simply the dump site? The controlled nature of the abdominal wound certainly suggested the latter.

'Anything to suggest she was killed where she was found versus being left there after the attack?'

Kailisa indicated with a gloved finger that Kate should change her position and stand with him on the other side of the body. She usually felt frustrated by his economical use of words as a medium of communication but she wasn't entirely sure that she was ready for what he had to say.

'Here. Lividity marks on the side of the face, upper arm and the left hip. At some point soon after her death she was lying on her left side. At the scene she was on her back.'

'So she was displayed? He killed her somewhere else and then left her to be found?'

'Along with the clothing from the lower half of the body.' Kailisa pointed towards a series of photographs of the scene which were laid out on a counter top which ran along one wall of the mortuary.

Kate walked over to the images and studied them. The woman's body was supine, naked from the waist down with the legs together. The lividity mark on her left hip was clear in the picture as was the abdominal incision. How long had she been there before Cawthorne made his grisly discovery?

She turned to ask Kailisa the one question that she knew he always hated.

'Any idea of time of death?'

He'd removed the stomach and was in the process of examining the contents.

'She was in full rigor mortis when she was brought in which suggests that she'd been dead for between eight and twenty-four hours. Body temperature indicated around the middle of that range, making adjustments for the overnight temperature on Saturday night. The stomach is empty of solids but contains a liquid which smells like coffee. Obviously I'll need to have it tested.'

'So sometime between Saturday morning and Saturday afternoon seems likely?'

Kailisa concurred.

It fit perfectly with the last known sighting of Melissa Buckley. And the last person to have seen her alive was her husband. Kate snatched off her gloves, picked up her phone and rang Hollis.

# Chapter 4

Hollis glanced at the screen of his phone and then flicked the answer icon into the red. He knew that he'd be in for a bollocking later but that didn't matter now. What mattered was the woman in front of him; the one who had been trying to mess up his life for the past few weeks. Suzanne Doherty.

She'd been out of prison for four months. He knew because he'd been keeping track of her, surreptitiously of course, and had been aware of her release date. He wouldn't have bothered if it hadn't been for the letter. That fucking letter which made him want to curl up with shame and embarrassment. She'd addressed it to Doncaster Central and he'd been handed it as he'd signed on for work on a chilly spring morning. He remembered that morning vividly as his last moment of peace.

The contents weren't especially worrying; she wanted to see him when she got out, to make amends for how she'd treated him. It was the usual guilty bullshit that he'd seen a couple of times during his late teens and early twenties. His own fault really. He'd been the one to accept her olive branch when at age seventeen, she'd reached out to him. His adoptive parents had always been open with him and had always answered his questions as patiently and as fully as they could, but it wasn't enough. At seventeen Dan Hollis had wanted answers to the big questions. He wanted to know who he was and where he came from. His memories of his life before the adoption were hazy, even though he'd lived with his biological mother until he was seven years old, and he felt a need to try to flesh out what he thought he remembered.

He'd met up with Suzanne in a pub two days after he'd turned eighteen. She said that she'd wanted to buy him his first legal drink and looked devastated when he told her that his dad had already done that – he made sure that he called his adoptive parents mum and dad just to spite her; he hadn't wanted to make it easy. They'd talked and she'd explained her situation; that she hadn't been old enough to cope with a child and that she'd tried her best but it had all been too much. But, now she was older, she wanted to make it up to him.

Dan had asked a few questions about her life and she was open about her two terms in prison – one for drugs the other for soliciting – but it was hard to hear, as a teenager, that his genes came from somebody who was so messed up, and he'd ended up walking out.

They'd tried again after he'd joined the police force but, just as Dan felt like they might be making progress, she dropped her bombshell. She couldn't, or wouldn't, tell him who his father was. For that, he loathed her.

Now she was back in his life. Insinuating herself into cracks and corners, 'bumping into' him after work or 'just passing' his flat. She seemed to be everywhere and the last thing he needed was for his colleagues to find out who she was. The stress had been affecting his sleep and he knew that he'd been drinking far too much but he seemed to be powerless to keep her out of his head. And out of his life.

This morning had been by far the worst though. He'd just been on his way to try to track down the last of the three women that Ryan Buckley had mentioned in his statement, taking the stairs two at a time and smacking the door open when there she was, waiting right outside the back entrance to the police station.

'Danny!' she exclaimed brightly as though she were surprised to see him. 'Fancy meeting you here.'

He stalked off towards his car hoping to out-stride her but he could hear her heels pecking out an insistent rhythm on the tarmac behind him.

'Wait up. I need to talk to you.'

She grabbed the top of his arm and he whipped round, resenting her touch, her voice, her presence in his life. '*I* don't need to talk to *you*!' he yelled.

She flinched back and then smiled at him. 'Course you do, Danny. I might have some news for you.'

He sneered at her. 'Too little too late. Just fuck off.' He'd dropped his voice to a near-whisper, aware that one of his colleagues could appear at any minute. What would they make of this tiny woman who had obviously got him riled up? She was petite, both in height and frame, and her too-tight clothes were too young for the fifty-year-old woman he knew her to be. The short denim skirt and sparkly maroon crop top would have looked wrong on anybody over fifteen and in daylight they looked as out of place as a morning suit at a football match. Her fake-tanned face reminded him of an old leather sofa that had been in the sitting room of a house he'd shared as a student, lined and worn, and her hair was a wispy, white-blonde mess in need of a brush or a hairdresser. She looked like one of those mummies that had desiccated over centuries but still had hair and discernible features.

Her eyes were very much alive though. There was a taunt in them. She knew that he'd be embarrassed by her and that he wouldn't want any of his colleagues to overhear their conversation. Her grin widened as his phone rang but he didn't take the call.

'Come on, Danny. Five minutes.'

She wasn't going to go away and he couldn't be seen talking to her outside the nick.

'Okay, okay,' he sighed. 'Five minutes. I'm working. Get in the car.'

He pressed the remote and the Kia Sportage chirped at him; opening the driver's side door he nodded to Suzanne. 'Get in.'

She shook her head. 'How do I know it's safe? You could take me anywhere, do anything to me. And you'd get away with it. You're a copper.'

She was right. He could drive her into the middle of nowhere, kill her, dump her and stand a good chance of not being caught, but he wouldn't do that because, as she said, he was a copper.

'Just get in,' he said. 'We'll sit here. I won't even put the engine on.'

Suzanne looked at him sceptically but she reached out and opened the car door, keeping her eyes fixed on him as she eased herself inside. Despite the anger he felt, Hollis almost laughed at the idea that this woman didn't trust him. *She* was the one following *him* around; *she* was the one harassing *him*.

'So what do you want?' he asked, plonking himself down in the driver's seat and turning to face her. 'I assume it's money.'

She grinned at him exposing teeth that were nearly as discoloured and ruined as her face. 'Nice car this,' she said, running one hand along the leather seat. Must've cost a few bob.' Hollis didn't respond as she flipped down the sun visor and grinned at her reflection in the vanity mirror. 'You always were the clever one weren't you?' she continued. 'I just need a few quid to get myself set up.'

'Set up?'

'I need somewhere to live, Danny.'

He cringed at her use of the familiar name. Nobody ever called him Danny, not even his parents. He'd got into fights about it at school, taking on boys who were bigger and stronger just because he didn't want anybody to remind him of *her*.

'Don't call me Danny. I'm not a kid anymore and I can see right through you. Why the hell should I give you anything?'

Her eyes narrowed, snakelike, but the smile stayed firmly fixed on. Hollis could see that she was calculating how far she could push him, and how much she might be able to get out of him.

'I need a couple of grand. I've found a flat and I need a deposit and a couple of months' rent until my benefits kick in. I'll pay you back when I can.'

Hollis snorted. 'Pay me back? How the hell are you going to pay me back? Everything you get will go on booze or drugs. Or are you going to earn a few quid turning tricks like you used to?'

Suzanne turned in her seat and stared out through the windscreen. 'I only did that because I had to,' she said, quietly. 'I had to feed you, buy you clothes. I didn't want to have a kid, but when you came I did my best to look after you. I used what I had. I wasn't much more than a kid myself so it's not like I had a choice, is it?'

Her wheedling tone of self-pity only made him angrier; more resentful.

'You could have given me up sooner. That was a choice. I could have been settled with a decent family instead of being fed scraps and living in rags. And even when I was getting sorted out you just couldn't leave me alone. Do you think I don't remember that day you took me out of school and the police came? Have you any idea what a trauma like that can do to a little kid? I was happy to see you. You were going to take me to the fair and then I was put in the back of a police car. I had no idea what was going on.' He felt himself trembling as he remembered his anger and confusion.

'Oh poor little Danny,' she mocked, turning to face him with a sneer. 'Did his mummy mess him up? Well you're doing all right for yourself now by the looks of things. It can't have been that bad.'

Hollis didn't respond. He couldn't. To speak would be to reveal the rage that was simmering inside him and he wasn't going to let her know how much she was getting to him. 'Why don't you just wait for your benefits and then get a flat?' he said, trying to ignore her jibe.'

The sneer became even more pronounced. 'Oh, come on, Danny. You know how it works. No address, no benefits; no benefits, no address. I've been sleeping on a friend's sofa but she won't let me use her address to make a claim.'

'And you think a landlord will give you a flat because you're waving a couple of grand around and might get some housing benefit at some point in the future?'

'He might if he owes me a favour or two,' Suzanne responded with a lewd wink.

Hollis felt physically sick. He opened the car door a crack to let in some fresh air and let out Suzanne's cloying perfume.

'Not a chance,' he finally said, the words and the air clearing his head. 'Why the hell would I give you anything? It's not like you ever did anything for me apart from abuse me and torment me. Just get out and leave me alone, you junkie whore!'

'Oh, Danny – don't be like that. Just a couple of grand and your colleagues in that shiny new building will never know that you're the son of a "junkie whore".'

His hand, resting on the door handle, itched to punch something. *So that's her game,* he thought, *blackmail.* 'I don't care,' he lied. 'Tell who you want. It makes no difference to me.'

Suzanne opened the car door about to get out and then froze as she watched a figure cross the car park about fifty yards in front of them. Hollis followed her gaze to where DCI Raymond was heading for his Volvo. 'Wait till he's gone,' he instructed, grabbing Suzanne's wrist.

She turned back to face him, the fake smile back. 'So you *are* ashamed of your dear old mum are you? Well you know what to do.'

Hollis dropped her wrist as though it had burnt him. 'I've told you, no. Tell who you want. My parents live in Chesterfield. They're the ones who raised me and taught me right from wrong and thank God they did. Fuck knows what would've happened to me if I'd stayed with you.'

She shrugged, completely unmoved by his outburst, and opened the car door fully. 'We'll see, Danny. You might not be bothered about people knowing about me but they might see you a bit differently if they find out who your dad is.'

She slammed the door and trotted off across the car park, a look of triumph plastered across her face.

# Chapter 5

'Where the hell are you?' Kate snapped, answering her phone. 'I rang you because I need you to get over to Selby's Garage with me ASAP.'

Hollis mumbled something about dropping his phone leaving Kate to wonder exactly where he'd dropped it and not really wanting the details. The important thing was that he was able to do as she'd asked.

'Look, I don't need to hear it,' she continued. 'It's her; it's Melissa Buckley. And Kailisa confirms murder. And rape. Meet me at the garage in half an hour. Can you do that?' She knew that her tone was borderline patronising but she wasn't used to any of her DCs messing up, least of all Hollis. She climbed into her Mini and set off in the direction of the town centre.

Selby's Garage occupied a large corner unit at the end of a street of terraced houses on the north side of Doncaster. Being only a ten-minute walk from the town centre, Kate wasn't surprised to see cars lined up two-deep in the yard with another two up on raised hydraulic lifts. Obviously business was good. She drove past the main entrance and pulled in on double yellow lines part way down the street watching for Hollis's Sportage in her rear-view mirror. She needed to talk to Ryan Buckley but she needed Hollis as a witness and a recorder. It wasn't going to be an easy interview and she needed a safe pair of hands to make notes and observe every nuance of the man's face and body. Now she was starting to wonder if Hollis had been such a good choice. Something was obviously bothering him. Kate had never seen him less than immaculate even after hours of night-time observation or a visit to a dirty crime scene, but his appearance and manner earlier had been a shocking contrast with the man that she thought she knew.

She'd also never seen Dan drink more than a couple of pints of bitter but she'd smelt alcohol on his breath this morning, which suggested he'd had a good skinful the previous night and his unshaven appearance and surly manner were worrying. If it had been O'Connor she would have shrugged it off; she knew that he liked a late night and his drinking prowess was legendary but her three DCs were usually early-to-bed, eager-beaver types.

Her phone rang. 'I'm behind you,' Hollis said, in his best pantomime villain voice.

Slipping the phone into the pocket of her jacket, Kate got out of the car and spotted Hollis about fifty yards away, close to the garage. She raised a hand in greeting and walked towards him, grabbing his arm and dragging him further down the street.

'We need to play this carefully,' she said, foregoing any form of greeting. 'The body's definitely Melissa Buckley and it looks like a brutal attack. According to Kailisa we're looking at a time of death which fits Buckley's story. We're also looking for the kill site because Kailisa thinks that she was dumped in the park after being left somewhere else for a couple of hours.'

Hollis's eyes lost focus as he processed the information. 'So he could have killed her at home and then rung round her friends before dumping the body?'

'He could have. Or she could have left for work exactly as he said and somebody else killed her.'

'Somebody she was meeting?'

'That's what we need to find out. I've not heard anything from Barratt yet about the car or her colleagues so we'll have to see what we can find out. Come on.'

She allowed Hollis to lead the way into the office area of the garage, relying on all the stereotypes about men and cars to get them the information that they needed. A young woman was sitting behind a desk which was almost completely swamped by manuals and piles of greasy paper. She glanced up at them, light glinting dangerously off her nose stud. 'Help you?'

Her hair was dyed a deep black and matched her eyeliner and nail polish. Red lips were a stark contrast in a Goth-girl-pale face and her black t-shirt was emblazoned with a CD cover for a band that Kate had never heard of.

Hollis showed his ID and explained that they were there to talk to Ryan Buckley while the woman's disinterested stare never wavered. All she was lacking was a mouthful of gum to snap at him. Eventually she turned in her seat, opened a glass partition in the wall behind her that led into the cavernous work area and yelled, 'Ryan! Coppers for you!'

*Not much chance of catching him by surprise,* Kate thought.

A large figure in grimy overalls appeared from beneath a Ford Ka. He glanced in their direction before muttering something to one of his colleagues who was in the process of removing something from beneath another car. Buckley got a nod in response and Kate recognised a boss-employee relationship in the gesture.

'Have you found her?' Buckley asked as soon as the door closed behind him, shutting out some of the sounds of electrical tools and too-loud Radio One.

'Is there somewhere we can speak in private?' Hollis asked the receptionist.

'Break room,' she said, pointing to a Portakabin standing beside one of the two huge workshop doors.

Buckley led the way, his overalls straining at the seams as he climbed the steps and ushered them into a box-like space kitted out with a sink, a fridge, a kettle and an assortment of mismatched chairs, most with overflowing stuffing or torn fabric. Every surface seemed to be covered with oil or grease, much of it obviously well-ingrained from years of dirty hands and overalls. There was a small, square coffee table in the middle of the space, covered in car magazines and an array of chipped mugs. The room smelt of men; of hard, physical work, sweat and an underlying odour of cigarettes, which obviously predated the smoking ban.

'Seat?' Buckley asked, pointing to the least offensive derelict armchair. Kate shook her head and leaned against the wall next to the door allowing Hollis to take the seat, which was too small for his long limbs. Buckley sprawled on a rickety office chair which was missing a wheel and had been repaired with what looked like a dog's rubber ball cut in half.

'Have you found Mel?' he asked again.

'We think so,' Kate said and for a second the man's face brightened until her tone registered.

'No.' He shook his head. 'I don't want to hear this.'

'Mr Buckley, Ryan,' Kate said gently. 'The body of a woman was found on Town Fields yesterday. She matches the description of your wife, including the scar and the moles on her back. We'll need you to formally identify the body but it's very likely to be her. I'm very sorry.'

She watched as the man in front of her seemed to implode. He drew his limbs inwards towards his core, hands over his face, elbows on knees, his huge bulk shuddering with shock and barely contained grief. Hollis turned to look at her – the question clear in his eyes. Was this man their murderer? Kate always liked to watch intently whenever she had to deliver news like this. She tried to assess the reaction, the initial response, and the first few words, to try to establish whether the recipient was faking. She didn't get that feeling from Ryan Buckley. The slow-motion curling in on himself reminded her of a baby hedgehog she'd once found as a child. It had tried to turn itself into the smallest ball possible for protection and comfort and Buckley seemed to be having a similar response, making himself a smaller target; bracing himself against any further blows from her or Hollis. And, unfortunately for him, there *was* more to come.

He looked up at Kate, eyes suddenly full of hope as if a new thought had just struck him. 'What was she doing on Town Fields? She went to work. Do you think it might be somebody else? Somebody who looks like Melissa?'

Tears magnified his blue eyes, contrasting starkly with his tear-darkened lashes.

'I'm sorry, Ryan. There's no real doubt. You gave us a really good description.'

His face went blank as though he hadn't heard or couldn't process her response.

'How?' he asked. 'How did she die?'

'At the moment we think she was murdered.'

He winced at the word, his head flinching back. 'That can't be right,' he said. 'Who'd want to kill Mel? It doesn't make any sense. It's probably not her.'

Kate took a deep breath. 'Ryan. We need somebody to identify the body; to confirm that it is Melissa. Do you think you can do that? Do you want me to contact somebody who can come with you?'

Buckley shook his head. 'No. It needs to be me. No point in upsetting her mam or her sister if it's probably not her. Where do I have to go?' He stood up and looked at the door as if he was expecting them to take him straight away.

'She's at the DRI, the Doncaster Royal Infirmary,' Kate said. 'But it probably won't be until tomorrow. I just wanted to let you know that we think we've found her because I knew that you were worried sick about your wife.'

He stared at her wide-eyed like a child eager to please a parent. 'I *was* worried sick. I rang round everybody I could think of. I tried to find her.'

Kate wasn't sure whether he was trying to convince himself or her so she let him continue.

'They all said no, they hadn't seen her. I know we'd had a row but she'd never stayed away that long before. I tried to find her. I really did.'

The tears were back, spilling down his cheeks, but he seemed oblivious to them, lost in a scenario where he was the hero desperately searching for his missing wife. He settled back into his chair and looked from Kate to Hollis.

'You married?' he asked. Hollis shook his head.

'Best thing I ever did, marrying Mel. Some of her mates told her that she was too good for me – probably true – but she never made me feel like that. She's always really interested in people, likes a natter with anybody. She was a Goth when I first knew her. Came in to pick up her mam's car and got chatting with Charley on reception about music. I came in with the keys and they were in their own little world. She had to pack all that in when she started on the trains though – they have a strict uniform policy. She…' He looked round as though he'd suddenly remembered where he was, and why. One hand drifted to the arm of the chair and his fingers began to peck aimlessly at the filthy velour.

'Ryan?' Kate squatted down in front of him and leaned in close. 'I know this is really difficult but we want to find whoever did this to Melissa. Is there anything that you can tell us, or anything that you think you should have already told us that might help?'

Silence. The man stared onto space, completely lost.

Kate's phone rang cutting through the stillness of the room like a siren. She fumbled it out of her pocket. Barratt. 'Ryan, I really need to take this call. If you think of anything please, please tell DC Hollis.'

She pushed open the door, and gratefully sucked in a lungful of fresh air. 'Barratt? Got anything?'

She trotted down the rickety wooden steps of the Portakabin and huddled against a high brick wall that protected one side of the property, listening as Barratt filled her in on what he'd learnt.

'Two things. First – Melissa Buckley wasn't rostered to work on Saturday, it was a day off and she'd booked it a week ago. Oh, and there's a staff locker room where the work clothes are kept so leaving home in her street clothes wasn't unusual.'

'What's the other thing?'

'Melissa's car. It's parked on one of the streets near Town Fields. Uniforms are knocking doors in the area as we speak to see if anybody saw her on Saturday but it's a busy spot – a large nursery for under-fives, a dentist, a couple of shops. They might get lucky, though. It might have been fairly quiet at the weekend – the nursery and the dentist are only open for a couple of hours in the morning.'

'Forensics checking out the car?'

'Yep. I rang it in to Raymond and he okayed it straight away. I knew you were at the PM and I didn't think it should wait until I could clear it with you.'

'No. You did the right thing. Where are you off to next?'

'I thought I'd have a look at where the car was found, see if anything jumps out at me.'

A sudden thought struck Kate. 'Matt, was the car found anywhere near where the body was discovered?'

'Nope. Opposite side of the fields.'

She'd been trying to imagine Buckley using Melissa's own car to dump the body and then simply abandoning the vehicle in a nearby street. It would have been sloppy, but very convenient. Or had Melissa been visiting whoever had killed her and they'd dumped her body as far away from their home as possible? Too many unknowns.

*** 

'Ryan, did Melissa know anybody who lived near Town Fields? A friend, a family member?' Kate asked as soon as she stepped back into the fug of the Portakabin.

He looked at her and frowned. 'Not that I know of. Why?'

'Was her dentist there?'

He shook his head. 'She goes to the one in Rossington, same as me.'

'And you don't have children?' she asked, thinking about Barratt's list of businesses in the area where the car was found.

Buckley froze. His facial expression hardened and his eyes narrowed. 'No. No, we don't have kids.'

There was something there. Kate wasn't sure what, but she'd managed to push a button without realising it. Something about the subject of kids had got Ryan Buckley very wary. 'Did you want kids, Ryan? Did Melissa?'

'Of course. Everybody wants kids, don't they?' He looked at Hollis for confirmation but the DC kept his face neutral.

'So you were trying?' Kate asked, thinking of the fake caesarean scar.

The tears were back. 'We were doing more than that. We were having IVF. That's what we argued about before she left. It wasn't working and she'd started talking about using a sperm donor. It was my fault, see? We wanted to keep trying with the IVF but it would have cost us a fortune. I said something about it being a waste of money and she took it all wrong. I didn't mean that having kids was a waste of money... I just didn't think it was going to work for us. She was furious. She stormed off and... and...' His words were muffled by hiccupping sobs.

Kate kept hearing Kailisa describe the wound in Melissa's abdomen as 'ritualistic'. Was this the answer? Buckley didn't want his wife using another man's sperm to get pregnant so he strangled her and then made the cut to rid himself of the idea that somebody else's baby was inside her?

'Ryan,' she said gently, 'I think we need to have another chat back at the police station.'

# Chapter 6

'Coffee?' Kate asked, plonking the cardboard cup on Cooper's desk. The younger woman smiled gratefully. Short and blonde with freckles, it would have been easy to mistake Sam Cooper for a teenager. She looked much younger than twenty-seven, but her intellect was way beyond her years and that was why Kate valued her input.

'Found anything?'

Cooper took a long swig of coffee before replying.

'Not a thing. I've managed to track her car on CCTV from where she joined the A638 to where she turned off Thorne Road. Time stamps show that she left home at around 10am and turned off Thorne Road about half an hour later. We know where her car ended up so the CCTV really doesn't add anything.'

Kate sipped her own coffee trying to make sense of Melissa Buckley's behaviour. There were a few commercial properties in the area but Ryan had already ruled out the nursery and the dentist. She must have been meeting somebody, or visiting one of the buildings in the streets around Town Fields but who and where?

'Okay. How about the car park for the sports facilities? Anything on that from the night that the body was left or the morning it was found?'

Cooper sighed and tapped her keyboard.

'Have a look,' she said, pushing her chair away from her desk so that Kate could see her monitor more clearly. 'Can't see much during the night as it's not lit apart from an outside light on the main changing block and that only lights up about ten square feet of car park.'

She tapped another key and the blurry darkness flickered and started to dissipate as dawn broke.

'There's Duncan Cawthorne,' she said, pointing at a figure climbing out of a large 4x4.

Kate watched as he removed cones, balls and bibs and left the car park, out of view of the camera. Sam sped up the footage until two police cars arrived.

'It gets a bit busier after this as people start to suss out that something's going on.'

A few people arrived and started to mill around the cars. Small groups, twos and threes, gradually forming larger groups whose members split off as others arrived. Nobody stood out. Nobody looked like they shouldn't be there. There were joggers, dog walkers and a couple with two small children and a football.

*Was he watching?* Kate wondered. *Standing in the crowd enjoying the chaos that he'd caused?* 'Thanks, Sam,' Kate said. 'Can you start digging into her phone records? I'll text you the details. And her bank account.'

In the corridor, Kate bumped into O'Connor who was slouching along with his hands in his jeans pockets and his head bowed, looking despondent. His shirt was wrinkled and his mop of red hair looked like he'd been outside in a high wind. Kate was often surprised by her DS's lack of interest in his own appearance, especially when compared to the two other men on her team.

'No luck, Steve?'

He glanced up at her, clearly startled to see her. 'Not a thing. Nobody can remember seeing anything suspicious. It sounds like there weren't too many girls out that night. Might still be a bit chilly.'

'So why the long face? Can't be the first time you've drawn a blank on a line of enquiry.'

He shook his head. 'It's not just that. There's been a bit of a shift of allegiances out there. Some of the regulars have moved on. There's somebody new sniffing around and I don't think it's good news.'

Kate understood O'Connor's concern. He spent a lot of time cultivating his contacts and even the slightest shift in loyalties and agreements could mean that he had to start again with new faces, new problems and new villains.

'I'm sure you'll suss it out,' Kate said. 'And while you're here, could you have a word with Sam. She's digging into the Buckleys' financial situation and you're good at spotting the dodgy stuff.'

He gave her a grin and pointed to the ceiling. 'Upstairs first,' he said. 'I'm starving. You can't deny a man his lunch.'

'Course not. Get Sam a burger as well – I bet she's not had anything since she came in this morning.'

Hollis was waiting for her in the observation room. He still looked rough but he gave her a smile and gestured towards the glass. 'He's been there for half an hour. I've checked with his boss and Buckley was definitely at work on Saturday when Melissa was last seen. Got in at around eight and stayed until just after one. I've sent somebody round to Melissa's sister to ask her if she or her mum can ID the body. Kailisa's finished so they can do it this evening. I thought it best to get it done just in case we need to keep him.'

Kate nodded her approval. Buckley's revelations about the IVF treatment had chimed with the fake caesarean wound and Kate wasn't fully convinced that Buckley wasn't the killer. Did he suspect that Melissa was having an affair or even possibly carrying another man's child? She studied the man sitting at the table in the next room. He seemed stronger than he did in the earlier interview, more determined. His head was raised and he was staring straight in front of him, the muscles in his jaw clenching and unclenching as he waited. He was certainly powerful enough to be their attacker but what was his motive?

'Right, let's go,' she grabbed an empty folder from the desk and marched down the corridor.

***

Buckley scowled up at Kate and Hollis as they entered the interview room. He'd agreed to accompany them to Doncaster Central but

Kate wasn't sure how he'd react when she cautioned him. She was surprised when he listened to the formulaic phrases dispassionately. He made no objection to the interview being recorded and didn't ask for legal representation.

'So, Ryan,' Kate said. 'Do you understand why you're here?'

'Because you're not doing your job properly?'

The belligerence was shocking after the pathos of his initial reaction to his wife's death. It was almost like he'd turned into a different person. She ignored his insult.

'Ryan, we need to ask you some more questions because of some things that were discovered at the post-mortem.'

He shook his head. 'How do you know it's even her? I'm supposed to be identifying her body.'

Hollis opened his mouth, presumably to let Buckley know that his sister-in-law and her mother had now been asked to perform that unpleasant task, but Kate silenced him with a shake of her head.

'We'll get to that later,' she said. 'I really need you to answer some questions about your IVF treatment.'

He screwed up his face in disbelief. 'What the hell has that got to do with what happened to my wife?'

'That's what we want to find out,' Kate said.

Buckley looked around the room, his eyes lingering on the mirrored glass on one wall. 'Am I under arrest? Because, if not, I don't have to be here, do I? You can't keep me here if I don't want to stay.'

'True,' Kate said. 'But, if you decide to leave, it might make me wonder why. We need your help and, if you had nothing to do with what happened to Melissa, there's no reason why you shouldn't co-operate. I understand that you're upset and I know that this is really difficult but I need to try to work out what happened to your wife.'

He tapped his teeth together nervously, an insect-like clicking, looking from Kate to Hollis, visibly trying to decide whether or not to run. Kate watched as his face relaxed; he'd clearly realised that staying was the more sensible course of action.

'Okay,' he said. 'But if I don't like what you're asking, I'll leave. Or you can arrest me and throw me in a cell. To be honest I'm not much bothered either way.'

He pushed his chair back slightly from the desk as though he wanted to create as much distance as possible between himself and their questions, then waited for Kate to continue.

'I want to know more about the IVF treatment, Ryan. Specifically how long you've been having it and where.'

'Why? What's that got to do with anything?'

'There are some injuries on the body we found which initially led us to believe that the woman might be pregnant,' Kate said, trying to make her tone as apologetic as possible. Buckley just stared at her.

'She wasn't,' Kate continued.

Buckley exhaled loudly.

'Would you have expected her to be?' she asked, gently. 'Did the last round of IVF work?'

He shook his head and lowered his eyes. 'None of it worked,' he admitted. 'Too many problems.'

'With you or her?' Hollis interjected. Kate was glad that he'd been the one to ask the question. Buckley might feel more comfortable admitting his fertility problems to another man and she hadn't been sure how to broach the subject without putting his back up again.

'I tell people it's me but really it's both of us,' Buckley muttered. 'She's only ever had irregular periods and my er… sperm… has low motility. Slow swimmers. I think it was more to do with me than her though.'

That poured cold water on Kate's theory that Melissa had been trying to get pregnant with another man. If she had problems too there was little likelihood of that happening so not much point in her trying.

'So you tried IVF? Was that your first course of action?'

He snorted derisively. 'Do you know how hard it is to get IVF on the NHS? We had to go through loads of rounds of AI, artificial insemination, before they'd even consider us. And then you get three goes and that's it. We'd had our three goes. Mel suggested that we go private. She'd found a clinic in Sheffield but it was five grand a time. We don't have that sort of money.'

'So that's what you argued about, on the day she left?' Kate prompted.

Buckley nodded miserably. 'I told her that I thought it was too much. That if it wasn't going to happen naturally then we could look at adoption but she wouldn't have it. She was determined to carry our child.'

Kate believed him. She'd never been in the same situation but she'd had a few friends who had been determined to have a child and who had been willing to do just about anything to get pregnant. Much as she loved her son, Ben, she'd never felt that all-consuming need to have a baby. She'd been happy when she'd found out that she was pregnant and would still do anything for her son but she genuinely couldn't claim a biological *need* to be a mother.

'I need you to go through events of last Friday again, Ryan,' Kate said. 'You argued and she slept in the spare room. Can you remember any details of the argument?'

Buckley shook his head. 'It was horrible. She said that she was going to withdraw money from our savings for more IVF and I tried to get her to stop and think about it. She took that as me trying to tell her that I wanted to give up. Called me a few choice names and blamed me for her not getting pregnant. She even said that she'd have been better off marrying somebody else. Somebody who was more of a man.'

'Did she mention anybody by name?'

Buckley shook his head. 'It was more general. It's not like there's a long list of ex-boyfriends to choose from. Not as far as I know. She made me feel like shit and then she walked away.'

'And you're sure that she was still at home when you left for work on Saturday?'

'I told you, she was still in her dressing gown. We didn't say much to each other but I could see that she was still mad at me.'

'And then what?' Kate prompted. 'You went to work?'

'Didn't really see much point in doing anything else.'

Kate was trying to work out the timeline. Buckley had been at work on Saturday morning at the time the CCTV footage showed Melissa's car being driven along Thorne Road; his colleagues had confirmed that he'd worked on Saturday morning until 12.30 and that he'd been there all the time apart from a 'brew break' at around 10am. But he could have left the car somewhere close to his work and then driven it across town while he was on his break. It would have only taken him fifteen minutes to drop the car off and walk back to work. They needed to pin down the details of his movements. Kate jotted a note to Hollis. A quick phone call could put Buckley in the clear. Hollis glanced at her instructions and left as Kate announced his departure for the tape. He was replaced by a police constable who stood by the door until Hollis returned.

The DC passed Kate a note.

*Breaks taken in break room. Two others present. No opportunity to move car.*

Another dead end. They had no reason to keep Buckley, let alone charge him with anything.

'Okay,' Kate said. 'I know I asked you earlier but have you any idea why Melissa's car turned up on a side street near Town Fields? Can you think of anybody who lives in the area that she might have met up with?'

'I've been thinking about that. When we used to go to the hospital, especially for the counselling sessions, Mel liked to park down there. She enjoyed the walk, said it gave her time to prepare and then time after the appointment to shake off the hospital smell. Could she have had an appointment that I didn't know about?'

*It was possible,* Kate thought. The car had been found less than ten minutes' walk from the DRI. Had Melissa been pursuing another avenue, exploring other options? If so, how had she met her killer? Unless it was somebody at the hospital.

'Ryan,' she said. 'I'm going to need the names and contact numbers of everybody that you and Melissa dealt with at the hospital. Doctors, consultants, counsellors, everybody you can remember. I'm going to request Melissa's medical records so hopefully there'll be plenty of information there. And I want to know about her social media activity. Was she on Facebook? Twitter? Instagram? I'll need passwords if you know them, or any suggestions. And you mentioned ex-boyfriends. Any names would be helpful.'

The man sitting across from her was much calmer than when they'd begun the interview. He'd watched intently as Hollis had made notes, keen that the DC hadn't missed anything but now he was sitting with his hands on the table and his head lowered.

'Where is she?' he asked.

'Melissa?'

He nodded and Kate saw tears spill from his chin onto the greasy denim of his jeans. She watched as they soaked in, adding yet another dark stain to the pattern of oil marks.

'At the DRI.'

'Can I see her?'

'I think we can arrange that,' Kate said. 'But it'll be tomorrow.'

'But it is her?'

'I'm certain that it is. The scar and the moles match exactly.'

'I'd better take somebody with me. I don't want that responsibility. What if it's not her, or I'm not sure? Can you imagine? I think I'd always have some doubts. Death can do funny things to your head. I remember when my dad died, it didn't seem real. Still doesn't sometimes.'

Kate let him ramble. He seemed to need some sort of release, some catharsis and his inane mumbling was calming him down. They had no reason to arrest him, no evidence that he'd done anything other than fight about money with his wife and if that was grounds for arrest she'd have to haul in half of Doncaster.

Gradually, Buckley seemed to run out of things to say, his posture corresponding to his tone as he grew quieter and seemed to shrink in on himself again. It was time to let him go. She stood up, allowing Hollis to tell him that he was free to go, and headed for the door.

***

'Well, what do you think?' Hollis asked as he followed her down the corridor.

'Gut feeling?'

Hollis nodded eagerly, his blond fringe bobbing as he inclined his head.

'It's not him. There's no motive. He was at work on Saturday when Melissa was last seen, and it's not just his word – we've got her car on CCTV and he couldn't have been the one driving it.'

'Doesn't mean that Melissa *was*.'

Kate shrugged. 'If it wasn't Melissa Buckley in the car then it could have been anybody. But it wasn't her husband because he was at the garage. You've just checked his alibi and it's watertight.'

'Now what?'

'Now, we need to try to work out what the hell she was doing in the Town Fields area on Saturday. And if she went to the hospital, what for and who did she see there? And I think we'll probably need to talk to Melissa's family.'

*I'd spotted the ambulance as I was finishing my early morning jog and I deliberately altered my route so I could get a closer look. The car park was full of vehicles; liveried police cars and white vans with the South Yorkshire Police logo more discreetly placed on the drivers' doors, as though they didn't want to be obvious about why they were there. I knew though. They'd found her.*

*It was what I wanted, of course, but the reality gave me a slight frisson of fear. I was vulnerable now. If I'd made a single mistake I'd be caught. But I hadn't made a mistake. Everything had been exactly as I'd planned. Perfect.*

*I joined the growing crowd of onlookers, careful to stay outside the range of the CCTV camera, and asked an elderly man what had happened. I watched as a stretcher was removed from the rear of one of the vans and carried towards the display site. That's how I thought about it – the display site. I'd left her there so that she would be found quickly and my handiwork, my message, wouldn't become corrupted.*

*She'd been so trusting. Poor little Melissa. I wasn't sure exactly when I'd first planned to kill her but the resemblance to the other one must have played a huge part. I almost did a double-take the first time we met but, when I looked a bit more closely, the similarities were superficial. Melissa was younger, more alive somehow and less desperate. At first.*

*It had happened suddenly but I couldn't recall the exact circumstances. One minute I'd been pretending to pay attention while she spoke to me and the next I was thinking about wrapping my hands round her neck. Once the image was in my mind I couldn't shake it. Every time I saw her all I could think about was strangling her. And then my fantasies became more detailed. I wanted to cut her as well. To show her that she was no different from everybody else; she didn't deserve special treatment.*

*She'd looked stunning that morning. That was the other thing. She had so much going for her. A decent man, a steady job, close friends and family and she was a looker. I bet that she'd been popular at school and had taken it all for granted. So when I'd seen how immaculate her make-up was and how carefully she'd styled her hair I'd known that this was going to be the day.*

*The shock in her eyes as I'd grabbed her was almost funny. They did a strange popping out thing as though she was a surprised cartoon character. And then her face had started to go red and I'd smelt coffee as she gasped for breath. I'd watched her face until she'd lost consciousness then I'd ripped off her trousers and knickers. She was still alive. Barely but still there. I continued squeezing and pounded into her until I was sure that she was dead. Only then did I feel release.*

*The blade had been a beautiful pale blue in the hazy light of mid-morning. It was flawless, sharp and mesmerising. I had no hesitation at all, it felt like somebody was guiding my hand, steadying it. The flesh felt odd, waxy, even though I knew that I must be imagining it because she'd only been dead for a few minutes. But that didn't put me off. I carved my signature smile into her belly then knelt back to admire my handiwork.*

# Chapter 7

She was waiting for him again the next day as he left via the back door in search of the pool car that Kate had ordered. After they'd allowed Ryan Buckley to leave the previous day they'd got caught up in phone interviews and only now had time to finally talk to Melissa Buckley's mother and sister. This time Suzanne didn't waste any time on pleasantries, looking him up and down like he was something nasty that she'd stepped in.

'Got anything for me?' she sneered and he could see that she already knew that he wouldn't co-operate.

'Course not,' he said, pushing past her. 'I told you yesterday that I'm not playing your stupid games. If you want money get a real job and earn some like the rest of us.'

She snorted in amusement. 'Call this a real job? Hounding innocent folk and not managing to catch any of the real villains. You're all the same. Can't believe that my son turned out to be filth.'

He rounded on her, his face so close to hers that he could smell the alcohol on her breath. 'Don't ever call me that. I'm *not* your son.'

She didn't move. Instead she let him have his say and then leaned in even closer. He could see make-up caked into the lines on her face, fooling nobody, and the different shades of her hair, unnatural blonde after a half inch of pale grey which dated her like the lines in a cut tree trunk. 'Oh, you're mine all right,' she spat. 'But who else made his contribution? Isn't that what you'd like to know? Who shot his load in my tight little teenage twat and landed me with you? It might not just be my genes you have to contend with; maybe you're grown from bad seed on both sides.'

Dan shook his head in disgust. 'I don't care. He's probably just another sad sack of shit that I'm better off without.'

He turned back to the car park and started to walk away, not trusting himself to be physically close to her any more. He needed to get away from her poison and her spite. And he needed to be well away from her when Kate came out of the door; he couldn't begin to imagine how his boss would react to seeing this creature that claimed to be his parent. Risking a glance back at her he tried to assess her with a stranger's eyes. She looked like exactly what she was; an ageing whore. Her denim skirt was too short, showing ladders in her tights which were climbing up her thighs and her vest top did nothing to conceal her stick-thin arms and scrawny shoulders. The fake tan didn't extend much beyond her neck giving her an odd two-tone appearance, as if her lower body was in shadow and her head was in sunlight.

'He's a copper,' Suzanne shouted, as he turned to walk away. At first Dan thought she was talking about him to somebody else – but then he realised what she meant and stopped dead.

'Thought you'd enjoy that,' she cawed behind him. 'Must be his DNA in you not mine. Nobody in my family would ever think about doing what you do.'

Dan took a deep breath and turned to face her. 'Are you trying to tell me that my father is a police officer?' he snarled.

Suzanne grinned. 'Not just an ordinary copper. He's high up. Much higher than you.'

Hollis shook his head, disgusted with her lies. 'Bullshit. If he's so high up why aren't you bothering him about money instead of me? I'm sure, whoever he is, he'd be happy to pay to see the back of you.'

Suzanne's face cracked into a wide grin. 'Why do you think I'm here? I thought I might bump into you, but I've got other fish to fry.' She winked at him and started to walk back towards the door, the tapping of her heels drilling into his brain like a migraine. What was she saying? That his father worked at Doncaster Central?

'You're lying!' he shouted after her. 'You're making it up to get to me.' And it was working. He was standing in the work car park shouting at a middle-aged woman. Christ, he hoped that Kate was still busy upstairs; she couldn't see him like this.

Suzanne turned back to him, raised her shoulders in an exaggerated Gallic shrug and gave him a tight smile. 'Am I? You're the copper – prove it.'

'I don't need to,' Hollis said. 'Because I don't give a toss. Stand there all day if you like. I've got work to do.'

He walked towards a pair of dark grey Audis, pressing the button on the key he'd been given and watching for flashing lights to indicate which car he'd been allocated. The one on the right. He grasped the handle of the driver's door and risked another glance at Suzanne as he eased it open. She'd gone. Either she'd been lying about waiting for somebody else or she'd given up. Unless... perhaps somebody had seen her and let her into the building. Or she'd met up with whoever she'd been waiting for and he'd walked her round the corner out of the way. Either way, there was little chance of Kate bumping into her.

He dug his phone out of his pocket and texted his boss the registration number of the car and then settled into the leather seat to wait. The visit to Melissa Buckley's mother and sister was a formality really, to see if either of them could add anything more to what was still a very sketchy impression of Melissa's life. He'd managed to contact the third friend on the list that Ryan had given him. Ellie was on holiday in Gran Canaria and had left her phone switched off for the first day so that she could 'chill'. He hadn't told her about the body, just that Melissa was missing but Ellie had seemed genuinely shocked by the news. She knew about the IVF and didn't have a bad word to say about Ryan Buckley despite being privy to some of Melissa's rants about him. Hollis actually wondered if Ellie had a bit of a thing for her friend's husband. The other two names that Buckley had jotted down after the first interview had yielded nothing.

This wasn't a visit that he was looking forward to. He knew that Kate valued his insight and his compassion but he was feeling neither insightful nor compassionate at the moment. If he could only think of a way to get rid of Suzanne, his life would get back into its regular groove, but he couldn't seem to get her out of his mind. When he tried to sleep, her face dominated his thoughts and her words seemed to echo around the cavities of his skull; so he drank. It started as a couple of beers but last night he'd polished off a whole bottle of wine. And still it wasn't enough.

She had information about him that nobody else did and he was trying not to let it bother him. What did it matter if he never knew the identity of his biological father? He couldn't have wished for better adoptive parents so why should he care? Except he did. He had always felt incomplete, even within the security of a loving family, he'd always wondered where he came from. He remembered Suzanne because she'd been around when he was growing up, but when he thought about his father, all he saw was snowy static like a badly tuned television set. It wasn't just a blank, it was something hard to focus on and headache-inducing.

Now she was trying to tell him that his father was a police officer. Why would she do that? To get under his skin probably; to taunt him and laugh at his discomfort. But a small part of him was curious. Could she have met somebody on the police force when she was seventeen and working as a prostitute? Somebody who might have taken advantage of her, or even been a regular client? He thought about the men who worked in various roles in the building. It would have to be somebody who was in their fifties at least and, as a lot of long-serving officers tended to retire before they were sixty, there weren't many candidates that he could think of. There was a desk sergeant who might be the right age – Hollis couldn't remember his name – and one of the custody officers. There were a couple of superintendents who were coming up to retirement and there were probably at least a few older officers in traffic. It might be somebody even higher up in the food chain; he really had no idea.

He glanced in the side mirror and saw the door of the police station open. Kate. He needed to clear his head and focus on the task ahead; it wasn't fair to interview grieving family members if he wasn't a hundred per cent committed to helping them. And then another movement drew his attention. The DI was holding the door open for somebody – a man who was going back inside the building.

Suddenly Hollis was struggling for breath as a memory punched him in the gut. Suzanne had seen Raymond walking across the car park and had frozen *before* he'd told her to duck down in her seat. The DCI was in the right age range and he'd been in his office when Dan had left. Why had he suddenly popped outside at the same time that Suzanne had disappeared? He shook his head trying to clear it of the suspicion that was threatening to overwhelm him. Was DCI Raymond his father?

# Chapter 8

'What's up with you?' Kate asked as she plonked herself on the passenger seat of the Audi and closed the door. 'You look like a wet weekend in Cleethorpes.'

Hollis gave her a ghost of a smile and started the engine. She studied his face in profile as he seemed to be making a point of not looking at her: checking his mirrors, looking behind him as he pulled out and then studying the traffic before he eased them onto the main road.

'Seriously, Dan, what's up? You've not been yourself for a few days now. I'm going to keep asking until you tell me something. You seem to stink of booze every other morning and I don't know when you last had a haircut but I think it's overdue. It's not like you. I'm worried.'

He still refused to look at her so she took her phone out of her pocket and started to check her emails. If he wasn't going to tell her then she wasn't going to pretend that everything between them was normal. Two could play the not talking game. Silence was a tactic that they often used in interviews: most people had the urge to fill it with something. But she knew that Hollis would see straight through her attempt to get him to talk.

'Where to?' he asked eventually.

'Thorpe. Crosslands Estate. Melissa's mum and sister should be back from the hospital.' She kept her answers brief, terse, hoping that he'd break the tension when he realised where they were going. Thorpe, and especially the Crosslands Estate, held a lot of memories for both of them. Kate had grown up there, leaving during the miners' strike of the 1980s when her father had moved the family further south. More recently the estate had been the scene of a series of child murders which had almost cost Kate her life and then a case involving a suspicious 'mercy' killing. It seemed like she couldn't escape the place for long; it always drew her back.

'Which street?'

'I'll direct you when we get there,' Kate said as Hollis reached out to programme the satnav. She knew those streets as well as she knew the rooms in her flat and probably a lot better than any GPS device. She knew the feel of the concrete pavements against tender knees, the crunch of the cinder paths and overpowering smell of sun-warmed privet hedges.

They drove through Balby and Warmsworth in silence, Kate allowing Hollis time to decide if he really didn't want to talk or just couldn't decide how to tell her whatever was on his mind.

As they reached the water tower at the end of Warmsworth 'drag' he slowed down and turned his head towards her. 'Okay,' he said. 'There is something wrong but it's personal, family stuff. I know I'm a bit distracted at the moment and I know I've let a few things slide but I'm working on it and trying to sort it out. If it gets in the way of the job then I'll tell you and you can make me take some personal time or something. I don't want time off and I don't think I need it but it's not something I can talk about.'

*At least it's a start,* Kate thought, *an admission that things aren't all right.* She had to respect Hollis's right to his privacy. Even though their relationship bordered on friendship, she was his boss and she couldn't get too involved in his personal misery, whatever the cause. He didn't talk about his family much. She knew that he was an only child and that his parents lived on the outskirts of Chesterfield but that was all. She'd decided that if he wanted her to know anything else that he'd tell her but he hadn't been any more forthcoming and there wasn't much she could do about that except allow him his privacy.

'Next left then second right,' she said, as they approached the estate. She'd let the matter lie – for now.

***

Rachel Stead lived in a corner house two streets away from where Kate had grown up. Probably bought from the council in the 1980s, it was a sturdy brick-built semi with a long strip of garden down one side and a small paved driveway at the front, currently occupied by a silver Nissan Micra. Kate eased past the car and knocked on the door without waiting to see if Hollis was following her.

The woman who opened the door looked so much like Melissa Buckley that Kate hesitated for a second before introducing herself and Dan. There was no way that this woman was Melissa's mother, she was barely into her twenties, and she confirmed this by introducing herself as Bridget, Melissa's sister. She led them down a bright hallway to the kitchen at the back of the house where an older woman was sitting at the table, hands wrapped around a mug of tea. In her fifties, Rachel Stead bore little resemblance to her daughters. Her closely cropped cap of grey hair may have been dark at some point but it was impossible to tell and, as she raised her face to look at the two police officers, Kate noted that her eyes were blue rather than the deep brown of her daughters.

'I'll put the kettle on,' Bridget announced, gesturing to the empty chairs at the table. 'Have a seat.'

Kate watched as Hollis folded his long legs under the table then sat down next to him. Rachel had put down her mug and was rolling a tissue between her fingers, turning it into a sausage shape and then nipping off the narrow ends before spreading it out and starting again.

'You understand why we're here, Mrs Stead?' Kate checked.

The woman nodded. 'You want to ask about our Melissa.' Her gaze remained fixed on her hands.

'I know that this is really difficult.'

A mug slammed on the counter top behind Kate and she turned to see Bridget scowling at her, her unmade-up face pink with anger.

'What's bloody difficult is sitting here making endless cups of tea while whoever killed my sister is still out there,' Bridget said.

'And I doubt that there's anything that my mam or me can tell you to help you find this fucking murderer!'

Rachel dropped the tissue that she'd been squeezing and glanced up at her daughter. Her face was narrow and pinched-looking with deep wrinkles carved down the sides of her mouth. Kate knew that she was roughly the same age as Melissa's mother but the other woman looked at least a decade older as she admonished her younger daughter.

'Bridget! I won't have you using language like that in my house. The police are here to help.'

Bridget continued to glare at Kate and then she sneered, her pierced upper lip curling towards her nose in disgust. 'Here to help,' she muttered, turning back to the kettle and the mugs.

Kate noted her skinny black jeans, held up with a thick, black leather belt and the ripped dark T-shirt which exposed a sleeve of tattoos on her left arm. It looked like both girls had gone through a rebellious phase: Melissa with her multiple piercings and Bridget with her Goth clothes and tattoos. Bridget still needed time to grow out of hers, it seemed.

'I saw her, you know,' Rachel was saying. 'I went to see our Melissa at the hospital yesterday evening. Ryan was already there. He said he'd been questioned again but you'd let him go. He'd not been in to see her when I got there so we went in together. I knew it was her as soon as I saw her. She didn't take after me; neither of them did. Favoured their dad. He was dark-haired like them. Ryan was in bits when he saw her. He's a waste of space in a lot of ways but he really loved our Melissa.'

Hollis took out his notebook and pencil as Bridget plonked mugs of tea in front of them. Kate realised that she hadn't asked how they liked it and had obviously decided that weak and milky was a decent offering. Kate asked her to sit down.

'Before we start,' she said. 'I'm really sorry about Melissa. I can't even begin to understand how you're both feeling but I want you to know that we're doing everything we can to find out who did this to Melissa and to bring them to justice. We're following a number of lines of enquiry including trying to trace her movements from Saturday. If you know anything about where she might have gone after she left home, it would be a good idea to tell us.'

The two women exchanged blank looks.

'No idea,' Bridget said, taking a sip of her tea. Kate noticed that her fingernails were well shaped and painted a glossy black. 'We've talked about it but nothing comes to mind. If she wasn't going to work or meeting one of her friends then we're as clueless as you seem to be.'

The antagonism was back in her tone and a challenge flashed in her clear brown eyes.

'We spoke to Ryan,' Kate continued. 'He said he thought that she'd gone to work, but we found out that she wasn't rostered to work on Saturday.'

More blank looks. They had no idea where Melissa had been, that much was obvious. Time to try a different line of questioning.

'Did you know that Melissa and Ryan were having IVF?' Kate asked.

Rachel smiled enthusiastically. 'They'd been trying for a baby for ages,' she said, her face suddenly much more animated as she thought about the possibility of grandchildren. 'They'd been through some treatment that hadn't worked.'

'AI,' Bridget interjected.

'Aye, that was it. Then they started trying this IVF. Spent ages at the hospital; appointment after appointment. Turned out that there was something not quite right with both of them. Funny, I'd have put money on it being Ryan. Thought Melissa would take after me. If we didn't take precautions, Pete only had to look at me and I'd fall pregnant.'

'Mum!' Bridget protested.

Rachel coloured as she realised what had taken her off topic. 'So, yes we knew all about it.'

'And you knew that they'd gone as far as they could with the NHS?'

Rachel nodded unhappily. 'They were going to have to pay if they wanted another try. I told them that I'd help if I could, but I've not got much. Most of what Pete left me went into this house because the girls were grown up by then.' She looked round the kitchen possibly regretting spending money on home décor when it could have gone towards providing the next generation of her family. Next to her, Bridget rolled her eyes.

'I think it just wasn't meant to be,' Rachel continued. 'I talked to Melissa about her other options, adoption, fostering, even offered to be her surrogate but she was hell-bent on having her own child. It was all she ever talked about.'

'And what about Ryan?' Kate asked. 'Was he as keen?'

The two women exchanged a glance that Kate couldn't read.

'He was keen,' Rachel said. 'But Melissa told me that he didn't want to spend a fortune on a private clinic. They'd argued about it a few times. I can sort of see his point – it's not like they had much money. That house cost them a fortune. Paid over the odds, I think, but Melissa had her heart set on it. Ended up with a fairly big mortgage.'

*Interesting*, Kate thought. Rachel was painting a picture of Melissa as being somebody who was single-minded and used to getting her own way. What had Ryan's role been in all this? Did he just go along with her for a quiet life?

'Did she arrange a private clinic? Or private counselling?'

Both women shook their heads.

'They'd only just finished at the DRI,' Bridget said. 'They were still talking about it, trying to decide what to do next.'

Hollis looked up from his notebook. 'But, is it possible that Melissa had gone behind her husband's back and arranged something else? Even if she was just exploring her options?'

Kate could have kicked him. It was the wrong question at the wrong time and she could see by the way Rachel's face suddenly closed down that he'd effectively ended the interview.

'Are you asking if my sister was deceitful?' Bridget asked, scowling at the DC. 'Mel loved Ryan and wanted to have a baby with him. They were in it together. Why would she go behind his back?'

Hollis smiled, seemingly oblivious to the sudden change in atmosphere. 'I'm just asking whether she might have taken matters into her own hands and made an appointment that her husband wasn't aware of.'

'So you're saying that she deserved this because she went behind Ryan's back?'

Hollis held his hands up in front of him, palms out. 'Of course not. But we need to know where she went on Saturday.'

'And you think what… that she might have been seeing somebody else? Trying to get pregnant with another man and then pass the kid off as Ryan's?'

It was a possibility that they had discussed but it had no place in this interview and Kate was horrified that Hollis had managed to plant the seeds of that idea in the minds of Melissa's mother and sister.

'Look, there's nothing else that we can tell you,' Rachel said, standing up. 'We don't know where she went on Saturday. She loved her husband and she was a good person. She's the *victim* here, *not* the one to blame.'

'We know that, Mrs Stead,' Kate said, desperately trying to repair the damage. 'What my colleague is suggesting is that, out of frustration, Melissa might have explored the private medicine option without consulting her husband. Just getting the facts. She might have wanted to know all the details before she presented them to Ryan.'

Rachel just stared at them; the damage was done. There was nothing to be gained from continuing the interview. Much better to leave the family to their grief.

\*\*\*

'What the fuck was that?' she asked Hollis as soon as they were back in the car. He hunched over and put his head on the steering wheel.

'I know,' he mumbled. 'I'm sorry. We didn't seem to be getting very far so I wanted to move things along. It was the wrong call.'

'It was fucking disastrous,' Kate said. 'What's wrong with you? You're one of the most sensitive interviewers I've seen and you go and do something as stupid as that. Do I need to take you off this case? Because I will. Your head's not in this at the moment and, whatever's going on, it's not as important as finding out who killed Melissa Buckley.'

He leaned back in his seat and closed his eyes.

'It's my mum,' he said. 'She's back.'

Kate stared at him, baffled.

'Where's she been?'

'Prison.'

'I thought she was a librarian in Chesterfield? How did she end up in prison?' Hollis didn't talk much about his family but Kate was fairly sure that she'd remembered this detail correctly. She couldn't imagine what a librarian could have done to warrant a custodial sentence.

He raised a hand and wiped it across his face, pinching his finger and thumb into his eyes as though he'd got a headache.

'My biological mum. I'm adopted. My adoptive parents are the most decent people you could ever wish to meet but the woman who gave birth to me is a nightmare.'

'In what way?'

'She's trying to blackmail me,' Hollis said, his voice trembling. 'She wants money for a flat. If I don't get it for her she's threatening to tell you and probably Raymond that she's my mother. She thinks that I can't stand the embarrassment.'

'Well you obviously can,' Kate said. 'You just told me.'

Hollis sighed. 'There's more. This morning she told me that if I didn't get her the money then she'd ask my father. My biological father. I don't know who he is – she won't say – but I think it might be somebody we work with.'

Kate checked her watch. They needed to get back to Doncaster Central and liaise with the rest of the team but she wanted to hear

Dan's story. Now he was finally talking to her, she could at least listen to what he had to say.

'I'll drive,' she said, opening the door. 'You need to tell me exactly what's been going on.'

They swapped sides and Kate started the engine.

'It gets worse,' Hollis said.

'Go on.'

'I think my real father might be DCI Raymond.'

'Shit,' Kate said, pulling away from the curb. She was starting to understand why Dan had been looking such a mess lately.

# Chapter 9

The grey sky hung over Doncaster like the threat of Armageddon as Kate steered the car back into Doncaster Central car park. The humidity had increased and the air felt alive with static electricity.

'Looks like we're in for a thunder storm,' she said as she locked the car and followed Hollis to the back door of the police station. He mumbled something inaudible and Kate, behind him, sighed heavily. The drive back from Thorpe had given the DC just enough time to fill her in about the details of his birth mother and her recent involvement in his life.

Kate had no idea what to make of Suzanne's story that Hollis's father was a high-ranking police officer but she could see the effect it was having on her colleague as he yanked the door open and jogged up the stairs. He'd gone from despondently slouching in the passenger seat of the car to a tight ball of anger which seemed as likely to break as the coming storm.

In the team office, O'Connor was conspicuous by his absence, but Cooper was tapping on her keyboard and Barratt was swinging on his chair as he spoke to somebody on the phone. He glanced up as Kate approached and stuck a finger in the air indicating that he needed a minute before he could speak to her.

She sat at her own desk and logged on to her computer to check her email. Two from Raymond asking for progress updates. She glanced at his office door. He was at his desk, on the telephone, his free hand karate-chopping the air as he spoke. Kate studied the lines of his newly slim face and the shape of his head. Was there a hint of Dan Hollis about the jaw and the hairline? She wasn't sure, and it certainly wouldn't have crossed her mind if Dan hadn't mentioned it. It seemed extremely unlikely but Kate knew how Dan could get once a thought had lodged in his brain. Normally she appreciated his terrier-like tenacity but this was going to eat him alive if he allowed it to dominate his thoughts.

There was an email from Sam Cooper about Melissa Buckley's phone records which Kate opened and skimmed but she decided that she'd be better off having Sam explain her findings. The numbers and allocations didn't mean much to her.

'Sorry about that,' Barratt said, spinning his chair 180 degrees so that he was facing her. 'Preliminary forensics on Melissa's car. There's nothing odd so far, apart from the fact that we don't know where the key is as her handbag's missing.'

'Thanks,' Kate said, trying to hide her disappointment. She'd been anticipating fibres or maybe an unusual footprint on the mat in front of the passenger seat but life was never that straightforward. She could always hope though.

'Sam, talk me through what you've got.'

Cooper grabbed a pile of papers from her cluttered desk top and handed them to Kate. 'Bank statements corroborate Buckley's account of their finances. They weren't hard up but going private for IVF would have really stretched them, especially if it didn't work first time. They have a joint account and both pay their wages in. She has an ISA with a few grand in it, he claims to have no savings and I've found no reason to doubt him.' She paused, grabbed the bottle of water next to her keyboard and took a swig as the others waited patiently.

'Phone records are mostly unsurprising. Calls to Ryan, her mum, her sister, work, her friends...'

She was building up to something – Kate could tell – the drink had been a nervous tic to try to draw attention from herself or to give her time to prepare for the reaction of the others when she did the big reveal. Never comfortable in the spotlight, Sam had a number of mechanisms for deflecting the focus but sometimes what she had to say was just too important.

'There is one anomaly in her phone history,' Sam continued. 'There's a number that I haven't been able to trace.'

'How come?' Barratt asked. Sam's forensic IT skills were legendary and it was rare to hear her admit defeat.

'It's an unregistered mobile.'

'Have you tried ringing it?' Hollis suggested. Cooper gave him a *duh!* look.

'It's switched off, goes to generic voicemail. I haven't left a message, just in case.'

Cooper had done exactly the right thing. If this number was connected to Melissa's killer it would be unwise to let him know that he was the focus of police attention.

'Okay, we need to ask Ryan and Melissa's friends and family if they recognise the number. What about CCTV from the hospital on the day Melissa went missing? Anything?'

Sam shook her head. 'The DRI won't release footage from inside the hospital, we might have to get a warrant. There's a camera in the car park which shows part of the path to the main entrance and a traffic camera a bit further along Thorne Road that shows part of the pavement leading to the hospital. O'Connor looked at the first and I did the second. Nothing there. If she went to the hospital that morning then she dodged both of those but there are a couple of other ways she could have approached so this isn't conclusive.'

'Have you rung the IVF clinic to see whether she had an appointment that day? Are they even open on a Saturday?'

'They are – ten till three. They won't tell me, at least not over the phone. Patient confidentiality. Again, we might need a warrant to access her records.'

'She's dead,' Kate said, stating the blatantly obvious. 'They should co-operate. I think I'd better get over there. Face-to-face might yield better results.'

She looked around at her team. Melissa Buckley had been dead for three days and they were no nearer to finding out what had happened to her. Spirits were still fairly high though, despite their lack of progress.

'Barratt, with me to the DRI. Sam, ring round Melissa's friends and family and see if anybody knows who that phone number belongs to. And keep digging into her financials. There might have been another account, try under her maiden name.'

'What about me?' Hollis asked.

'Go back to Town Fields. Have a look around. You've got a good eye for anything unusual. See what strikes you.'

Frowns of bewilderment all round from her team. She hadn't admitted as much but Kate had effectively given Hollis the afternoon off.

***

Kate dropped Barratt off at the main hospital entrance, sending him inside to pursue CCTV footage from Saturday morning in the hope that whoever was in charge might be more open to persuasion face-to face. The Doncaster Fertility Clinic was situated in the grounds of the Doncaster Royal Infirmary but was separate from the main hospital and had its own parking area. A red-brick building, it looked like it owed more to Doncaster's Victorian industrial heritage than to the utilitarian 1960s concrete structure that was its neighbour.

Kate parked as close to the entrance as she could and tried to imagine what brought people like Ryan and Melissa Buckley here. It wasn't something that she had experienced personally. She'd always been sure that she wanted children but, after Ben's birth, Garry, her ex-husband had seemed disinterested and distant. Kate had made the decision for both of them that one child was enough and, in retrospect, it had been a sound choice. Garry had had his first affair when Ben was three years old. Blaming the pressures of work, parenthood and Kate's long hours with Cumbria Police he'd begged for forgiveness without really accepting responsibility. Kate had tried to forgive but the trust was broken and she could never quite manage to forget the brutal impact of such a betrayal. The second affair was with a teaching assistant at the school where Garry worked as a PE teacher. This one had been short-lived and apparently traumatic for Garry. Kate had listened to his sob story with antagonism rather than sympathy but had stayed in the family home for her son who idolised his father.

Garry was now living with a woman half his age and they had a toddler. Kate couldn't help but feel a little bit sorry for the woman but, in a way, she was grateful that Garry had been taken off her hands. And she would always be glad that they hadn't tried for more children in an attempt to paper over the cracks in their marriage. Ben had a baby brother and Kate was free to get on with her own life. She regretted the years when that life barely included her son but now, about to finish his second year at Sheffield University, Ben was closer to her – literally and emotionally.

The building looked even more like a Victorian mansion as Kate approached and trotted up three gritstone steps to a porch tiled in terracotta and black chevrons. She studied the door, half expecting to see a bell pull next to it but, instead, a handwritten sign told her that the 'Door sticks – push hard'. She smiled at the irony of the instruction on the door of a fertility clinic before placing her hand on the brass door knob and giving a firm shove.

She'd overestimated the amount of force needed to open the door and almost stumbled as she tripped across the threshold, much to the amusement of a receptionist who smirked at Kate's dramatic entrance.

'Can I help you?' the receptionist asked, trying to hide her smile.

'Yes,' Kate said with a grin. 'I'm looking for my dignity.'

The receptionist shook her head. 'Sorry about that. A lot of people read the sign and end up coming in like a SWAT team. Do you have an appointment?'

Kate reached into her pocket for her warrant card. 'I don't. But I'd like to speak to whoever's in charge, if that's possible.'

The smile disappeared as the woman studied Kate's ID. 'Can I ask what this is about?'

She looked up at Kate, obviously trained to put clients at ease but clearly uncomfortable with the situation. She was young, probably mid-twenties with long blonde hair swept back into a tidy pony tail. Her make-up was slightly overdone for work but Kate could see the tiny crater marks of teenage acne beneath her foundation, perhaps explaining the excessive coverage. Her green eyes were curious but wary as her hand hovered over the telephone next to the keyboard on her desk.

'I'd like some information about a couple who were patients here. It's in regard to an ongoing investigation so I really can't discuss the details.'

'I'm not sure that anybody would be able to help,' the woman said. 'All our *client* information is strictly private.'

'If I could just speak to whoever is in charge,' Kate persisted, 'I'm sure that I could get the information that I need and be on my way.'

The receptionist glanced at her computer screen and tapped her keyboard. 'The centre director, Mr Beresford, is in a meeting at the moment. If you could come back later…'

Kate had had enough. 'I'm sorry,' she said, her tone contradicting her words. 'You obviously don't understand. I'm involved in a murder enquiry and there may be a connection to this facility. If you could inform Mr Beresford that I'm here I'm sure that he'd rather answer my questions than be faced with three members of my team and a warrant to search each and every file in the building.'

She wasn't sure that she'd be able to get a warrant that quickly but it sounded impressive and the receptionist obviously agreed because she'd picked up the phone and started to frantically punch in numbers. Kate stepped away from the desk, pretending not to listen as the woman apologised to whoever was on the other end of the phone and then dropped her voice to little more than a whisper. The words 'police', 'murder' and 'warrant' were clearly audible and Kate allowed herself a smug smirk – her bluster seemed to have worked.

'Mr Beresford will be with you shortly,' the receptionist said, coldly. She was obviously irritated that her authority had been undermined. 'If you'd like to take a seat…'

The woman pointed to a huddle of chairs grouped around a bay window, intimate and unobtrusive. Kate plonked herself down on the seat closest to the reception desk, stretched out her legs and crossed them at the ankles, hoping to give the impression that she was willing to wait, but not for too long.

Less than five minutes later, a door to her left opened and a figure stepped through. Over six feet tall, lean but muscular like a marathon runner, Beresford was an imposing figure. His dark hair was smoothed back from his forehead revealing a prominent widow's peak and his face was clean shaven. He raised perfectly shaped eyebrows at the receptionist who inclined her head in Kate's direction. Beresford extended one improbably long arm as he approached, hand fully extended to shake Kate's.

'Edward Beresford. I manage the facility. I understand you'd like to speak to me.' His tone and expression were as formal as a character from a Georgian period drama. Kate tried not to wince as her fingers were crushed in an excessively hard grip which told her exactly how much he didn't appreciate being dragged from his meeting. Beresford's dark suit and crisp white shirt oozed stature and authority; he was clearly a man used to being in charge.

'Could we go somewhere private to talk?' Kate asked.

Beresford studied her for a second as though her request was the most outlandish thing he'd ever heard, then his face creased into a smile which failed to reach his eyes. 'Of course,' he said and led the way into a short hallway and then up a flight of steps. The Victorian mansion theme didn't extend beyond the reception area, Kate noticed. The carpet in the hallway and on the stairs was industrial grey and the walls were white – obviously intended to scream 'clinic!' at clients who might have been duped into thinking that they were in a plush hotel. The only indication of the building's former glory was the highly polished dark-wood banister which flanked the main staircase.

'In here,' Beresford said, holding a door open and ushering Kate inside. 'Please excuse the mess.'

The room was obviously Beresford's office. A smoked-glass computer desk dominated one corner, complete with an ergonomic chair which wouldn't have looked out of place on the bridge of the Starship Enterprise. Two walls were shelved and the shelves were stacked with books from floor to ceiling. Kate couldn't read many of the titles on the spines but she could see enough to realise that they were organised carefully into some sort of filing system. They were all upright, nothing out of place.

Under the window, a low table and three easy chairs provided an informal seating area, which Beresford indicated with an outstretched hand.

'Please, sit,' he said, perching on the chair furthest from the door. Kate sat opposite him trying to rid herself of the image of a praying mantis as he leaned closer.

'I'm sure your receptionist explained why I'm here,' Kate said. 'I'm investigating a murder and there appears to be a connection between the victim and your clinic.'

'A connection?' Beresford tilted his head suggesting disbelief.

'The victim and her husband had been undergoing fertility treatment here. It's possible that she may have had an appointment on the day her husband reported her missing.'

'Surely her husband would be aware of such an appointment.' Beresford looked sceptical. 'The vast majority of our clients come in with their spouses. And, even if this woman did have an individual appointment, I fail to see how I can help you.'

*He obviously isn't going to make this easy,* Kate thought. 'I'm trying to track her movements and it's possible that she came here. If you can confirm that she had an appointment, then I can fill in another gap in the timeline.'

'But you understand that client records are confidential?' Beresford said with a regretful smile. 'It would be a breach of trust, not to mention my ethics, to break that confidentiality. The work we do here is very sensitive and it is important that our clients are guaranteed privacy.'

Kate felt like she was playing chess with a grand master. She made a move and he countered, she tried again and he blocked her. He didn't seem to realise that she had the power to knock all the pieces off the board and declare a win if she chose to.

'Mr Beresford,' she said, struggling to keep her tone of voice as non-threatening as possible. 'I can guarantee you that, in the circumstances, a simple confirmation would neither compromise your ethics nor break the trust of a dead woman. But it might help us to solve a brutal murder.'

Beresford's face contorted with distaste at Kate's bluntness.

'But her husband is still alive, I presume, and I have to respect his—'

'Her husband is distraught. He's the one who told us about their fertility issues, he's the one who led me to this clinic. All I need to know is whether the dead woman had an appointment here on Saturday. It's obvious that you feel unable to help so, as I explained to your receptionist, I'll come back tomorrow with a warrant and a colleague who can get all the information that I need from your IT system in about thirty seconds.'

She stood up and strode across the room to the door. Checkmate.

'Wait,' Beresford said.

She turned round and saw that he'd moved over to his desk.

'Give me a name.'

'Melissa Buckley.'

He tapped three keys and leaned in to peer more closely at the screen. 'No. Nothing for Saturday. At least nothing medical.'

'Medical?'

'We have a fully integrated service here,' Beresford explained. 'Our clients receive medical treatment and counselling. We treat NHS and private clients in exactly the same way and offer exactly the same level of care.'

The keyboard rattled as he typed something else.

'The Buckleys had completed three cycles of IVF treatment. The Doncaster Hospital Trust won't fund any more for a couple their age and with their issues. We are one of the most generous trusts in the north of England. Many will only fund a single cycle. The Buckleys would probably have been advised to have further counselling to enable them to consider their options for the future, but no such appointment has been made for either party.'

'Either party?' Kate asked, surprised. 'Couples have separate counselling sessions?'

Beresford looked up at her. 'Occasionally. It can be beneficial for one partner to talk freely without having to consider the needs and opinions of the other.'

This was becoming much more complicated than Kate had anticipated. She should have done some research before blundering in like the new sheriff in a Wild West town.

'Perhaps,' she said, sitting down again. 'You could talk me through the process. It might help the investigation if I can understand what the Buckleys were going through.'

'I don't see how,' Beresford said. 'I thought you only needed to know whether Mrs Buckley had an appointment. You've had your answer.'

Kate sighed. 'It's more complex than that,' she admitted. 'Without going into detail I can inform you that there were certain irregularities discovered during the post-mortem which suggest a link between Melissa's murder and her fertility issues. If I can understand the process it might help me to understand how and why she was murdered.'

Beresford's eyes were bright with curiosity and he licked his lips quickly, lizard-like, as he leaned forward. 'Irregularities?'

'That's all I can say. I'm sure that I can find somebody to explain IVF to me in simple terms but, as I'm here, and you're an expert…' she held her hands out, palms up as if to suggest that it would be foolish of her to squander this opportunity.

Beresford stared at her, frowning slightly as though trying to work out if Kate was trying to trick him. 'All right,' he said, finally. 'Where would you like to start?'

Forty minutes later Kate felt as if she knew everything she'd ever need to know about hormone injections, sperm washing and intra-vaginal egg harvesting. After a lengthy explanation of the process, she'd been able to persuade Beresford to provide a list of people who the Buckleys would have dealt with on their many visits to the clinic. This consisted of Beresford, a counsellor and two nurse clinicians. There were obviously reception staff and technicians but Ryan and Melissa's dealings with those would have been on a much less personal level and Beresford had assured her that, beyond collecting samples, the role of most of the staff would have been minimal. Kate had insisted that he include these 'minor players' on the list, just in case.

She took a picture of the names with her phone and emailed it to Cooper along with an instruction to go home and get some rest. For once she chose to take her own advice, and decided to head back to her flat and, hopefully, Nick.

# Chapter 10

'Right, that's your last one,' Dan said, placing the two drinks on the table. The woman sitting in the corner of the booth gave him a bleary grin as she grabbed for the drink and took a big gulp.

'That's what you said last time,' she said, lips loosened with drink, spraying tiny droplets of Bacardi and Coke onto the grimy table top.

He slid onto the bench seat opposite her and took a swig of his pint. They'd been here for nearly two hours and she was no closer to giving him the information he wanted. He'd spent a good part of his afternoon tracking her down – time that he should have been spending on the murder of Melissa Buckley – and he was starting to regret his decision. The boss had as good as given him the afternoon off but he still felt bad about using police resources to find an address and phone number. He'd even had a quick peek at her criminal record. Not as extensive as his mother's but there were two old convictions for shoplifting and three for soliciting. She'd managed to stay out of prison though, which was more than he could say for her sister. She bore a striking resemblance to Suzanne: similar age, similar haggard features, similarly inappropriate clothes, but, where Suzanne was blonde, Michelle was chestnut brown. They shared the same fortnight's growth of grey roots though.

Dan couldn't quite believe that the woman across the table from him was his auntie. He had other aunties – his adoptive mum had two sisters – and they were nothing like Michelle. He remembered her vaguely from his childhood as a woman in her twenties with a big laugh and a nasty temper. He had an especially vivid memory of being marched home by Auntie Michelle when he was six years old and had been caught stealing a handful of bubble-gum from the local shop. The shopkeeper had rung home and Michelle had been there. She'd grabbed him by the neck and pushed him in front of her all the way, her foot making occasional contact with his backside as she screeched at him for being stupid enough to get caught. He had no concept of morality at that age but he knew that most people thought stealing was the crime – not getting caught for it.

She'd been drinking steadily since he'd arrived at the pub, an anonymous chain establishment on the edge of Doncaster's entertainment complex. Hollis wasn't too worried that any of his colleagues would be frequenting the bowling alley or the multiplex cinema at this early hour, so he thought the pub was a safe bet for a couple of hours of anonymity. What he hadn't anticipated was the influx of families eager to take advantage of the 'kids eat free mega deal'. He'd managed to find a quietish booth as far away from the kiddies' play area as possible but their hushed conversation was still punctuated with shrieks of delight and equally loud yells from irate parents.

Michelle had put down her drink, her third double since she'd arrived, and was watching him as he tried again to think of a way to get the information that he wanted from her. Kate had often told him that he was a sensitive interviewer with good instincts about people but, in the hour that they'd been here, he'd not managed to get much out of Michelle apart from the usual pleasantries and a lot of unwanted information about her children. He really wasn't in the least bit interested in the exploits of his 'cousins' except to make sure he knew their names in case he ever had to arrest one of them. It seemed that 'our Jamie' was something high up in a used car dealership and 'our Shane' was between jobs after getting sacked from the biscuit factory. Michelle hadn't said so but Dan got the impression that he'd been sacked for doing something dodgy involving boxes of broken biscuits and a back door.

'You've spoken to your mam a fair bit then?' Michelle asked.

Dan nodded. 'It's not like I want to talk to her but I can't seem to get rid of her.'

Michelle wrinkled her nose at his belligerent tone. 'Well, she is your mam and she did miss out on seeing you grow up. Only to be expected that she'd want to know you're all right. She didn't know them folk that you ended up with. Taking you away like that so she couldn't see you. Where was it? Nottingham?'

'Chesterfield,' Dan said. 'It's not like it was Australia.'

'Yes, but your mam had her troubles and by the time she'd sorted herself out that couple had adopted you. Not much she could do after that. I know she got in touch when you turned eighteen though.'

Dan thought about correcting her. It was *him* who'd made contact with *Suzanne* not the other way around. A choice he regretted more with each meeting. 'We didn't really get on,' he said. 'I thought it might be good to know where I come from but she didn't really want to tell me much.'

Michelle took another gulp of her drink. 'Well, it was a difficult time for her when you were born. Our parents had chucked us both out and she was practically on the streets. You can't blame her for not wanting to go over all that again. Best forgot.'

She stared at the table top, lost in her thoughts, or struggling to make sense of her memories. Dan wasn't sure which, but he knew she was stringing him along and he knew why. It was probably the first time Michelle had been offered free drinks with no strings attached and she seemed determined to take advantage of his generosity. He'd told her twice that the next drink was her last one but they both knew that he'd keep going back to the bar until he'd got the information he wanted. Or until Michelle passed out.

'So, what did you want to talk to me about?' Michelle said, raising bleary blue eyes to his, eyes that reminded him of his own, and Suzanne's. He knew that he needed to play this carefully, his training kicking in as he tried to gauge the best way to get the information that he wanted. If he asked Michelle directly who his father was he was giving her the opportunity to deny any knowledge or, worse, to lie. He needed to tread carefully.

'I just want to know what Suz… my mum was like when she was younger, when she had me. I remember her a bit but it's all a bit hazy. I thought you could fill in some of the gaps and tell me what she was like as a kid, as a teenager.'

Michelle grinned at him as though his request was the most natural thing she'd ever heard. Her dark hair was coming loose from the elastic band that she'd used to hold it back and a few strands dropped across her eyes. She stuck out her lower lip and blew upwards to dislodge them before draining her drink. 'Oh, the stories I could tell you, Danny Boy. She was a right one, your mam. Little bugger, she was.'

He waited for more but she remained silent, slowly spinning her glass round on the drip mat. Dan took the hint and went back to the bar. Orange juice for himself and just a single for Michelle this time. He needed her to be vaguely coherent.

'So, Suzanne was a little bugger,' he prompted, putting the fresh drinks on the table and sitting back down, 'In what way?'

For a second, Dan thought he might have misjudged this woman. The glance that she gave him was shrewd, almost reptilian, until she raised her glass to her lips and smiled sadly. 'Always after the lads. I blame my dad. All she ever wanted was his attention but he had no time for any of us. I think that's why she acted up all the time. I hate to say this about my own flesh and blood but she was a bit of a tart. She'd go with anybody if they bought her a can of beer or offered her a packet of fags.'

This wasn't what Dan had wanted to hear. If his mother had slept around, the chances of him narrowing down probable candidates for his paternity were slim.

'Sounds like she was a bit of a sad case,' Dan suggested.

'You know, I think you're right. She wasn't a bad lass, she was just sad. And she went with the lads to try to make herself feel better.' She nodded to herself as if this was a sudden revelation.

'So there wasn't anybody special?'

'Oh they were all special.' Michelle chuckled and slurped her drink. 'You been watering this down? It doesn't taste as strong as the last one.'

'Nope. Still double Bacardi and Coke. You must be getting used to it. You'll be asking for triples next.'

'Not a bad idea, lad,' Michelle said, winking at him lewdly. 'If you weren't family I might think you were trying to get me drunk and take advantage of me.'

Dan tried to supress a shudder at the thought of touching this crone. 'There must have been steady boyfriends though? Lads she saw regularly.'

'One or two,' Michelle agreed. 'One or two. There was one lad broke her heart. Got what he wanted and told all his mates that she was a slag. Nearly killed her that did. Little bastard.'

'What was his name?' Dan asked. 'I might be able to use my contacts, get him done over.' He heard the words, in his own voice, but he felt oddly disassociated from them. He wasn't the sort of person who could or would have somebody 'done over' but he sensed this might be the way to impress Michelle and get her to share more information with him.

'John somebody. Roberts? Robertson? Ibbotson? Oh, I dunno. It was a long time ago and besides he's dead now. Car crash while he was drunk. Nearly killed a woman and two kids as well. Good riddance, I say.'

It wasn't much but Dan made a mental note of the possible names. If this John had kids, a DNA match might be possible.

'What about when she had me? Was she still seeing this John bloke?'

Michelle tilted her head and looked at him as though this was the first time she'd seen him. 'Oh, no. John dumped her when she was about fourteen. She'd moved on to older men by the time she got pregnant with you.'

'Older men?'

'She liked authority. One was a soldier. A sergeant. His mam lived on our estate and he moved his wife and little lass in with her. He used to be around a fair bit when he wasn't away with the army. Nearly thirty he was when he got involved with our Suzanne. Dirty bastard.'

'What was his name?'

'Alan? Or Ian? I dunno. It's all a long time ago. York. His last name was York, like the city.'

This sounded more promising.

'And then there was that copper.'

Dan suddenly felt like somebody had thrown a bucket of ice-cold water over him. 'Copper?'

'Aye. A young policeman. Nice looking he was. I met him once. Only a bairn himself. He was quite taken with our Suzanne. Until he found out what she was doing for money, I suppose. Not many men would put up with that. Still, she had to live and jobs were scarce.'

'What was his name? Can you remember?' Dan asked, trying to conceal the tremble in his voice.

Michelle shook her head.

'Benny? Bobby? Billy? Summat like that. I don't think she liked him that much but he made her feel safe when she was on the streets.'

Dan could barely hear her, his mind ablaze with this new information. He could picture the name plate on the DCI's office door. 'W. Raymond'. He knew that the W was William. Billy Raymond? Could it be true?

*She was surprisingly light when I picked her up as though, her spirit having left, her corpse was an empty shell. I don't believe in an afterlife, or a god, or any of that stuff but I was acutely aware of a difference in the body. Whatever had made Melissa 'Melissa' had gone. This slack jawed, bug-eyed thing bore very little resemblance to the woman that I'd known. I was disappointed in a way. I wanted it to be her; it was important to my message, but what I was left with would have to do.*

*I considered taking all her clothes off but I soon realised how impractical that was. Her limbs had stiffened quite quickly and I thought I'd probably have to cut the remaining clothes off her, which didn't hold much appeal. Instead I'd decided to leave her naked from the waist down so that it was obvious what had been done to her. I took her handbag and her phone and hid them in my wardrobe. I also checked her pockets for any means of identification – I didn't want to make the job of the police too easy – then I wrapped her in bin liners and carried her out to my car.*

*My original plan had been to bury the bodies in my garden. There was much less likelihood of being caught that way, but then there was no likelihood of anybody seeing what I'd done – or understanding it. So I'd decided that I wanted Melissa to be found. I wanted somebody to read the clues and to work out why I'd felt compelled to get rid of her.*

*I drove down a small road that ran along the quietest side of the huge open area of Town Fields and parked next to the railings which separated the field from the street. The chances of being seen were slim as all the buildings had been converted to commercial premises: a school, a dentist, various offices. It was always a bit of a ghost town after dark. A quick look around and it had been a simple matter to lift the body over the fence. Then I walked round to a gate, slipped through it and posed the body exactly how I'd wanted it to be found, complete with her trousers and knickers neatly folded by her side. I'd hoped that the message was clear; that people would finally begin to understand that some things in life were a privilege. And if I didn't have that privilege I was going to do something about those whiners and moaners who thought they could have anything they wanted.*

*After I'd arranged the body, I drove home and slept like a baby until my alarm at eight o'clock when I got up, dressed and set off for a jog. Then the real fun had started. It was such a buzz blending into the crowd and listening to their theories and suppositions. Some thought it was a child's body that had been found – as if I'd do that – and others assumed it was a prostitute. But nobody even got close to the truth. That it was an ordinary woman – just like some of them, or their wives or sisters – and she'd got exactly what she deserved.*

# Chapter 11

Kate looked down at the list of jobs that she had to assign. Most of them involved interviews with staff at the fertility clinic and with Melissa Buckley's friends and colleagues but none of them looked even close to a lead. Barratt hadn't made much progress at the DRI. It looked like Beresford was telling the truth, that the Buckleys would have seen a lot of technicians but none for any length of time.

The case was about to enter its second week and she didn't feel any further forward than she had when the body had been discovered. Kailisa's lab report was back and it confirmed that Melissa had drunk coffee prior to her death and that she hadn't had a recent injection of any of the fertility hormones she'd been using. It seemed that she'd given up on trying for a baby, at least for a while. The report also confirmed the rape and the absence of semen or lubricant. It was this fact that she decided to throw at her team to get them thinking.

Raymond had finally allocated them a proper incident room for the case and Kate had asked for a meeting there first thing. She'd bagged a chair at the head of the table, plugged in her laptop and waited. She was surprised when O'Connor appeared first, looking relatively fresh. It wasn't like him to be early for anything.

He gave her a sheepish smile and pulled out a chair. 'I know, I know. I must have wet the bed if I'm in this early.'

Kate smiled back. It was a standing joke on her team that the first one in was always accused of having wet the bed – except Kate of course. None of them would have had the audacity to suggest such a thing about their DI. 'You had coffee?' she pointed to a drip machine that had been set up on a desk near the door. 'It's not great but it's hot and wet.'

O'Connor smirked and seemed about to make a smutty joke when Barratt burst through the door. He looked from Kate to O'Connor and grinned. 'What's up with you, Steve? Wet the bed?'

O'Connor gave him a two-fingered salute and loped over to the coffee machine as Hollis came in followed by Cooper.

'Black one sugar for me,' Cooper said and was rewarded with another of O'Connor's hand gestures – only one finger this time. Despite his pretended irritation, O'Connor followed Sam's instructions and plonked a steaming mug onto the table in front of her.

'Dan?'

Hollis looked up at him, his expression blank. 'What?'

'Coffee?'

Hollis shook his head and slumped further down in his chair. Kate could see that he'd probably had another rough night. His eyes were bloodshot and underlined by dark patches and his skin looked slightly grey and dehydrated. He'd managed to shave but there were two dots of tissue paper on his neck where he'd cut himself and there was a tiny drop of blood on the collar of his shirt.

Team assembled, Kate took a breath and ran a finger over the trackpad of her laptop, bringing it to life. She turned on the projector, allowing the others to see the image that was displayed on her screen. It was a close-up of the wound in Melissa Buckley's abdomen.

'Right. Here's what we know so far.' She gave them an account of Kailisa's findings, the interviews that had already been conducted and her suggestions for moving the investigation forwards. As she was concluding her introductory comments she looked up to see Raymond hovering in the doorway, obviously following her every word. She paused but he gestured for her to continue.

'The obvious anomaly is the rape,' she said. There was evidence of brutal penetration but no semen or any indication that a condom was used. Thoughts?'

'He used an object? Or a sex toy?' Barratt suggested.

It was what Kate had been thinking.

'Problems with that hypothesis?'

'It could mean that we're not looking for a man. A reasonably strong woman could have overpowered Melissa, strangled her and then sexually assaulted her as she was dying and unable to fight back.' O'Connor's face was grim as he presented his theory and Kate knew that it wasn't just because of the brutal attack. He'd doubled their pool of suspects. Until now she'd assumed that the attacker was male but the new findings meant that she couldn't rule anybody out purely based on their gender.

'Right. Open minds needed. We don't seem to be getting very far in terms of finding a viable suspect so let's think about motive.' She flicked back to the photograph of Melissa's abdomen. 'Why would somebody do this? Specifically this wound. It must mean something to the attacker that isn't obvious to us so what is it?'

Silence. She hadn't expected a flood of suggestions but just one to get them started would have been helpful.

Finally Cooper said, 'Jealousy?'

'Explain.'

'Could be somebody who can't have kids for whatever reason so they're sending a message that other people shouldn't have them either.'

'So why Melissa? She was struggling to conceive. Might her attacker have known that? If it was purely jealousy surely he or she would have gone after somebody who was already pregnant.'

Cooper shook her head. 'Not necessarily. Obviously we need to think about opportunity. This person might not have had access to a pregnant woman. There's something personal about the way he… or she… has cut Melissa. I don't think that she was snatched off the street, and the timing isn't right for that. Very few people are taken in broad daylight.'

The others nodded in agreement.

'She knew him,' Barratt said. 'Or her. Whoever did this got close enough to strangle her without disabling her first by hitting her over the head or something. Whoever this was, I think Melissa knew them and maybe even trusted them.'

It made sense. Kate made a note on the pad next to her laptop. *Trust?* 'So it could have been somebody who was jealous that Melissa was able to get help with her fertility issues? Somebody who knew what she was going through?' It felt possible but not quite right. What they were suggesting seemed to point to a friend of Melissa rather than a stranger but surely she would have mentioned to Ryan that she was meeting up with a friend. Why the secrecy? Still, it was all they had at the moment.

'So where does that leave us?' Kate asked. 'Where do we go next?'

'Re-interview friends and family,' Hollis suggested. 'Find out exactly what they knew about Melissa's medical history and when they last saw her. We thought we were looking for a man when we did the initial interviews but that's changed. Everybody that she knew is now a potential suspect. Shit. That's a lot of people.'

'Social media,' Raymond said from the doorway. The others turned to look at him and Kate noticed Hollis turn a shade paler as he realised that the DCI must have been listening for a while.

Raymond stuffed his hands into the pockets of his trousers and took a step forward into the room. 'Check her Facebook, Instagram, Twitter. See who she confided in. You've got some of the account passwords from Buckley. Check her email as well if you can get in.'

Kate tried to keep her facial expression neutral. It wasn't like the DCI to interfere and she couldn't ever remember him interrupting a briefing. She didn't want to resent his presence but it was hard not to feel like he was checking up on her, making sure she was doing her job properly.

'Cooper, that's your department,' Kate said. 'I know you've managed to get into her email and Instagram. Keep on with the others – especially Facebook. Check Messenger and see who she was chatting with and what about. And keep on with that unknown phone number.'

Sam scrawled something in her notepad and stood up to leave.

'Hang on. Did you find another bank account for Melissa?'

'Nope. There's just the ISA – about seven grand – and there's her joint account with Ryan.'

Kate turned to O'Connor. 'Steve, did you find out anything about the Buckleys having any dodgy loans?'

O'Connor scowled. 'Nope. Tried a few people but nobody had heard of the Buckleys. I was out last night again talking to some of the girls around Town Field. Still haven't found anybody who saw anything on Saturday night. There's not as many girls out at the minute though. Like I said, I think there's somebody new on the scene and it's like they're all a bit wary.'

Kate filed the information away in her mind. A new pimp or a dodgy punter could change the dynamic of a tight group of working girls – she'd seen it before – and it might be worth pursuing, although she didn't think that Melissa Buckley had been mistaken for a prostitute in broad daylight on a Saturday morning. She'd get O'Connor to sniff around when he got a chance.

'Right. Jobs. Hollis, with me to the DRI. I've got two lists of people the Buckleys saw at the hospital; one from Ryan and one from a Mr Beresford who runs the fertility clinic. They don't quite match up but between us we should manage to cover both. Go and find us a car.'

Hollis left followed by Cooper. Barratt and O'Connor hovered around the desk awaiting instructions.

'You two go back to the list of friends and colleagues. I want formal statements from all Melissa's friends and I want to know who she was close to at work. Find out who she confided in, who she'd fallen out with, who secretly fancied her. Whoever killed her is probably already on a list of contacts somewhere – we just need to figure out who he is.'

'Or she,' said O'Connor with a grin. 'Don't forget *she*. It's important to be inclusive in these PC times.'

Kate waved her hands at them both, shooing them from the room.

Raymond was still standing next to the door, his expression unreadable.

'Was there something else?' Kate asked.

'Have a seat for a bit. Let's have a chat, Kate.'

Alarm bells ringing full force in her head, Kate pulled out a chair halfway up the table and sat down, watching as Raymond sat down opposite her. There was something off about his manner – and he hardly ever called her by her first name. He'd been different for a few weeks – quieter and more reflective. Whenever he'd called her into his office she'd been surprised that his customary belligerence had been toned down and his manner towards her had recently bordered on the paternalistic.

'You might have noticed a few changes,' he began. 'I've seen how people are looking at me. Different haircut, lose a bit of weight, smarten up your clothes and suddenly people think there's something wrong. Well there is and there isn't and I thought you ought to know.'

He took a deep breath and tried a smile that didn't seem to fit his mouth very comfortably.

'You remember I had a few days off last month?'

Kate nodded warily, imagining a range of unpleasant scenarios.

'I had a bit of a scare. A minor cardiac event. *Not* a heart attack but close enough. Diana was terrified and she gathered the kids together like they were expecting me to conk out but the doctor said it was most likely exacerbated by stress.'

It had been unusual for the DCI to have time off. Kate had assumed it was either a short, and much needed, holiday or some personal time. She'd had no idea that he'd been ill.

'So,' Raymond continued. 'I've started to lose a bit of weight. Had to buy some new suits. Thought I might as well get a decent haircut as well. Diana likes it shorter. She says I look ten years younger. I feel about fifty years older but I can't tell her that.'

He was rambling and Kate got the sense that he was going all round the houses to avoid revealing the real point of the conversation.

'Sir, I...'

He held up one of his huge, bear-paw hands to prevent her from interrupting.

'Kate. I've put in for early retirement. I'm leaving in a few months. This job's had the best of me and I feel like I owe it to Diana to give her whatever's left. I thought you should hear it from me rather than on the office jungle drums. And I'm feeling a bit nostalgic, like an old fool, so that's why you might find me taking a more active role in this investigation. I don't want to step on your toes, I just want to be involved, on the ground, one last time.' He paused, his eyes flicking from left to right as though he was checking a script that he'd memorised. 'If you feel like I'm getting in the way I want you to tell me. This is your case, work it your way but I'd like to be included whenever it might be practical for both of us. Okay?'

'Okay,' Kate said, trying to make sense of what he'd just told her. Heart attack. Retirement. Involvement. It was a lot to take in. 'I'll do my best to make sure you're part of it.'

Raymond smiled gratefully.

'And, sir? It can't have been an easy decision. Your wife is a lucky woman to have somebody who would give up all this.' She pointed to the photograph of Melissa Buckley that was still displayed on the screen.

His smile broadened into a grin.

'Lucky? She's bloody frightening, Fletcher. Frightening and *very* persuasive.'

# Chapter 12

Her head still reeling from Raymond's revelation, Kate slipped into the passenger seat of the pool car.

'Everything okay?' Hollis asked. 'You look a bit off. Raymond have a go?'

'No, nothing like that. Just trying to keep a lot of information in my head. This case is getting on top of me a bit. I can't believe we're no closer to finding out who killed Melissa. We don't even have one viable suspect.'

Hollis put the car in gear and eased out of the parking space. 'That's what today's about isn't it? We've refocussed. There's somebody on our list of names who knows something. There must be. We all agree this isn't random so all we need to do is find the link between Melissa and her killer.'

'Ah,' Kate said. 'That's all. I don't know what's taking so long then if it's that easy.'

She could tell from the fixed way Hollis was studying the traffic, and his careful movements when he changed gear, that she'd offended him. He'd only been trying to lighten the mood, to instil a flicker of hope and she'd snapped his head off. 'Hey, I'm sorry,' she said. 'I shouldn't let it get to me like this.'

Hollis continued to stare through the windscreen.

'How's things with you? Have you found out anything else from your… mother… your birth mother?' She stumbled over the question unsure about which term to use for the woman who was making her DC's life a misery. He'd turned up to work looking hungover again and his contributions to the briefing hadn't exactly been stellar.

'I met her sister last night. Thought she might be able to give me a bit more information.'

'And?'

'And it's just made things worse. It seems that my *mother* had a lot of male attention from around the age of fourteen. Started early apparently. Michelle hinted at all sorts of issues with their dad which I don't want to even think about. There were a few lads her own age and a couple of older men when she turned sixteen. At least she was legal when she got pregnant with me.'

'Older men?' Kate asked. 'How old?'

Hollis indicated again and pulled them into the main DRI car park. 'One was a soldier who lived on the same street,' he said, slowing down and scanning for an empty space. 'The other was a police officer.'

'You're in the wrong place,' Kate said. 'Sorry, I should have told you. Go round the side – there's another place to park, nearer the clinic.'

Hollis huffed in frustration and leaned his arm across the back of her seat as he reversed.

'So the sister remembers a police officer. That suggests your mother isn't lying.'

'It gets worse.'

Kate stayed silent waiting for him to explain.

'She said that his name was Benny or Bobby or Billy. She claimed that she couldn't remember.'

Kate knew that DCI Raymond's name was William and she'd heard him referred to as Bill on a number of occasions. Never Billy though, but people often chose different versions of their name as they matured. She'd been Cathy until she was nearly seventeen. Now she hated it and always snapped her sister's head off if Karen accidentally called her anything but Kate.

'Do you think it's him?'

Hollis shook his head. 'I honestly don't know what to think. I just wish that she'd stayed away. I don't need her in my life and

I don't want all this uncertainty. What difference will it actually make if Raymond is my biological father? It's not like I'm a kid. Why would he even be interested?'

'I thought you wanted to know. You said that's what she's holding over you. At least you'd have that certainty. And you could do a lot worse.'

'Is this it?' Hollis asked, ignoring her final statement as he pulled into the clinic's parking area. 'Interesting old building.'

Kate got the message. Hollis could only talk about the issues with his mother in very small bursts. She understood that. Anything else would have been too much for him to deal with and she had to respect his right to privacy.

'Looks like an old mansion, or *The Addams Family* house. A bit creepy for a medical building. Christ, it could be the morgue.'

'Well, it's not. But wait until you meet the crypt keeper.'

A light shower had them running across the car park to the shelter of the building's porch where Kate almost slipped on the polished surface of the red tiles. Hollis grabbed her arm, holding her steady as she regained her balance and she was reminded of his role in her team. He was often the voice of reason, the solid reliable one when the others were throwing out all sorts of outlandish theories and ideas. He was dependable. She'd trust him with her life just as she had once trusted him with that of her son, Ben. If he was the one struggling, she owed it to him to be there, to pay attention and to help in any way that she could.

'Thanks,' she mumbled, pulling her arm free of his hand. 'Nearly made a right tit of myself.'

He smiled at her and, just like that, they slipped back into their roles, the conversation in the car forgotten – for now.

*** 

A different receptionist from the one Kate had met before greeted them from behind her desk. This one was tall and slim with closely cropped dark hair and a less than welcoming expression. Kate had phoned ahead before leaving Doncaster Central just to be sure that

Beresford had organised access to his staff as she'd requested. He'd answered in the affirmative but hadn't sounded pleased about it and he'd obviously passed on his lack of enthusiasm to the receptionist.

'Can I help you?' the woman asked, her tone more pleasant than the faint scowl that hovered around her eyebrows. She'd obviously realised that they weren't clients.

Kate showed her ID and asked for Beresford.

'Is he expecting you?'

'He is,' Kate confirmed, thinking *he'd better be.* The woman picked up the telephone receiver, pushed a key and turned her back on Kate and Hollis making it impossible for them to hear her murmured comments. Shaking her head at the receptionist's obvious attempt to signal her distaste for their presence, Kate tapped Hollis on his arm and indicated the chairs where she'd waited before. She wasn't going to be kept standing around until Beresford deigned to grace them with his presence.

Hollis took a seat opposite her and removed a crumpled sheet of A4 paper from the breast pocket of his suit jacket. He unfolded it and read aloud.

'We're looking for Janice Hoult, nurse physician who would have harvested Melissa's eggs, Tim Matthias the therapist and Pauline Dorries who was responsible for Ryan's *sample*.' Kate noticed that Hollis blushed slightly as he said 'sample' rather than sperm. Obviously he was one of those men who felt uncomfortable discussing the workings of their reproductive system. If he'd managed to lighten up a little on the way back to Doncaster Central she'd make sure to tease him about it.

'I think that should cover it for today,' she said. 'I spoke to Beresford at length yesterday and he was reluctant to co-operate at first but when I threatened to turn Sam loose on his computer system he finally gave me the information I needed. I've got addresses for the three we're seeing this morning, plus Beresford. Dorries and Matthias live near Town Field but that doesn't help us as we know that Melissa's body was kept somewhere else. We have no idea where she went after parking her car.'

'What about the technical side?' Hollis asked. 'There must be lab technicians who do all the science stuff.'

'On another list,' Kate said. 'Barratt did some preliminary work at the main hospital. This one is all the people who would have had face-to-face dealings with the Buckleys. Beresford said that they like to keep the contact as personal as possible so the team who dealt with Ryan and Melissa is quite small. We'll talk to the technicians after these interviews.'

'Receptionists?'

'Good thinking,' Kate said. 'There are at least two and they would have been the first people the Buckleys met when they arrived here. I just hope they got a better welcome than we did.'

Kate strolled over to the reception desk and leaned casually on the polished wood. 'I'm sure you know why we're here,' she said to the receptionist, her tone carefully conversational.

The woman nodded, lips tightly pinched together. She couldn't quite hold Kate's stare, her eyes skipping away to the left and then refocussing as though she thought that her inability to look at Kate would indicate guilt. Kate had seen this many times before – it was nerves. A lot of people, regardless of their innocence, when faced with the prospect of speaking to the police almost instinctively felt, and consequently acted as if, they were guilty.

'You'd have met the Buckleys?'

Another nod.

'Many times?'

'A few. I job share with Amy. We both end up meeting all the clients at some point.'

'Do you remember Melissa and Ryan Buckley?'

'I do. Nice couple. He was a mechanic – I remember him sometimes coming in straight from work in his overalls. I think she worked on the trains. They'd have been coming here for about a year I think – maybe a bit longer.'

'And did you form an impression of them, as a couple?'

'Nice enough, I suppose. I don't have much to do with the clients beyond greeting them and telling them to go through to their appointments.'

Her expression had relaxed and she sat back slightly in her chair, obviously on comfortable ground now.

'So they didn't stand out in any way?'

The woman's eyes lost focus and shifted from side to side as though she was trying to remember something but then she shrugged and looked back at Kate.

'I remember feeling a bit sorry for them. They were a bit younger than most of our clients, in their twenties, and they'd obviously been struggling with their issues for a long time. I think they'd probably used up all their options in terms of NHS care. Shame really. If it was up to me I wouldn't limit it to three goes – it's cruel. I think, if you're desperate for a baby then the system should—'

'DI Fletcher,' the door to the hallway had opened and Edward Beresford beamed at her, interrupting the flow of the young woman behind the reception desk. 'I hope Kellie has been co-operating with your enquiry.'

He winked at the woman who flushed and immediately found something interesting on her computer screen.

'She has,' Kate confirmed, irritated that the man's presence had interrupted her conversation with the receptionist. 'Just getting an impression of what brings people to your facility.'

Hollis jumped up and strode over to them.

'My colleague,' Kate said. 'DC Hollis. He'll be assisting me when I interview your staff. I hope that's not a problem.'

Beresford looked Hollis up and down, almost as if he were assessing whether he could beat the younger man in a fight, before shaking his hand. Kate wondered which one would have the tightest grip. She wasn't surprised to see Beresford pull away first.

'Not at all. I assume then that *you* won't mind if *I* sit in on the interviews?'

Kate had expected this. During their previous encounter she'd formed the impression that Beresford was a man who liked to be in control and the receptionist's reaction had confirmed this. He wouldn't like the idea that *his* staff were discussing the clinic without him being able to vet their comments, or at least be present so that he could clarify or explain anything negative that might be said.

'That won't be possible,' Kate said brusquely. 'If any of your staff feel the need for support they are within their rights to ask for legal representation, otherwise what they tell us is confidential.'

'But I—'

'Mr Beresford,' Hollis said. 'My role is as recorder. These are not formal interviews so I'll just be making notes rather than a tape recording. If it's not possible for us to conduct these interviews in a private room without interruption then we will gladly arrange for your staff to come to Doncaster Central and be interviewed there, potentially under caution. I know which I would prefer but I'm happy to give them that choice if that's what you want.'

Kate studied the two men as they held position, neither willing to give any ground. Hollis was taller but his slim frame seemed willowy next to Beresford's muscular physique; Kate had no idea which man she'd bet on in a wrestling match but she'd back Hollis every time in an argument about appropriate police protocol.

Beresford gave him a broad grin and held his hands out, palms up, in submission. 'I only want what's best for my staff,' he said.

'I understand that,' Hollis replied. 'But we want what's best for our investigation and, when we're talking murder, *our* rules apply.'

'So, if we can get started,' Kate said, trying to break the tension between the two men. She appreciated Hollis's formality and intractability but now they were just wasting time and it looked like it could be a long day.

'Of course,' Beresford said, turning back to the door and holding it open, allowing Kate and Hollis through to the hallway.

# Chapter 13

Beresford led them to the door of a downstairs consultation room, flicking the notification sign from 'available' to 'occupied' as he turned the handle and ushered Kate and Hollis inside. The room had obviously been rearranged for their visit. Three comfortable, low chairs had been stacked on top of each other and pushed up against a coffee table – obviously the interviews weren't meant to be cosy. A desk dominated the space beneath the window with two plastic chairs on one side and two on the other. Beresford made a point of removing one of the chairs that faced the window and taking it out into the hallway.

'I hope you don't mind,' he said when he came back. 'I've rearranged the room to make it more conducive to your business. If you'd like to get comfortable I'll have Janice Hoult paged.'

He left, closing the door firmly behind him, leaving Kate and Hollis to plan the first interview. Kate immediately went behind the desk and moved one of the chairs so that it was sitting at an angle to one of the desk's shorter sides. She then shifted the single chair so that it was facing the one that she had just moved with no desk between them.

'Where do you want me?' Hollis asked.

'Just sit there,' she said, pointing to the chair that she'd left in place. It would enable Hollis to rest on the desk while he made notes.

'What's this?' he asked as he plucked a buff folder from the desk. He passed it to Kate who opened it and sighed heavily. She should have expected this from somebody as organised as Beresford. The folder contained a single sheet of paper and on it, neatly typed, was a schedule for the interviews. Beresford had allowed thirty minutes per person.

'It's our schedule for the morning,' she said, passing it to Hollis. 'What should I do with it?'

'Leave it in the folder and stick it over on that coffee table. I've got the order that we're seeing the staff in, but we won't be sticking to Beresford's time limits.'

Hollis followed her instructions and then positioned himself behind the desk. Kate checked her watch. According to Beresford's plan they were due to see Janice Hoult at 9.30; Kate's watch said 9.27.

'Three minutes,' she said to Hollis with a grin. 'I bet she's exactly on time. Can't imagine her boss allowing tardiness.'

At 9.29 there was a tap on the door. Hollis grinned at Kate and said, 'Come in.'

The woman who walked through the door glared belligerently at Kate and then at Hollis. She was tall, much taller than Kate and had her mousy blonde hair scraped back in a severe bun. Minimal make-up did little to hide the deep wrinkles around her mouth and eyes and her uniform was inadequate cover for her bulky frame. She looked like an Olympic shot-putter gone to seed.

'Have a seat,' Kate said, indicating the only vacant chair.

Janice sat heavily as if she'd suddenly been relieved of a great weight and looked from Kate to Hollis. 'Who's in charge?' she asked.

'That would be me,' Kate said, keeping her tone light. 'I'm Detective Inspector Fletcher and this is Detective Constable Hollis. I'm sure that Mr Beresford has told you why we're here.'

'He has. And, while I'm sorry about the murdered woman, I don't see what I can do to help. I'm very busy and I don't really have time for what I assume is just a formality.'

'Why would you assume that?' Kate asked.

Janice smiled, shark-like. 'I know that Melissa Buckley was murdered. I'm assuming there was some sort of sexual assault – there usually is in these cases – so you'll be looking for a male perpetrator. As you can see, I'm not your man.'

Kate heard a muffled snort from Hollis but kept her eyes fixed on the woman in front of her.

'That's a lot of assumptions,' she said calmly, despite the simmering anger she felt towards this arrogant woman. She wondered if all Beresford's staff had to attend his own special charm school before he allowed them to work in the clinic. 'Perhaps you can try to open your mind a little and answer some of our questions. Even if we were looking for a man it's possible that you may have information that might lead us to him.'

Janice cracked a tiny hint of a smile obviously approving of Kate's manner. 'Okay then. But I don't have long.'

Kate flipped open her notebook and glanced down the list of questions she'd made the previous day. Most of them were quite straightforward but she wasn't going to let Janice get away with quick answers. Not that she had any reason yet to suspect that the woman had anything to hide, she was just irritated by her manner. 'Have you worked here long, Ms Hoult?'

'Nearly ten years.' The response was clipped. Just enough information in the shortest space of time.

'Perhaps you could talk me through your role at the clinic. I have a basic understanding of the IVF procedure but I'd like to be clear about exactly what you do.'

'Is that relevant?'

'Trust me, everything I ask is relevant. Every little detail could be helpful.'

She sat back while Janice explained how she was involved in the harvesting of a woman's eggs and the implantation of the embryos. Janice didn't add much to Kate's understanding but Kate could tell that she'd got the other woman rattled by the way she rushed through the process, clearly keen to get back to the *real* questions.

'So this would be how you had contact with Melissa Buckley?'

'Yes. I performed one harvest and three implantations. Each implantation was two embryos.'

'Only two? I thought women usually had three or four?'

'Melissa Buckley was young. The chances of an embryo being viable are much higher in younger patients. We wouldn't want to be impregnating women with quadruplets unnecessarily.'

'So you met Melissa at least four times?'

'I met her *exactly* four times,' Janice confirmed. 'She would have been briefed on the procedure by Mr Beresford and counselled by Tim Matthias prior to the initial harvest.'

'And Mr Buckley?'

'Also four times. We encourage partners to be present.'

'What impression did you get of the Buckleys?'

Janice shook her head as though the question was meaningless. 'They seemed like a pleasant couple. He held her hand throughout. I got the feeling that they both wanted a baby. Nothing unusual.'

'You never heard them argue? They didn't fall out at all?'

'Nope. Not in my presence.'

Kate glanced down at her list of questions. 'Do you have children, Ms Hoult?'

'What?'

'Kids. Do you have any?'

'I don't see—'

'Please, if you could answer the question it would be very helpful,' Kate prompted, smiling encouragingly.

'I have two, both boys.'

'Conceived naturally?'

'I don't… I can't believe…' she spluttered her face contorting with outrage. 'Does Mr Beresford know that you're asking these sorts of questions?'

'Mr Beresford assured us that his staff would co-operate fully with our investigation. I can assure you that this question is relevant,' Kate said, enjoying the woman's discomfort.

'Well, not that it's anybody's business but both my boys were conceived naturally. My husband and I were lucky.'

'Do you know of any staff here who have also made use of your services?'

Janice looked aghast. 'Of course not. That would be highly unethical. If anybody working here had fertility issues they would be referred to another clinic. We can't treat our own, it's not allowed.'

'And you wouldn't know of anybody having such issues?' Kate continued.

'No.'

Kate looked at Hollis who was still scribbling in his notebook. 'Anything further to ask, DC Hollis?'

They'd rehearsed this. Kate was to ask the general questions about the role of each member of staff and to bring up the fertility issue. Hollis was to ask the most important question almost as an afterthought to catch the interviewees off guard.

'Where were you on Saturday afternoon and evening?' Hollis asked.

Janice Hoult was completely unphased by the question. 'I was here until three o'clock, then I went into town to meet my husband for a bit of shopping and dinner. Saturday night is our "date night". We ate at the Indian on the market square – we're regulars so somebody there will be able to confirm that. We got home just before ten. The babysitter will remember that because we always get back in time for her to get home and do a bit of revision before bed.'

'I'll need phone numbers for your husband and the babysitter.'

Janice retrieved her mobile phone from the pocket of her tunic and read out the numbers.

'Is that all?' she asked as Hollis made a note of the information.

'For now,' Kate said.

Janice Hoult nodded once as though satisfied with the way she had handled the interview and then left.

'Well?' Hollis asked as Janice closed the door behind her.

'Can't see it,' Kate said. The woman had seemed brisk and professional *and* she had what appeared to be a strong alibi. Kate also didn't feel convinced that a woman could be behind the brutal attack on Melissa Buckley but her training and her instincts were sometimes in conflict and she was aware of the need to keep an open mind. Perhaps it was prejudice or possibly intuition but, when she pictured the injuries inflicted on Melissa, she imagined a male perpetrator filled with hatred.

'Who's next?' she asked Hollis.

'Tim Matthias, the therapist. I doubt he'll tell us much – patient confidentiality and all that.'

Hollis was right. Kate didn't expect the therapist to give much away about the Buckleys' personal circumstances. She was about to suggest that they focus on the man rather than his role but a knock on the door prevented her from speaking.

'Come in,' Kate called and an imposing figure stepped into the room. Tanned and bald, Tim Matthias was slightly taller than average and his perfectly tailored grey suit did little to disguise his muscular legs and broad chest.

'Have a seat,' she said, gesturing to the chair opposite her own. Hollis introduced them both and explained his role while Matthias settled himself in his seat, one ankle on the opposite knee, hands loosely resting on his thighs. He undid the button on his suit jacket, revealing a luxurious blue lining.

'How long have you been here, Mr Matthias?'

'Nearly two years. I moved up from a private clinic in Staffordshire. I wanted to do more in the NHS rather than only treating private patients.'

*Very worthy,* Kate thought. *Bet the new job didn't come with a pay cut, though.*

'So this position was a sideways step?'

'Promotion actually,' Matthias admitted. 'I'm the senior counsellor here.'

*Not so noble after all.* 'Can you explain your role at the clinic?' Kate asked.

Matthias smiled at her, revealing teeth that were either naturally perfect or expensively capped. The smile deepened the wrinkles around his eyes and Kate realised that he was older than she'd first imagined and rather attractive when he wasn't frowning.

He gave her an outline of his duties and where his role fit into the IVF process. All very precise and clinical.

'How well did you know Melissa Buckley?'

'As well as I know any of my clients,' Matthias responded. 'Obviously we develop a therapeutic relationship over a period of weeks or months.'

'And her husband, Ryan?'

'Much the same. I always saw them together. Some couples prefer individual sessions but the Buckleys opted to see me together.'

'So you never saw either of them on their own?' Kate asked.

'No. They *both* attended every appointment,' Matthias said slowly and deliberately as though explaining to a small child. Kate ignored his patronising tone. He seemed very composed, self-contained and at ease with the situation and Kate didn't want him to feel like he had the upper hand.

'Where were you on Saturday?' she asked, instead of waiting for Hollis to jump in. Kate wanted to unbalance him; to challenge his obvious equilibrium.

'I was at home for much of the day. I probably went for a run and then spent time in the garden or working on the house.' He was completely unruffled by her question, leaving Kate wondering if Janice Hoult had briefed him when they passed in the corridor.

'Alone?'

'Sorry?'

'Do you live alone?' Kate said slowly, mimicking his earlier tone.

'Yes. So there's nobody to verify my movements on Saturday.'

'And you were at home all day?'

Matthias thought for a second. 'Not all day. In the afternoon I volunteer at a local youth group, The Dropzone. I do a bit of counselling with teenagers.'

Matthias had been in no hurry to reveal this verifiable part of his alibi and again, Kate felt like he was teasing her. There was something very controlled about his tone and his body language and she got the distinct feeling that he was drip feeding her the information she requested.

'Do you have children, Mr Matthias?'

For the first time he looked unsettled. If Janice had found time to brief him she obviously hadn't mentioned this question.

'No,' he said, shaking his head and settling his features in an expression that Kate read as puzzled. 'As I said, I'm single at the moment and I don't have children from *any* of my previous relationships.' His intonation suggested that he had women throwing themselves at him on a regular basis.

'So it's a conscious choice? You haven't met the right woman yet?'

'It's a conscious choice, yes. If or when I have children I want the circumstances to be right.'

'Can you give me your impression of the Buckleys?' Kate asked. 'How did they seem as a couple?'

Matthias shifted position, uncrossing his legs and folding his arms across his chest. Kate could see from his body language that he wasn't going to tell her anything of significance.

'Much like any other couple who come here,' he began. 'Desperate but hopeful. They talk about their dreams for the future, their plans for the children that they hope to conceive. Sometimes they talk about the strain that their fertility issues put on the relationship.'

Kate noticed that he was speaking in general terms, deliberately avoiding being specific about Ryan and Melissa.

'And Melissa? What did you make of her?'

'In what way?'

'Did she seem more or less keen than her husband?' Kate asked. 'More desperate?'

'I really couldn't say,' Matthias fudged, leaving it unclear whether he didn't know or didn't want to comment. Kate looked over to Hollis.

'Anything else?'

'I think that's all,' Hollis replied, scanning his notes. There wasn't much else Kate could ask. Matthias had made it clear that he wouldn't discuss specific clients and he'd told them his movements on the day that Melissa disappeared.

Kate stood up. 'Thanks for your time, Mr Matthias. We'll be in touch if there's anything else we need to know.'

'I'm sure you will,' Matthias said as he opened the door.

# Chapter 14

'Well, he was a bit odd,' Hollis said as soon as the door had closed behind the therapist. 'Arrogant, I thought. And that stuff about not wanting kids until the "circumstances" are right. I hope he doesn't tell his clients that.'

'He probably just compartmentalises,' Kate said. 'We all do it. I'm sure some of your personal views conflict with some of the things we end up having to do as coppers.'

'I suppose.'

'Did he seem familiar to you?' Kate asked. 'There was something about him that rang a bell and I can't work out what it was.'

'Nope. And his record's clean. Maybe you met him on another case – he might have been a witness. Easy to check later.'

Kate wasn't convinced. She usually had a good memory for names and faces and she was sure that she would have remembered somebody as distinctive looking as Tim Matthias. Perhaps he just reminded her of somebody.

'Pauline Dorries next,' Hollis said. 'I'm not sure how much she'll be able to tell us but she's the only other employee who had consistent contact with the Buckleys.'

Kate felt disheartened. The fertility clinic was the only feasible lead that they had but it felt very tenuous, especially after the first two interviews. These were professional people doing a job that helped others. What if she was wrong about there being a link? All they had was a wound suggestive of a caesarean section – that could mean something to any number of weirdos. It didn't have to be connected with the clinic.

Her mood wasn't improved by their next interview subject. Pauline Dorries was a tiny grey-haired woman in her mid to late fifties dressed in the same type of pale blue tunic and dark trousers that Janice Hoult had been wearing. She sat down without waiting to be invited and scowled at Kate.

'Well?'

'You do know why you're here?' Kate asked.

'I know it's something to do with the body of that woman that was found on Town Fields. What I don't know is what it's got to do with me.' She crossed her legs and picked a speck of fibre from the knee of her trousers.

'That's what we're hoping to find out,' Kate said. 'You met Melissa and Ryan Buckley. What did you make of them?'

Dorries shook her head. 'I didn't make anything of them. They were just another couple trying like hell to have a baby. I only spoke to Mrs Buckley briefly and then met her husband on a couple of other occasions.'

'How did they seem?'

'Seem? Like everybody else I meet in this place. Tired, frustrated and embarrassed. I don't know what you've been told but all I do here is make sure that the men are comfortable, that they have everything they need to produce their sample, then I take it off them, label it and send it to the lab.'

'So you don't spend any time with them?'

'No more than necessary.' She glanced at Hollis. 'Most of the men just want to get it over with and their wives do their best to be supportive but they don't really want to talk about it either.'

Kate was puzzled. Why had Beresford included this woman in the list of interviewees if she couldn't tell them much? Then she remembered his office and the almost pathological tidiness of his work space. He was being thorough. Kate asked Pauline about her own children – three, all conceived naturally – and her whereabouts on the previous Saturday – home with her family – before thanking her for her time and allowing her to leave.

'Waste of time,' Hollis muttered, finishing his notes and snapping his notebook closed.

'Probably,' Kate admitted. 'I think Beresford's just being thorough.'

'Is that why his name's not on the list?'

Kate smiled. She'd thought about that. After speaking to Beresford the previous day she suspected that he thought his part in the investigation was over. Time to let him know that he'd underestimated his own importance – if that was possible.

'His name might not be on the list but we need to speak to him before we leave.'

'Shall I go and find him?' Hollis asked, starting to get up.

'No point,' Kate said. 'I have a feeling that he'll come to us. He likes to be in control and he won't be happy until he's personally seen us off the premises. I think we'll just wait.'

Hollis sat back down and opened his notebook while Kate thought about what she wanted to know from the clinic's director. So far all he'd given her was a response to her question about a possible appointment for Melissa on the day she went missing and access to his staff. Now Kate needed him to answer the questions that she'd been asking others all morning.

Her patience was rewarded with a tap on the door less than ten minutes later.

'Everything okay?' Beresford asked, peering round the door. 'I thought you might be finished by now.'

'Nearly,' Kate said. 'Would you mind coming in and having a seat?'

Beresford looked baffled but he complied with Kate's request, sitting down opposite her and looking at Hollis who was sitting with pencil poised above a page of his notebook.

'What's this about? Was there a problem with one of my staff?'

Kate noticed the proprietary 'my'. 'Not at all,' she reassured him. 'I just need you to answer some questions. You would have been in contact with the Buckleys and you have admitted that you met them on at least one occasion. I think it wise that you answer the same questions as your staff. Unless you have a problem with that?'

Beresford stared at her, the outrage clear in his startled expression. 'You want *me* to answer questions?'

'We're interviewing everybody who had contact with the Buckleys,' Kate said, mildly. She was trying to sound reasonable but she could see that he was deeply irritated by her request.

'I suppose that's sensible,' he conceded, crossing his legs and straightening the crease in his trousers. 'Can we make it quick though? I'm already running late today.'

Kate found that hard to believe. Beresford struck her as a man who planned everything, down to the most minute detail. What he really meant was that she was holding him up and he didn't want his day's timings to be thrown off by her questions.

'I'll be as quick as I can,' Kate said. 'Firstly – how well did you know the Buckleys?'

'As well as I know all our clients. I do the initial assessment, meet with them and discuss their needs. After I explain what the clinic can offer I pass them on to the appropriate specialists.'

'And you meet all your clients?'

'Oh yes,' Beresford said with a self-satisfied smile. 'I pride myself on a personal service. I'm their first point of contact and I like to think that I can be approached if any difficulties arise.'

'And do they? Do difficulties tend to arise?'

He took a deep breath and Kate sensed that she was trying his patience.

'Rarely. Not in the Buckleys' case.'

'So you didn't see them after your initial assessment?'

Beresford shook his head.

'No. As far as I'm aware my staff handled everything to their usual impeccable standards.'

'You seem to have a lot of faith in your staff,' Kate observed. 'A lot of trust.'

Buckley didn't respond but kept his eyes firmly fixed on Kate's. She could tell that he was trying to work out where she was going with the question.

'A lot of them work weekends, is that right?'

'We open on Saturday mornings for private clients. Obviously I'd like to offer the same service to our NHS-registered couples but that isn't in my bailiwick. I can only do as instructed by the NHS trust.'

Kate heard Hollis splutter, presumably at *bailiwick,* so she tried to cover the noise with another question. 'Do you work on Saturday mornings?'

'Sometimes,' Beresford said. 'If a couple needs their initial assessment at the weekend then, yes, I come in.'

'Were you working last Saturday?'

'No.' He obviously wasn't going to elaborate unless prompted.

'So where were you?'

'At home. I took part in Parkrun, finished by half past nine – a personal best time this week. Then I went home for a shower, caught up on some work and spent the rest of the day pottering.'

'Pottering?'

'Tidying the house, cutting the grass, that sort of thing.'

'Can anybody verify this?'

Beresford's face flushed. 'You're asking if I have an alibi?'

Kate didn't respond, waiting for him to fill the silence.

'I don't have to be here,' he said, getting to his feet and looming over Kate. 'I'm supposed to be running this facility not answering pointless questions.'

Hollis stood up, using his height to grab the other man's attention. 'Please sit down, sir,' he instructed. 'We're only doing our job. We've asked your staff the same questions and they were more than co-operative.'

Beresford looked at Hollis then back at Kate and she saw the tension in his body relax. He smiled shakily. 'I'm sorry,' he said. 'It's just… I'm really busy and I need to get on.'

He sat back down, fastidiously adjusting the creases on the legs of his suit trousers, one foot twitching manically as he crossed his legs.

'Do you live alone?' Kate asked again.

'I do.'

'And there was nobody with you on Saturday?'

A slight hesitation before he replied. 'No.'

'Mr Beresford, do you have children?'

'I have a son. He lives with my ex-wife.'

'So he wasn't with you on Saturday?'

Beresford shook his head. 'As I said…'

'I know. You were pottering.'

There was nothing else to ask him. It would be easy enough to verify his attendance at Parkrun and Kate already had his contact details. If there was any reason for suspicion it was possible that a neighbour might have seen Beresford on Saturday. Or not.

Kate thanked him for his time and allowed him to leave.

\*\*\*

'So. Another one with no concrete alibi?' Hollis observed, tapping his pen on the desk. 'And he's a bit odd.'

Kate smiled. 'You think everybody's a bit odd, Dan. But we certainly made him a bit uncomfortable. Notice the hesitation before he told us that he was on his own on Saturday? I think there's a story there. And the Dorries woman. Talk about unco-operative.'

The morning's interviews hadn't moved them any further forwards but she texted Raymond to let him know the results. She also messaged O'Connor to organise a full check of everybody's alibis – those who had them. Kate's gut was being irritatingly uncommunicative and Hollis's categorisation of Beresford as 'odd' wasn't very helpful. They had a list of technical staff from the main hospital building to work through and she wanted to contact the other receptionist, Amy. In Kate's experience, admin staff were often the most observant people in any organisation. 'Got the other list?' she asked Hollis.

He pulled a folded sheet of A4 paper from his inside pocket and passed it to her. There were nearly a dozen names. Easily an afternoon's work.

'Come on then,' she said. 'Let's see if we can find any more "oddities".'

# Chapter 15

Chloe checked her phone for the third time since she'd arrived at the bar. She'd been registered with the dating site for a couple of months but this was the first time she'd got the feeling that she might have connected with somebody worthwhile. The others had been okay. One had even been able to hold an interesting conversation that wasn't about himself, but Chloe thought that Max had the potential to be the real thing.

She looked again at his profile picture. The thick-framed glasses gave him an intellectual air – Siobhan had dismissed him as 'geeky' but Chloe and her flatmate didn't have the same taste in men – and his thick dark hair and neat beard suggested that he cared about his appearance. Chloe smiled to herself as she remembered their most recent online chat where he'd been keen to find out about her, but also open about himself and his background. He was such a change from the men whose idea of a chat was to brag about their jobs, their possessions or, worse still, their 'prowess'.

She looked around at the heaving crowd of weekend drinkers and revellers. Small knots of people clustered around tables and in the shadowy alcoves of the former church. Most leaned in towards each other, heads blown together by the force of the heavy bass of the loud music.

Chloe had been surprised when Max had suggested Madrigal's as a meeting place as it was one of her regular choices of venue for a first date. It felt safe and familiar and very public. The other men she'd met had either chosen venues which were quiet and intimate or they'd allowed her to choose. She'd selected a position off to one side, standing between two tables with a clear view of the entrance and a place to balance her drink – non-alcoholic of course – she couldn't afford to risk being out of control with a stranger, no matter how 'geeky'.

Another quick check of her phone – just to see what time it was – she wasn't going to revisit Max's profile for the fourth time in less than an hour. Half past eight. There was nobody in the bar who even vaguely resembled the man in the photograph. For the first time since she'd left home, Chloe was beginning to have doubts. They'd arranged to meet at eight and she'd deliberately arrived a few minutes late – no point in seeming too eager – but, as she'd scanned the crowd, she'd realised that her usual tactic had failed her, leaving her no other option than to wait.

Twenty to nine. Still no sign of him. Chloe sighed heavily and began to push her way through the bodies heading in the direction of the bar. She needed a proper drink now; something to take the edge off her disappointment and humiliation.

She'd just ordered a large gin and tonic when a familiar voice addressed the barman.

'I'll get that, mate. And a Peroni for me.'

She turned to smile at her saviour. Perhaps the night hadn't been a complete waste of time.

*\*\**

Chloe wasn't quite sure whose idea it had been to carry on to X-Ray but, when she'd checked her phone and had seen that it was still quite early, she didn't see any harm in having a few more drinks and a dance. The gin had loosened her inhibitions and the company of a charming man had made up for her earlier disappointment.

They'd chatted for over an hour before deciding to move on. Nothing serious, nothing heavy, just two people mulling over their lives, their likes and their dislikes. There had been no need for Chloe to rein in her drinking – it wasn't like she was out with a man that she'd just met online – so she'd happily thrown back two more gin and tonics. The alcohol had improved her mood and she'd barely thought of Max as she'd considered the merits of her saviour. It was good to have company, to talk to somebody who understood her situation, and she was happy to go somewhere for a dance – and a few more drinks.

She left first. Her companion obviously didn't want to explain why he said he'd follow her but she knew that he probably needed the toilet and didn't want to kill the mood by mentioning something so prosaic.

The rain was a surprise. It had been so warm for the past few days that she felt like she'd forgotten the weather could even change. Cursing her lack of foresight, she lifted her handbag over her head and ran up the street.

The bouncer barely glanced at her as she plunged through the doors of the nightclub and into the warm embrace of the trance music that was usually playing on a Friday evening. The club was fairly quiet as she followed the beat down the stairs to the basement room she preferred. The bar was a beacon summoning her deeper and she felt the music loosen her limbs as she walked across the dance floor towards the rows of bottles and bobbing heads. Chloe ordered a Coke with plenty of ice. It was stuffy in the brick cellar and she wanted something refreshing. She didn't regret the gin earlier but it could end up being a long night and she felt the need to try to keep a clear head. Leaving at closing time was always a bit of a scrum and she didn't want to get caught up in anything if she left on her own – which he fully intended to do.

'Hope there's vodka in that.' She turned towards the voice and smiled. After her earlier experience waiting for Max she had felt a flicker of doubt when she'd left Madrigal's on her own but the smile was reassuring and slightly apologetic.

'Thought I was going to get stood up again,' Chloe joked. His smile widened. 'As if.'

\*\*\*

She'd rather have spent some time dancing but they managed to find a seat away from the speakers and continued their conversation from earlier. After a couple of hours, though, Chloe sensed that her companion was losing interest. They'd taken turns buying drinks, Chloe asking for Coke when it was his turn to go to the bar and adding single measures of vodka when it was hers. The last one had made her feel a bit sick and she'd decided that it was time to leave. She stood up and felt the room tilt slightly.

'You okay?' he asked, frowning with concern.

'Just tired, I think,' she said. 'I'll be better after a walk to the taxi rank. The fresh air'll do me good.'

'I could walk with you?'

Chloe shook her head, the motion making her stomach reel. If she was going to throw up then she didn't want a witness.

She bumped into the walls on either side as she climbed the stairs and then, suddenly, she was outside. The fresh air made her head spin again but she managed to remain upright and turned in the direction of the nearest taxi rank.

Ten minutes later Chloe had no idea where she was. People passed by, giving her a wide berth as though she had something contagious, and she considered asking somebody for help. But who? How could she trust a stranger on the street at this time of night?

And then that voice again. 'Chloe? You're going the wrong way for a taxi. Here, let me walk you there.'

She mumbled something about him being her rescuer and snuggled closer when he put his arm round her shoulders.

'It's going to be okay,' he murmured. 'I'll look after you.'

# Chapter 16

'We've got another one,' Raymond's voice boomed down the phone line and through the stereo speakers of Kate's Mini.

'Another one?' Kate asked, leaning forwards slightly in her seat to make sure that the microphone picked up her voice.

'Another body. Like Melissa Buckley.'

Kate indicated left, pulled in to a bus lane and grabbed her phone. This wasn't a conversation that she could risk being overheard by anybody sitting next to her in traffic. She turned off the Bluetooth function of her stereo and tried to steady her breathing as vehicles zipped past her, their drivers honking and scowling.

'Where?' Kate asked.

'Trafford Lane industrial estate. Bin men found her this morning. Posed like the last one, same injuries.'

'Who's at the scene?'

'Barratt. He was in early so I sent him out there. I suppose your mate Kailisa'll be on his way and there'll be assorted SOCOs in attendance.'

Kate checked her watch. Just gone eight. She'd been on her way to Doncaster Central to check statements and follow up alibis. In the two days since she and Hollis had visited the DRI the investigation seemed to be grinding to an embarrassing halt. They desperately needed a break but not like this. They should have been better, more thorough. There shouldn't have been a second body.

'I'm on my way there,' Kate said, hanging up on the DCI and pulling back out into the traffic.

***

Trafford Lane industrial estate lay to the north of Doncaster, backing onto the canal. Kate remembered it from when she was younger and the first rush of out-of-town shopping had sprung up in the early 1980s. It had been a small area of warehouse-sized furniture and gardening stores, all of which had now either gone out of business or been bought out by the giants of the industry. Trafford Lane had become used mainly for storage by the larger retail companies and a small logistics industry had developed around their premises. There was still a large DIY warehouse which was open to the public and a small Gregg's bakery to service the workers in the various operations.

A line of blue and white police tape cordoned off a corner of one of the parking areas guarded by two vans and three liveried police cars. A refuse collection lorry was parked away from the other vehicles with a group of figures huddled around it. Kate could make out two men in dirty fluorescent yellow bibs and two others in police uniform. Easing her Mini into a marked parking area, she studied the scene. She couldn't make out where the body was from where she was sitting but she assessed the car park – trying to imagine it at night. There were two tall streetlights at the entrance and a CCTV camera was perched halfway up the one nearest to her. That looked promising until Kate realised that it was pointed directly towards the pavement and one of the wires was hanging loose, swaying gently in the faint breeze.

'Shit!' she cursed, getting out of the car. Still scanning the car park, she strode over to the operations van where she showed her ID to a young female PCSO who looked like she was only just old enough to have finished her A-levels. Her blonde hair was neatly scraped back into a bun beneath her cap and her face was devoid of make-up. The high-vis vest covering her body armour did little to disguise her trim figure.

The PCSO studied Kate's ID as though it were an ancient artefact from an unknown civilisation before handing it back to her with a practised smile. 'You'll want to see the body,' the young woman said. 'There's quite a crowd back there at the minute.'

'And I'm SIO on a similar case so it's important that you let me through.'

The woman blushed. 'Of course, ma'am.'

'It's detective inspector, not ma'am,' Kate said to the PCSO as she stepped round her.

Behind the ops van was a narrow alley, flanked on one side by the tall wall of one of the warehouses and, on the other, by a rusting chain-link fence which had lost most of its plastic coating and sagged like a damp spider web on a wet day. Kate grabbed a set of overalls from the back of the van and covered her clothes and shoes before proceeding into the gloomy gap between two industrial-sized refuse bins with bright red bases and rugged black plastic tops.

A group of figures huddled about halfway down the length of the building and Kate could make out Kailisa and Barratt as well as two other men who she assumed were SOCOs. She stood, watching, as they slipped evidence into paper bags, the only sound an occasional muttered instruction and the rustle of their protective suits as they brushed against the wall or the fence.

Barratt stood up as she approached, blocking her path towards the body.

'Want to share?' Kate asked him.

'Body of a female. Found this morning when the bin men came in on their rounds. The bins were at the end of this alley and, when they moved the second one, they saw her up here.'

Kate looked back down towards the car park. 'Were the bins locked?'

'No. I had the same thought. Why drag her up here when he could have just tipped her into one of the bins?'

'And?'

'She's displayed like the last one. Naked from the waist down. Same injury to her abdomen.'

'Can I have a look?'

Barratt stepped back, flattening himself against the wall to allow Kate to pass. Kailisa turned as she approached and she was almost sure that she heard him sigh.

'Detective Inspector Fletcher. How lovely to see you,' he said turning back to his examination of the body. 'Let me answer your questions as succinctly as possible.'

Kate smiled; despite his formal tone he appeared to be in the mood to co-operate.

'Female. Early twenties to early thirties. Well nourished. Fair hair, minimal make-up. Undressed from the waist down. Large incision to the abdomen. Bruises around the neck and throat with a possible hyoid fracture. Time of death as yet unascertained. Identity unknown.'

Just like Melissa Buckley.

Kate peered round the pathologist and was shocked at the similarity to the photographs of the last crime scene. The woman didn't bear any physical resemblance to Melissa but the similarities in the pose and the wound were striking. The body was propped up against the fence, legs pointing towards the warehouse wall. Her upper body was clothed in an expensive-looking short-sleeved blouse, the top two buttons open, displaying an ample cleavage. Her hair was strawberry blonde, carefully styled and looked recently cut, and her make-up, while subtle was expertly applied. Her face looked almost serene, eyes closed, head tilted slightly back, but the bruises around her neck screamed violence. As Kate shifted her gaze downwards she saw the damage done to the woman's abdomen, a long cut, about three inches below her navel. It looked identical to the one inflicted on Melissa but Kate knew Kailisa wouldn't commit to any similarities until he'd completed a thorough PM and the accompanying forensic tests.

'What's that?' she asked, leaning in for a closer look. The woman's feet were bare but there was something on her ankle.

'Tattoo,' Kailisa said. 'Looks like a Chinese character.'

'Any others?'

'There's another one on her wrist, small, discreet.' He reached out a gloved hand and turned the woman's left arm over revealing a stylised flower design on the skin below her palm. Outlined in black, it looked almost geometric.

'What is that? Some sort of flower?'

'It's a lotus flower,' Kailisa said. 'It has many meanings in Hinduism. Purity, beauty, fertility, prosperity.'

*Fertility,* Kate thought. *Coincidence?*

'Can you email me photographs of the tattoos, please? If we can't ID her we can try local tattoo parlours, somebody might remember the designs. The lotus looks unusual.'

'I'll send the photographs as soon as I get back to the DRI.'

Kate itched to reach into her jacket pocket and get her phone out but that would have involved unzipping her overalls and she couldn't risk any contamination of the scene.

'Anything else?' she asked. 'Jewellery? Other distinguishing marks?'

Kailisa gently eased a few strands of the woman's hair clear of one of her ears.

'A gold sleeper in each ear. Nothing unusual, nothing fancy.'

Kate stepped back, trying to imagine what attracted the killer to this particular woman. Was it the fertility tattoo or was it something else? She appeared to be well dressed although they would need to see the clothes from the lower half of the body to be sure. The make-up and jewellery suggested that she might have been on a night out, but her clothing was understated. Perhaps she was meeting somebody who was already known to her? She might not have felt the need to pull out all the stops for somebody who was familiar, especially if she'd been going for a meal or to the cinema.

That made sense. The previous evening had been Friday – traditionally a big night out but it could just have easily been a convenient evening for a more low-key date. Had her killer courted her first? Was this all part of his plan? Kate had a gut feeling that, if she could identify this woman, she might be much closer to finding her killer than she had been with Melissa Buckley.

'I need pictures of those tats as soon as possible,' Kate said. 'If I step back beyond the cordon to get my phone out of my pocket, can I use it?'

Kailisa frowned up at her. 'We're about to remove the body. Can it wait until I can send you the photographs?'

'No,' Kate said. 'I need to find out who she is. If I can ID her it might take us a step closer to the killer.'

Kailisa sighed. 'Very well.'

Kate retraced her steps, brushing past Barratt on the way and struggled with the zip on her protective overalls. It seemed to take her an age to remove her phone from her inside pocket and zip everything back up and she could almost hear Kailisa drumming his fingers on his instrument case.

'Sorted,' she said, stepping as close to the body as she dared. 'If you could just…'

Kailisa had anticipated her request and turned the woman's arm over again to reveal the tattoo. Kate snapped off three quick shots, two close-ups and one from further away to show the position of the design on the wrist.

'And the ankle.'

Kailisa stepped back allowing Kate a clear view of the Chinese character.

'Thanks,' she said. 'PM tomorrow?'

Kailisa smiled for the first time since Kate had arrived. 'Tomorrow is Sunday, DI Fletcher. I know police officers work long hours but I'm not obliged to follow suit. Monday morning will be soon enough.'

Kate grinned back. She knew that Kailisa would happily work on a Sunday if he had co-operative staff. He was just as dedicated as every member of her team when it came to seeking justice for murder victims.

'I'll see you then,' she said heading back down the alley.

Three emails and two phone calls later and she'd allocated jobs to each member of her team. Cooper and O'Connor were dispatched to various tattoo shops around the town and the outskirts; Barratt had opted to stay with the body until it was removed and then check through the statements given by the bin men; Hollis was on his way to meet Kate at ThInk!, Doncaster's largest and most popular tattoo studio.

# Chapter 17

'You never fancied one?' Hollis asked, scanning the designs that covered every wall of the cramped reception room.

'What makes you think I've not got one already?' Kate said.

Hollis squinted at her and shook his head. 'No. Can't see it. I doubt you ever had a rebellious phase.'

'I think my rebellion was more of the drinking and smoking type. I've never really had the urge to indelibly mark my body. What about you?'

'What, spoil this?' Hollis flattened one hand and ran it down the front of his body. 'You can't improve perfection, especially not with a tattoo.'

'I wouldn't say perfection,' Kate responded. 'At least you're looking a bit better today.'

Hollis's appearance had improved a little. When she'd met him he was freshly shaven and his suit looked neatly pressed, but he still looked hungover and in need of a haircut.

Whatever he'd been going to say in response was cut off by the appearance of a middle-aged woman from a door which obviously led to a back room. She was short and her slim figure was swimming in a pair of oversized dungarees under which she was wearing a white vest that revealed sleeves of artwork on both arms. Kate's first thought was that she'd escaped from Dexy's Midnight Runners sometime around the mid-1980s.

'Can I help you?' the woman asked, looking at Kate before giving Hollis a long once-over.

'We'd like to speak to you about some tattoos,' Kate began.

'Well you're in the right place. What is it you want? Matching? His and hers?'

Kate held out her warrant card. 'We don't want to get tattooed, we're trying to find out who might have been responsible for the artwork on a young woman. You are?'

'Jill,' the woman said. 'Jill Ogden, like Coronation Street. I own this place and do a lot of the work.' She stuffed her hands in the pockets of her dungarees, her face suddenly serious. 'You're trying to identify somebody, aren't you?'

Kate gave her the usual line about not being able to comment on an ongoing investigation, but she could see that Jill wasn't convinced.

'Fine. I know you can't tell me but if it's somebody local the chances are that she came in here at some point. We're the best in town and everybody knows it.'

'How many people work here?' Kate asked.

'Three. In the week we have a receptionist and another sketch artist – he'll probably be in later. It's only me this early on a Saturday though. If I get a customer, I just leave the door to the studio open so I can see if anybody else comes in.'

'Do you do many Chinese symbols?'

'A few. They were more popular about ten years ago, after the Celtic art phase. Then the Maori stuff came in. Now it's all either celebrity faces or fantasy stuff.'

Kate held out her phone. 'Do you know what this symbol is?'

Jill took the phone and used two fingers to enlarge the image.

'Woman. It's the Chinese symbol for woman. I've done loads of those. Did one really high up on a girl's thigh. Told her that by the time somebody saw it they'd have worked out what sex she was.'

Kate took the phone back and flicked through the images until she had the clearest one of the lotus flower. 'What about this?'

Jill's face froze.

'You recognise it?' Kate prompted. 'Is it one of yours?'

'No, it's not mine, but I know who did it. He was going to fill it in but he never got the chance.'

Kate heart rate gave a sudden jump. Could it really be this easy?

'Hazza, the other artist who works here did that. It's quite small, right?'

Kate nodded in confirmation.

'His girlfriend wanted a tattoo on her wrist. He said it wasn't a good idea. Wrists are like the neck, really hard to cover – I suppose you could wear tight cuffs but that's not great in warm weather. Anyway, he couldn't convince her otherwise so he said he'd do it if she kept it small. Did the outline in heavy black and he was going to shade it in in pale blues and purples but she dumped him before he got the chance.'

'Do you remember her name?'

'Course I do. Chloe. Nice lass. Probably a bit too good for Hazza. I always thought that he was her bit of rough.'

'Chloe what?'

The woman scratched an eyebrow. 'Same name as some celebrity. Or was it a newsreader? Shit, what was it?'

Kate waited, trying to rein her impatience.

'Welsh. That was it. I remember Hazza saying something about her being English and thinking it was hilarious. Chloe Welsh.'

Hollis took out his notebook and wrote the name down.

'And when was this?' he asked. 'When did she dump Hazza?'

'Two, three years ago. And she never did get that outline filled in.' Realisation struck. The woman went still as the full implication of the conversation sunk in. 'She's dead, isn't she?'

Kate and Hollis remained silent.

'I know you can't say but that's why you're here. Bloody hell. Hazza'll be devastated. Loved her, he did.'

'Do you have a contact number for Hazza?' Kate didn't want to get drawn into any further conversation about Chloe Welsh's fate. Jill groped in her pocket for her phone.

'It's his morning off and it's still early so he's probably in bed, hung-over. He lives in town on one of the streets off Thorne Road, up near the hospital. Sorry, I haven't got an address. I've got a mobile and a landline.' She showed Hollis the screen and he noted down the numbers.

'His name's Josh Harrington.'

'Whose name?' Kate was puzzled.

'Hazza. His real name's Josh Harrington. We call him Hazza because of his surname.'

*Not the most original nickname,* Kate thought as she thanked the woman and led Hollis back to where she'd parked her Mini.

'Shall I ring the others?' Hollis asked. 'Seems like a bit of a wild goose chase now we've got a name.'

'No.' Kate wasn't ready to pull both of her colleagues off the search for the dead woman's identity just in case Jill Ogden was wrong. 'I'll give O'Connor Sam's list and send Sam back to base. I think she'll be more use trying to find out anything she can about Chloe Welsh. I'll try this "Hazza" first though.'

She dialled the mobile number that Jill had given Hollis but it went straight to voicemail.

'Must still be in bed.' She tried the landline. Just as she was about to hang up somebody picked up the phone at the other end.

'Hello?' The voice was groggy and difficult to hear.

'Josh Harrington?'

'Who wants to know? If this is a sales call you can sod off.'

'Don't hang up,' Kate instructed. 'I'm a police officer and I need to talk to you about your ex-girlfriend Chloe Welsh.'

'Is this a joke?'

'It's no joke, Mr Harrington. And I'd rather not do this over the phone. Jill Ogden gave me your number but she didn't have an address for you other than you live off Thorne Road somewhere.'

'I'm not giving you my address,' Harrington said, his voice much stronger now. 'How do I know who you are?'

Kate had expected this. 'I'll give you the number of my desk at Doncaster Central. Ring it and ask if I work there. Or ring Jill Ogden, she'll confirm that we've just spoken to her.' She gave him the number and told him that she'd ring back in ten minutes.

# Chapter 18

'Nice place,' Hollis remarked as they pulled up outside a Victorian house on a shady street that ran south off Thorne Road. 'Wouldn't have thought tattooing would be very lucrative.'

Harrington had rung back within Kate's ten-minute deadline and given his address. She and Hollis had driven separately to Doncaster Central where Kate had left her car, allowing Hollis to drive to their destination.

'It's probably been knocked about inside,' Kate said. 'Flats and bedsits. The building's probably all fur coat and no knickers.'

She led the way up the laurel-shrouded path to the imposing front door and her suspicions were confirmed as she scrutinised a row of labelled door bells. She pressed the fourth one down and the main door opened, with a buzz, into a dingy hallway which smelled of cooking with an underlying hint of cat pee.

'Maybe it's not such a nice place,' Hollis mumbled.

Two scuffed and peeling doors led off left and right with an imposing staircase dominating the middle of the hallway. Kate checked the doors but they were numbers one and two so she started to climb the stairs which wound round to the upper floors. The stale smell seemed to dissipate as they climbed higher and the next floor was brighter – lit by a skylight in the landing to the second floor.

'There,' Kate pointed to a door at the foot of another staircase. It looked like the ones below, shoe marks near the base where it had probably been held or kicked open and the paint around the lock and handle a peeling off-white.

The door was slightly ajar so Kate pushed it open. 'Mr Harrington?'

'In here.' The voice came from a room at the end of a short hallway. Kate pushed open the next door to reveal a crowded sitting room which smelt of cigarette smoke and something sweeter, possibly incense, possibly cannabis. A sagging sofa faced a huge flat-screen television. Beneath it was a games console – four handsets lay clustered around an overflowing ashtray on a grimy-looking coffee table. Kate instinctively checked the contents of the ashtray and noted that the smell definitely wasn't incense.

A small figure was hunched on the sofa; tracksuit bottoms and a grey hoodie doing nothing to disguise his slim frame or the trembling in his limbs.

'Josh?'

The man looked up at her and Kate saw grey slashes of tiredness beneath his eyes. She introduced herself and Hollis and looked around for a seat. Taking one of the straight-backed chairs next to a compact dining table she nodded towards the other, indicating that Hollis should sit down. The last thing she wanted to do was intimidate the witness before they'd had a chance to talk to him properly. With the light from the window behind her, Kate was able to get a better look at Josh Harrington. She was surprised at his stature, expecting a tattooist to be imposing, or at least a little unusual in physical appearance, but Harrington looked like a teenager awaiting a telling off from his parents. The only thing that put him in his twenties was a straggly beard that might have been called 'hipster' by somebody more generous that Kate.

'You understand why we're here?'

'It's about Chloe, int it?' Harrington responded, his grey eyes suddenly glassy with tears. 'She's dead, int she? That's what Jill told me.'

He'd obviously rung his employer back after he'd spoken to Kate. 'I suppose you want to know about me and her?'

Kate took out her phone and scrolled through to the pictures of the dead woman's tattoos. 'Can you confirm that this is your work?'

She passed the phone to Harrington who zoomed in on the first image – the Chinese character.

'It could be mine,' Harrington said. 'But lots of women get this design.'

'Have a look at the next one.'

He flicked the screen and the nervous twitching suddenly stilled, his breathing turning to shallow gasps.

'Josh,' Kate prompted gently.

'It's hers. I remember the shape of the petals, I gave them an extra bit of curve – redesigned the original pattern. She never had it coloured.'

'Jill Ogden gave us a description of Chloe, Josh. It matches a body that was discovered this morning. The tattoos confirm the ID.'

Harrington hung his head. 'And I suppose I'm a suspect, being the ex-boyfriend?'

'We just want to build up a picture of Chloe's life.' Kate ignored his question. 'You split up what, two years ago?'

'Nearly three,' Harrington said miserably.

'Why was that?'

He sighed. 'She dumped me. She was ambitious, you know? She wanted to get on. She'd decided that she was going to do a degree and she said I was holding her back. Said that she could do better than this.' He waved his hand limply in the air, indicating the state of the room. 'She said I was a waste of space and I wasn't making anything of my life. Probably right.'

Hollis had taken out his notebook and was jotting down Harrington's responses.

'And when did you last see Chloe?' Kate asked.

'I've seen her around. Pubs and clubs and that. But we've not really spoken since she dumped me. I suppose the last time was in The Lion a couple of months ago.'

'Who was she with? Was she on a date?'

'No, she was with a group of women. They were pretty rowdy. Looked like it was a hen night or something. No blokes.'

'And how did she seem?'

Harrington frowned at Kate. 'She seemed like she was having a good time. Laughing and that. I was a bit wasted so I'm probably not the best judge.'

Kate considered his answer. Could he have been enraged seeing her so happy and decided to do something about it? It was plausible; but three years later? That seemed a long time to wait. And how could he have known about Melissa Buckley's injuries and copied them? Unless he'd killed Melissa as well.

'We've not had time to find Chloe's family. Obviously we need to inform them. Do you have any idea who we can contact?

'There's nobody,' Harrington said. 'Her friends were her family. Her mum and dad were killed in a car crash when she was ten and her nan brought her up after that. The nan had a stroke a few years ago and died.'

'So who did she live with?'

'She shared a flat with a friend called Siobhan something when we were going out. I can give you the address.'

Kate tried to work out the implications of Harrington's revelation. Chloe could have been a lonely and vulnerable young woman – an easy target. But that didn't quite gel with a woman out enjoying herself surrounded by friends. It was time to get to the important questions. She turned to Hollis and raised her eyebrows indicating that they were about to start on the 'good stuff' and that he should note down *everything*.

'Josh, where were you last night?'

Suddenly Harrington couldn't meet her eyes. 'I was out with my mates.'

'Out?'

'We went to The Star and a couple of other places then on to X-Ray.'

'What time did you leave?'

'Two, half two. I'm not really sure. I'd had a fair bit to drink.'

'And did anybody see you leave? Did you leave with anybody?'

He shook his head. 'I didn't pull if that's what you're getting at. I told my mates that I was leaving, one of them might remember the time.'

'We'll need names and numbers.'

Harrington removed his phone from the front pocket of his hoodie and turned to Hollis. He gave the DC four male names and had to look in his phone for their mobile numbers.

'We were all pretty wasted,' he said. 'Not sure how much they'll remember.'

Again the shifty look.

'What about last Saturday?' Kate asked.

'Last Saturday?' he looked confused.

'Where were you last Saturday,' Kate repeated slowly.

'Same probably. Had a few drinks with my mates. That's what I usually do on a Saturday.

'And in the daytime?'

'Home in the morning. I'm usually a bit hungover after a Friday night out so it takes me a while to surface. Then I went to work.'

Kate looked around the room. There was enough seating for three or four people – and then there were the games handsets. 'Do you live here on your own?'

He looked suddenly relieved, as though Kate had thrown him a lifeline when he'd felt certain that he was going to drown.

'No,' he said on a huge exhalation. 'I share the flat with two other guys. Mikey's away for the weekend but Jack's around somewhere. He was still up when I got in this morning – he'll remember what time it was, he's not much of a drinker. I'll see if he's in his room.'

He went out into the flat's cramped hallway and Kate heard a sharp knocking on a door. Two more taps and Harrington was back.

'Must've gone out. I can give you his mobile number.' His eagerness to please was almost pathetic. He'd found a possible way out of his predicament and he was desperately clinging on to it.

Hollis took the number and Chloe's address and they left Harrington with an instruction to contact Doncaster Central if he thought of anything else that might help.

'He doesn't feel right for this,' Hollis commented as soon as they closed the car doors. 'I think his ex was right – a bit of a waste of space. Not sure he could be bothered to make the effort to kill somebody.'

Kate agreed. Harrington had seemed genuinely upset by their visit and there was no obvious link to Melissa Buckley. She'd resisted asking if he knew her in case he'd already heard about her case. She hadn't wanted him to make the link between the two murders and go running his mouth off in a drunken stupor.

'Let's try the address he gave us,' she said. Hollis checked his notebook and then slipped the car into gear.

# Chapter 19

The address that Harrington had given them was for a flat in a converted factory in Balby. More upmarket than Harrington's own building, this one had a glass entrance door which opened onto an airy vestibule. The door bells were in a row above a speaker, an additional layer of security, allowing residents to ascertain who was visiting.

Harrington had given the address as Flat 6 – the label next to the buzzer bearing that number was blank. Kate was impressed. If two women lived here they were sensible enough not to advertise their names to any casual caller. She pressed six and a metallic voice answered almost immediately. 'Hello?'

'Is that Siobhan?'

'Who's this?'

Kate introduced herself, approving of the woman's caution. She explained that she also had DC Hollis with her and that they wanted to talk about Chloe. After a second's hesitation they were buzzed into the foyer with instructions to follow the stairs up to the second floor. The building looked like quite a recent conversion. The paintwork was scuff-free and the cathedral-sized windows on each landing looked like they had been recently cleaned, allowing the bright afternoon sun to stream through to the industrial metal staircase.

The door to Flat Six was open. Kate tapped twice and a voice invited them in. Inside was as bright and modern as the entrance hall and staircase but with the addition of swathes of colour. The walls of the hallway were painted yellow and pale blue, and one was adorned with film posters from the 1990s. Tim Robbins, shirt blowing in a storm, leaned back to embrace the rain on an advertisement for *The Shawshank Redemption* and next to him, Keanu Reeves was a tall dark triangle on a poster for *The Matrix.*

'Through here,' the voice said, leading them into a large living room which made full use of the light from the two floor-to-ceiling windows. It could have been a Manhattan loft – if it hadn't had a view of the main road through Balby.

'Siobhan?' Kate asked.

The woman confirmed her identity and Kate reintroduced herself and Hollis. Siobhan looked pale, her pallor accentuated by dark, almost black hair. She was wearing a towelling dressing gown – white hearts dotted across a garish cerise. Her eyes flicked from Kate to Hollis – she was frightened. 'Has something happened to Chloe?'

'What makes you think that?' Kate kept her tone gentle, neutral.

'She didn't come home last night and she didn't text me. We always text each other if we cop off. Sometimes we even send pictures of the bloke or his address. Just in case.'

'So you think she might have met somebody last night?'

'Well, that's kind of what I assumed. Is she all right?'

Kate sent Dan to find the kitchen and put the kettle on while she sat next to Siobhan on the sofa. 'She's not all right. I'm very sorry, Siobhan – a body was found earlier this morning. We still need to find somebody who can confirm the identity but we're almost certain it's Chloe. It looks very much like somebody killed her.'

Siobhan was obviously trying to hold herself together but her chin trembled as she asked if Chloe had been sexually assaulted.

'It's too early to tell,' Kate said. 'There are a lot of tests to be done.'

Siobhan gave a small nod of understanding then stood up. 'Do you mind if I go and get dressed? It feels disrespectful to be talking about her like this with me slobbing about in my dressing gown.'

'That might be a good idea. Would you mind if we had a look in Chloe's room while you get yourself sorted? There might be something there that could help.'

'Second door on the right,' Siobhan said. 'I doubt you'll find anything. Chloe and me didn't have any secrets. We were like sisters.' Her voice broke on the final word and she dashed to the door of her bedroom, closing it firmly behind her. Kate collected Hollis from the kitchen where he was gazing out of the window waiting for the kettle to boil and shoved him towards the door of Chloe's room.

'She says it's okay if we have a look around. I doubt we'll find much but it's worth a try.'

Chloe Welsh's bedroom was much more spartan than Kate would have expected of a woman in her late twenties. The walls were cream as was the duvet cover on the double bed and a series of framed prints of views of world cities were the only pictures on the walls. No friends or family, Kate noticed. There was a wardrobe in light wood and a matching chest of drawers which served as a dressing table. The surface was littered with make-up and a mirror reflected the light from the tall window. Kate opened the top drawer – underwear and more make-up. The second contained tops and the third seemed to be a mix of sweatshirts and socks. Not very organised.

The wardrobe was similar. Dresses and trousers hung askew with no apparent system and the bottom of the space was awash with shoes, obviously thrown in and mostly mismatched. There was nothing here to give much sense of the woman that Chloe Welsh had been, beyond her chaotic approach to storage.

'Anything?' she asked Hollis who was standing behind her, leaning on the door jamb.

'Looks fairly conventional to me. No laptop or tablet? I would have thought if she was studying for a degree she'd have needed a computer.'

This was much more like the Dan Hollis she knew; shrewd and observant.

'It might be in the living room. I wasn't really looking.'

She sent Dan back to the kitchen and sat down on the sofa to wait for Siobhan, casting her eyes around for a computer. Lodged between an armchair and a side table she could see a neoprene case and a charger. Just what she was looking for. She considered leaning down to inspect it but they had no warrant and, for all she knew, it could belong to the other woman in the flat. Better to wait.

Hollis came in with a tray containing three mugs of tea placed carefully on coasters. Kate noticed that hers was strong with only a dash of milk – just how she liked it – Hollis was definitely back in the game. His eyes were drawn to the laptop case and he gave Kate a questioning look to which she shrugged in response. The quick shorthand gestures were familiar and reassuring.

Siobhan strode back into the room and sat down on a chair opposite Kate. She glanced at the mug of tea on the table near her elbow but didn't pick it up. She looked more composed, less vulnerable, now that she was dressed in skinny black jeans and a pink T-shirt and she'd obviously applied a little make-up but it didn't disguise the redness around her eyes or the sad droop of her mouth as she looked expectantly at Kate. 'I suppose you want to know about Chloe? What she was like, who she was seeing, that sort of thing.' Again, the trembling of the chin but she was obviously trying desperately to keep herself together.

Kate admired the effort and the amount of respect it demonstrated for her friend. She'd interviewed family and friends who could barely form a coherent sentence, so devastated were they by grief, but not this woman. She clearly wanted to help but she'd probably fall apart as soon as Kate and Hollis left and the enormity of her loss hit her full force.

'Can I take your full name,' Kate began.

'Siobhan Dunne,' the other woman responded.

'And how long have you and Chloe shared this flat?' Kate began.

'Four and a bit years. My dad's a developer and he bought the building. The flat's mine but Chloe pays me rent. It's minimal to be honest but she's a friend and it's not like she has much money.'

'You've known each other a long time?' Kate was careful not to use the past tense.

'A few years. We both worked in the same restaurant in town when we were in our late teens. Fabrio's?' Kate knew the place. It was well known in the Doncaster area for cheap and plentiful Italian food.

'Where do you work now?'

'I'm a junior buyer for the NHS. I travel a lot during the week but I'm always home for the weekend.'

'And Chloe?'

'She's been working at an organic farm shop off the Bawtry Road. Chilcott's. She's been there about two years. I don't think it pays well but it gives her time to study.'

Kate glanced down at the computer case. 'What was she studying?' There was no way to phrase the question in present tense. Siobhan obviously registered the shift as her eyes welled with tears.

'Psychology with the OU. She started eighteen months ago.'

'What about her social life? Did she have a boyfriend? Somebody steady?'

Siobhan smiled sadly. 'She gave up on all that when she got ill.'

'She'd been ill?' Kate wondered what could have been wrong that Chloe would put her life on hold.

'She was diagnosed with non-Hodgkins lymphoma three years ago. It really shook her up. That's a big part of the reason why she dumped her boyfriend, Josh. She'd been going out with him for ages but she knew he wouldn't have been strong enough to support her through it.'

'And was she still having treatment?' Kate asked.

'No that was all finished. She was lucky really. She had a lump in her neck but it turned out to be quite localised, it hadn't spread. She had an operation and then some radiotherapy.'

'Must've been a shock.'

Siobhan nodded. 'It was. She was terrified. Started making all sorts of provisions in case she didn't make it. She made a will and everything. Even had some of her eggs frozen in case she couldn't have kids after the treatment. She's only started dating again in the last few months. She'd been using websites and dating apps. Nothing serious, maybe once a fortnight. She said it was just for fun but it was good to see her thinking about the future. That's where she was last night, I think.' Her eyes widened as she realised the implication of what she'd just said. 'You don't think she went out with the person who… who… did this?'

'We really can't speculate at this stage. Can we just go back a bit? You said that Chloe had some of her eggs frozen?'

Siobhan smiled weakly. 'She was a planner. I think it was because her childhood was so chaotic so she always wanted to be prepared. I tried to talk her out of it, to be honest. I thought she'd have enough medical stuff to cope with without all that.'

'But she did it?'

'Yep,' Chloe sighed. 'Went to the hospital and got it sorted.'

'The DRI? Not to a fertility clinic?'

'No. I went with her. It was in the main hospital.'

Kate tried to hide her disappointment. For a few seconds there had been a glimmer of hope, a hint of a link to Melissa Buckley. 'And she's made no attempt to use the eggs?'

'Is this relevant?' Siobhan asked. 'It seems a bit personal.'

'Trust me,' Kate said. 'I wouldn't ask if it wasn't important.'

'She said that she might visit the fertility clinic to explore her options. I don't think she'd met anybody special, but she'd got the all clear and she wanted to know if she could still have kids naturally. I don't know if she went through with it, though.'

*There might be something in her email,* Kate thought, *or a letter somewhere in the flat.* They'd need Siobhan's permission to search but it seemed likely that they'd meet with little objection.

'Where did she go last night?' Kate asked. The link with Melissa had been established but it required further investigation. It could be a coincidence and they needed to follow every possible line of enquiry rather than get side-tracked.

Siobhan looked anxious. 'I have no idea. I was back late from Nottingham and she wasn't in when I got home. She'd been talking about meeting some bloke who worked in a bank but I don't know the details. She showed me his photo online – but everybody fakes them, don't they? He looked all right, a bit studious, glasses and a goatee, but she liked that type. She probably started at Madrigal's. That's where she usually meets online dates. It's often busy and very public, not many shady corners. She liked X-Ray as well but, if she wanted something quieter, she'd probably go to the Swan – they serve decent food and it's not too expensive. She never lets the man pay – said it led to all sorts of expectations.'

Hollis was scribbling furiously. Kate found herself warming to Chloe Welsh. She'd had a rough start in life but she seemed to know her own mind and she was also sensible about her expectations of men.

'Siobhan. When Chloe was using an online dating site did she use her phone or a computer?'

Siobhan glanced down at the laptop case. 'Both. Mainly her phone but sometimes, when she was writing an essay, she'd check her messages as a bit of a break.'

Kate leaned down and picked up the case. 'Is this Chloe's?'

Siobhan smiled. 'It's always lying about somewhere. She never remembers to put it back in her room. I keep telling her that I'm going to drop something on it one day, or trip over it but she never listens.' Her last word became a strangled sob. Kate could see that the reality of the situation was catching up with Siobhan and their window of opportunity might be closing.

'I'm going to send my colleague to get an evidence bag and we're going to take the laptop if that's okay? There might be something on it that could lead us to whoever did this to Chloe.'

Even to Kate's ears it sounded like she was trying to use Siobhan's loyalty to Chloe to gain access to potential evidence but she needed to act fast. If Chloe had met her killer online he might have already deleted his profile, which had probably been fake anyway. It was a slim chance but it was all they had.

While Hollis went down to his car Kate quizzed Siobhan further about Chloe's life but there was nothing out of the ordinary and, significantly, no obvious connection to Melissa Buckley other than the fertility clinic. Siobhan painted a picture of a young woman who loved life, despite the tragedy that had shaped her younger years, and was planning for a bright future.

She explained that a forensics team would need access to the flat and to Chloe's room and gave Siobhan her number in case she remembered anything else. Laptop bagged and signed for Kate left the girl slumped on the sofa with her grief.

Just as she was about to open the passenger door to Hollis's car Kate's phone rang. An unknown number.

'DI Fletcher?' It was Siobhan. 'I'd like to be the one to identify Chloe's body if that's okay. And the man that Chloe was thinking about meeting, the bank one? His name might have been Mike or Max, something like that.'

# Chapter 20

Sunday lunch had always been Dan's favourite time of the week when he'd been growing up. His mum had always started early, preparing the veg and putting the meat in the oven soon after breakfast. Lamb was his favourite but he didn't mind if it was chicken or beef because the 'trimmings' were always the same: crispy roast potatoes, mash, mushy peas, carrots and Yorkshire puddings. It was the Yorkshires that he'd looked forward to the most. Two with his meal and another one smothered in raspberry jam for afters. Since he'd been an adult he'd had Sunday lunch at pubs and restaurants but it was never the same. The Yorkshires were always too crispy and he'd never been offered raspberry jam.

He knocked on the door despite being told countless times not to bother; it just didn't feel right walking in now that he didn't live here anymore. It was the first time in over two months that he'd been back to his parents' house. He'd used the pressures of work as an excuse but the truth was, he'd been unsettled by the return of his 'real' mum and he didn't want to contaminate his parents' home with her poison until he'd managed to get it in perspective. He'd wanted to postpone the visit again but he was running out of excuses.

He hadn't seen Suzanne for a few days and he was starting to feel a bit better now he'd spoken to Kate. The nights were difficult though. The Buckley/Welsh case and the nagging doubts about his biological father's identity kept leading him back to the bottle and he was aware that his parents would probably be able to see and smell the evidence.

'Dan!' His mum threw open the door and pulled him into a hug. Not an easy task for her as she was only five feet two and he towered over her. She held him tight then pushed him out to arm's length so that she could get a better look at him.

'You're looking skinny. I bet you're not eating properly.' She scowled up at him, her deep brown eyes shrewdly assessing his face. 'Working too hard, knowing you. You look tired and I bet you were out drinking last night.'

Dan smiled down at her, feeling the warmth of her welcome seep into his muscles. As soon as he'd pulled his car onto the drive he'd started to relax and the hug had finished the job. No need to tell her that he was indeed drinking last night – but on his own and quite heavily.

Anybody who met his parents would have been able to see that Dan had been adopted. Maggie, his mother, was tiny and round. Her dark hair had faded to a distinguished grey as she'd aged and her battle with her weight was long since lost. His father, Joe, was also small but, where Maggie had padding, Joe had points and angles. His fair hair had receded to the point of invisibility and his blue eyes were lost under bushy eyebrows, as though his facial hair was overcompensating for the scarcity of its brethren on his scalp. He was peering over his wife's shoulder, grinning excitedly like a teenager who'd just got to the front of a queue to see a celebrity.

'Dan. Good to see you,' Joe said, finally managing to push past his wife and grab his son by the hand. Never very emotionally demonstrative, Joe had managed to convey as much affection with a handshake as his wife did with a hug. His hand was strong and warm, very much like the man who offered it.

'Come on through then,' Maggie was saying, leading the way into the kitchen. 'Do you want a cuppa?'

Dan declined, seating himself in his customary seat at the kitchen table. It was here that he'd sat every afternoon after school, doing homework or eating his tea while his mother fussed over him and told him how clever he was and what a good life he was going to make for himself. As a teenager, Dan had been sceptical about his mother's predictions rather than rebellious, but he had to admit that his mum had been right. He had done well at school and he was making a good life for himself – as long as he didn't allow other people to ruin it.

While his mum fussed over the final preparations for the meal, Dan told his parents a little about work, especially the last big case which had fascinated them at the time. Maggie had always been a firm advocate of the 'right to die' but a recent case of assisted suicide had been much more complicated than it first appeared and it had shaken some of her certainty. The case had been in court recently and Maggie had been following it avidly, her pride in her son apparent as she listened again to his account of his own role in bringing a killer to justice.

***

Lunch eaten the family sat in the cosy living room, Joe drinking his second can of lager of the day, Dan with a Coke and Maggie with a cup of herbal tea. Dan had tried to broach the subject of Suzanne while they had been eating but his mum had regaled him with stories of his cousin, Martin, who had just bought a camper van and was intending to renovate it and travel Europe for six months. Dan had smiled, tolerantly. He'd always been measured against Martin as they'd been growing up and, as Dan had turned out to be more reliable and a better scholar, Martin had always come up short. Dan hadn't seen Martin for years but a small part of him envied his cousin's laid-back approach to life.

Now, in the soporific after-lunch period, probably wasn't the best time to bring up his birth mother but Dan felt the need to warn his parents that Suzanne was causing trouble just in case she tried to draw them into her drama. There was no easy way to broach the subject so he went for the direct approach.

'Suzanne's back,' he said. 'She's been hanging around Doncaster Central spreading her bile.' He tried to keep his tone light but he knew that Maggie wouldn't be fooled.

'What does she want?' his mum asked, sharply, putting her cup down carefully and balling her fists as though preparing for a fight.

'The usual. Money.'

'You haven't given her any?' His dad was equally concerned.

'Nope. And I'm not going to. She got into my head for a bit but it's my own fault for allowing her to get to me. I'm feeling a bit better now.'

'What do you mean *"got into your head"*? Is she trying to play some sort of mind games with you?' Joe leaned forward in his seat and Dan could see that he was getting angry at the mere mention of the woman who had accidentally given birth to his son.

Dan hesitated. He'd never been much good at keeping secrets from his parents. He decided, as usual, that the truth was the safest option. He explained about Suzanne's insinuations and his own suspicions about Raymond.

Joe was shaking his head. 'I doubt that very much, son. I remember what she was like when you were little. I can't see anybody with any decency wanting to have anything to do with her.' He blushed as he realised the implication of what he'd just said. He obviously believed that neither of Dan's parents were any good. 'I'm sorry if that upsets you but it's the truth. Suzanne Doherty is one of the worst people I've ever met and it's hard to imagine her appealing to anybody with any sense. And, for what it's worth, I don't believe that kids have to turn out like their parents. You certainly haven't.'

'Oh, but I have,' Dan smiled at his father. 'Any decency and honesty is straight from you and mum. I'm a firm believer in nurture over nature because I'm living proof.'

Maggie nodded at him and took a sip of her tea. 'But, if she's back, Dan, you need to be careful. She's not to be trusted. Is that why you've stayed away for so long? Were you having trouble dealing with her?'

Dan knew that denial was pointless. He described his mental state when Suzanne had first showed up and his subsequent binge drinking. He knew that his parents wouldn't judge him and he trusted them to trust him to work out his own problems.

'You can't let her get to you, son,' Joe said. 'She's poison and she'll bring you down to her level. People like that always do. Rise above. You're better than her and you always have been.'

'Easier said than done,' Dan admitted. 'I'm still struggling a bit. It's the not knowing that's really getting to me. I wish she'd just be honest instead of playing her stupid games.'

'Perhaps you're better off not knowing,' Joe suggested. 'And I know you'd be better off without that woman in your life. You've not to let her get to you.'

Joe was right, Dan knew that, but it wasn't easy to distract himself from his doubts and uncertainties and he could see that his parents were worried about him.

The rest of the afternoon passed all too quickly for Dan. It was good to feel safe, good to feel like he belonged. Suzanne had tried to take that away from him and he felt the familiar resentment as he thought about how she'd tried to manipulate him. He distracted himself by talking about the Melissa Buckley and Chloe Welsh cases – in very general terms.

His mother was appalled but Joe was interested and put forward several theories about the killer which couldn't possibly work as he didn't have all the information. He'd watched a lot of crime dramas so some of his suggestions were a little too outlandish for Dan to take him seriously, but he'd obviously been intrigued by the idea that his son might be on the trail of a serial killer. Eventually, Maggie had to stop him from writing down a possible timeline for his imaginary murderer to have attacked both women.

'Too far, Joe,' she said. 'Dan's the detective, leave it to him. He'll catch the bugger.'

Dan left, wishing that he shared his mother's faith in his abilities.

# Chapter 21

Armed with profile details and potential passwords Sam logged onto her computer and navigated to the me4U website. Having never used online dating, she was curious about what it would entail and how it might work. She looked at the homepage, which promised 'more than just casual dating' and 'the potential for lasting commitment', and thought about what Kate had told her about Chloe Welsh. This didn't seem like the site for somebody who was just interested in having a bit of fun. The images were all of glowing heterosexual couples hugging, holding hands and sharing what looked like romantic dinners, all smiling and gazing at each other adoringly.

She clicked on the 'Search for a match' icon and was directed to login or sign up.

'Good,' she muttered. As she'd expected there was no access to personal profiles unless a fee was paid and details were submitted. She typed in the email address that Siobhan had supplied for Chloe and tabbed across to the password box. She had Chloe's DOB, childhood pet, favourite bands and some variations on passwords that Siobhan knew had been used in the past. Sam started with variations on the birthday. In her experience most people weren't very imaginative when it came to passwords and often used the same string of letters and numbers for everything.

She tried the date of birth forwards and backwards. Nothing. She glanced at the scrap of paper with potential passwords and tried again. This time she tried the dog's name – Rebel – no luck. She wasn't surprised. Most websites demanded a password that was a mix of letters and numbers and which contained at least one uppercase letter. She tried again with a capital R. Nothing.

Luckily this wasn't one of those sites that timed you out after three attempts. Sam glanced again at the DOB. This time she tried Rebel with 91, Chloe's year of birth.

'Bingo,' she muttered as the profile screen came up.

She clicked into 'Account' to see if she could find out how long Chloe had been using me4U and discovered that she'd only been a member for four months. She'd had a two-week free trial and obviously liked what she'd seen because she'd paid £19.99 per month for the next six months.

Toggling back to the profile page, Sam read what Chloe had written about herself. It wasn't quite what Sam had been expecting. Chloe's profile was restrained and candid rather than the usual fun-loving, good time, GSOH stuff Sam had seen on friends' profiles. She was struck by a few lines about Chloe's hopes for the future.

*Studying psychology at the moment. Hope to be a child psychologist because I love kids.*

Again, a little unusual. Had Chloe been looking for something more long-term despite what her flatmate said? The profile certainly suggested that she was serious and the choice of website was an indication that she wasn't just out to have a bit of fun.

Sam clicked on 'Matches'. There were three – none of them Max or Mike.

'Damn,' Sam muttered. She'd had visions of cracking the case with a few quick keystrokes, but then, when didn't she?

'What's this?' said a voice from behind her. O'Connor leaned over her shoulder to get a closer view of her screen and Sam tried not to shift her position. She didn't want to give him the satisfaction of knowing that he made her feel uncomfortable.

'Swapped sides, Sam? Looking for Mister Right?'

She faked a laugh. 'As if. I'm trying to find out who Chloe Welsh might have met on the night that she was killed. Her flatmate says it was somebody she met online.'

O'Connor snorted. 'And you think he used his real name? Who does that? I can guarantee you it was a fake name and a fake photo.'

Sam looked again at the three matches. Were they all fake? The names seemed quite normal. Chris, Tom and Darren. She made a note of each one but the information available was very thin. Name, age, occupation, interests, what they are looking for in a woman. There were no contact details and the 'location' was quite vague. Two had put Doncaster and another was based in Wakefield. She was about to go back to Chloe's profile to see what she'd put that might have attracted a killer when she noticed another tab. 'Matched'. This led to another list of three men. Another Tom, a Jamie and an Anthony. Beneath this, in grey, was a further match but this one simply said 'profile deleted'.

'Shit,' Sam said, turning to O'Connor. 'This could be him but he's deleted his profile. I wonder if there's any way to restore it.'

O'Connor looked sceptical. 'You could contact the company but I doubt they'd be willing to give away that sort of personal information. If they even store it in the first place. If he's deleted his profile it might be gone for good.'

Sam picked up her desk phone. She didn't accept that. In her experience, very little computer evidence was ever 'gone for good'. It all depended on who could be persuaded to look for it. She sincerely hoped that me4U employed somebody who might be able to help. If not, she was sure that she knew somebody, who knew somebody who would love to have a go at finding the information.

An hour later and a contact of a contact told her that he didn't know anybody who might have access to the information that she wanted. Sites like me4U didn't hold data on users who had unsubscribed. Dispirited, Sam sent another couple of emails and then considered her options. She might not be able to find out who the deleted profile belonged to, but she could try to hunt down Chloe's other 'matches'. She scanned Chloe's profile page again and clicked on the 'Chat' tab. Again one thread was shown as deleted but there were three others, one for each match. She began to read.

\*\*\*

'What've you got, Sam?' Kate asked. She could tell that the DC had found something from her barely supressed smile and the eager way she'd looked up as Kate had entered the office.

'Probably not much but it's worth checking out,' Sam responded. 'I've been digging into Chloe Welsh's dating profile and I've got a bit of information on three men that she met up with.'

Kate walked over to Sam's desk and dragged up a chair.

'Tell me.'

'She was careful. *Very* careful,' Sam began. 'There are three matches on the site and she chatted with all of them for a while before agreeing to meet. One gave her his mobile number as confirmation of his ID. She didn't like that very much so she didn't meet up with him. The other two both sent links to their Facebook pages so that she could verify their identities. I've got full names and addresses for both. One's Tom Garner – lives in Bessacar, works in Doncaster. The other's Anthony Davies – lives near Town Fields, works at the hospital.'

'Nice work,' Kate said, her mind already trying to process the information. These men needed to be interviewed as soon as possible, especially Davies. She rang O'Connor and Barratt, gave them the details and sent them out in search of Davies and Garner.

'I've got CCTV from Madrigal's and X-Ray. Took a while but you know my powers of persuasion. There's no guarantee that we'll find Chloe on there but it's worth a look. Dan's chasing up the camera from the car park where she was found. Turns out it's the local council and you know what they're like.'

Sam nodded as she held her hand out for the USB drive that Kate was holding.

'It's getting late, Sam,' Kate said. 'This can wait.' She saw Sam check her watch but she knew that there was no point in telling the DC to go home. She often worked long past knocking-off time if there was an active murder case. God knows what her partner thought.

Kate reluctantly handed Sam the drive and turned to leave. There wasn't much else that she could do. O'Connor and Barratt would report in in the morning and Dan was probably reviewing any CCTV footage he'd found. She glanced towards Raymond's office. The DCI was still there, sitting at his desk staring at the contents of an open folder. Kate considered knocking on the door and updating him but there really wasn't much to tell him at this point. Instead she grabbed her coat and headed for the car park.

# Chapter 22

There was a buzz in the incident room when Kate arrived the next morning. She was surprised to see that Barratt, Cooper and Hollis were already there and already drinking coffee. She'd asked to meet at eight and had made sure that she was fifteen minutes early but her team had obviously wanted to impress her with their findings.

O'Connor arrived before she could address the gathering, poured himself a coffee and then surprised her by making her one as well.

'Thought you might need this,' he said with a grin. Kate felt herself blush. She knew that she looked tired and she really didn't want to share the reason for her fatigue with the rest of the team. O'Connor had seen straight through her though – she almost expected a lewd wink and a nudge from him before he took a seat.

'Right you lot. Either somebody's been in the confiscated drugs stash or one of you has good news,' Kate said, dragging out a chair at the head of the conference table and slumping into it. 'I'm really hoping it's the latter. Barratt, you've got a gormless grin this morning, why don't you start?'

Barratt took a sip of his coffee. 'I interviewed Tom Garner last night,' he said. 'Nothing there really. He had one date with Chloe, public place, didn't go well. He hasn't seen her since. They met at Fabrio's where Chloe's well known. She used to work there. A waitress confirms the story. Garner left, Chloe ordered another glass of wine and had a chat with a couple of her ex-colleagues.'

'Same with Davies,' O'Connor chipped in. 'Had one date but, as he put it, there was "no spark" so they went their separate ways. She paid for herself which he appreciated. Said she was "a nice lass" but not really his cup of tea. A bit serious.'

Hardly conclusive, Kate thought, but nothing to suggest either man was their killer.

'Come on then, Sam,' she said, turning to Cooper. 'It must be you with the big news.'

Cooper blushed and tapped few keys on her keyboard.

'I would've rung last night but it was late. I took the CCTV footage home with me – Abbie was on nights, don't worry, she didn't see it – and I started having a look. I wasn't sure at first because I've not seen a photo but it sounded like Dan's description of him.'

'Him who?' Kate asked, baffled.

'Josh Harrington. Chloe's ex. Dan had a quick look this morning and he's ninety per cent sure.'

So they'd been playing without her. Kate didn't know whether she was annoyed or proud of the independence of her team but she was glad that they'd found something.

'Let's have a look.' She turned on the projector and they all turned to the whiteboard behind her. The footage was grainy and black and white and at first Kate couldn't work out where it was from. Then she recognised one of the buildings on the opposite side of the street from the camera and realised that it was from Madrigal's wine bar. People were milling around in the street, some entering the establishment, some leaving. Kate checked the time stamp. The footage was from just after eight o'clock on the previous Friday night.

'Here,' Cooper said, stopping the footage. She pointed to a figure then started the video again. A young woman approached and stopped just in the top corner of the frame. She took her phone from her handbag and seemed to be using it as a mirror to check her appearance before walking towards the camera and disappearing from view.

'That's Chloe Welsh,' Hollis said. 'You can see the lotus tattoo when she holds the phone up.'

Even if she hadn't seen the tattoo, Kate would have recognised the woman. She looked confident but not arrogant as she approached the wine bar and there was no suggestion that she was anxious or nervous about her meeting with whoever was inside.

Cooper pressed pause again. 'I'm going to fast-forward about fifteen minutes then see if you can spot what I saw.'

The people in the frame sped up, the effect almost comical, until Sam found the point where she wanted them to focus again.

'There,' she said, using the cursor to indicate a man approaching the door of the wine bar. He was wearing a dark t-shirt and skinny jeans and he swayed slightly as somebody passed him. His scruffy beard and messy hair were clearly visible. Kate could see that it was definitely Josh Harrington.

'Pissed,' O'Connor muttered.

'He looks a bit unsteady,' Sam said and Kate remembered the overflowing ashtray in his flat. The reason for his tottering gait might have been down to more than a just few pints of lager.

'Have you got them leaving?' Kate asked. Harrington being in the same bar as Chloe was hardly conclusive but if they left together, or if he seemed to be following her, that would be much more suspicious. Cooper fast-forwarded the recording again until the time showed 10.14pm. There were fewer people in the street and those that were outside had hoods or umbrellas up. The sky was much darker and the streetlights were on.

'I don't remember the body being wet,' Kate said. 'Can we find out if it rained for long?'

'A couple of showers,' Sam mumbled. 'I got caught in one when I went out for a run. It had stopped by eleven or so.'

'That might help with time of death,' Barratt said. 'Somebody should tell Kailisa.'

Hollis laughed. 'Do you think he doesn't know what the weather and temperature were like on Friday night and Saturday morning? Just because we didn't think about it doesn't mean he overlooked it. Trust me – he'll know everything there is to know about atmospheric conditions that night.'

Dan was right. Kailisa was due to perform the PM on Chloe's body later that day and she was certain that he'd have collated and probably colour-coded any relevant information.

'Here's Chloe,' Sam said, drawing their attention back to the CCTV footage. They watched as the woman took a couple of paces into the street and then backed up out of view. A second later she was sprinting across the road with her handbag held over her head. A few more people followed, two with hoods up and one with an umbrella as well as three men in shirt sleeves laughing at their own bravado as they defied the elements.

'And here's Harrington.'

He left the bar and crossed the road, seemingly oblivious to the weather. He looked even more unsteady on his feet and tripped slightly on the kerb as he crossed to the other side of the road and turned right, out of view. The same direction Chloe had taken less than two minutes earlier.

'Where do you think she's going?' Barratt asked. 'What's in that direction?'

'Taxi rank,' O'Connor suggested. 'Bus station.'

'X-Ray,' Sam said, tapping the keys of her laptop and changing the image in the screen.

The stage was different but the players were the same. Among the hoods and umbrellas Chloe could clearly be seen entering the night club, followed a few minutes later by Harrington.

'Does he follow her when she leaves?' Hollis asked. 'And can we get footage from inside? Or from Madrigal's?'

'They don't have CCTV inside either place,' Kate said. 'Not in the main bar or dance floor. There's a camera outside the loos in the wine bar and one in the corridor leading to the toilets in X-Ray. Sam's got footage from both.'

'There's nothing there,' Cooper said. 'The camera angle on the one from Madrigal's is weird like it's been knocked. It only shows a section of wall. The one from X-Ray is too dark. One of the lights was out in the corridor.'

'Druggies probably,' O'Connor interjected. 'They do that a lot in pubs and clubs. If somebody claims that they were offered drugs in the toilets it's impossible to see who went in and out. The management will realign the cameras but they'll be tampered with again in a few days.'

He was right. Kate knew that CCTV was hardly ever useful when it was from inside a drinking establishment. Too many people with too much to lose.

'Back to the early hours of Saturday morning,' Kate said. 'Is Harrington following Chloe when she leaves the club?'

'No,' Sam said. 'He leaves first. Look.'

She'd moved the footage on to 1.02 am and Kate watched as Harrington left the night club and turned left. He could have been heading home.

'What time did his flatmate say he got in?' Kate asked Hollis.

'Sometime after three.'

'So what was he doing for two hours?'

'Chloe leaves here,' Cooper said. The time stamp said 1.17am. Chloe seemed a little unsteady on her feet as she strode away from the camera and turned in the opposite direction to the one that Harrington had chosen.

'He didn't follow her this time.' Barratt observed.

'No,' Kate said. 'But if she was going to get a taxi home he would have known which direction she was heading in. He might have ambushed her somewhere. Pretended that it was a coincidence and persuaded her to go with him to his flat or somewhere else.'

'But he's going the wrong way.'

'Only when he leaves the club. What's to say he didn't change his mind and double back? Unless he passed directly in view of the camera we wouldn't know.'

Silence as they all thought about this possibility.

'But three years after she dumped him?' Barratt finally said. 'Why wait so long? If he was angry with her why wait three years to do something about it?'

'Festering,' Sam suggested. 'Or maybe he's seen her out with other men and his jealousy finally got out of control. Speaking of which there's nothing to suggest that Chloe was meeting somebody on Friday night. She goes into the bar and the club alone and leaves on her own as well.'

'Unless she was meeting Harrington,' Kate suggested. 'We need to get round there and see what he has to say for himself.' She checked her watch. Too early for Harrington to have left for work which was good. She didn't want to confront him with other people around. She still wasn't convinced that he'd murdered Chloe but he was lying about not having seen her recently. And if he was lying about that, what else hadn't he told them? Did he have a connection to Melissa Buckley that they'd missed?

*Chloe wasn't like Melissa. A single woman with a sad back story, Chloe was ideal. The first time we met she told me that she was finally ready to start dating again after her cancer treatment. There was something a little bit lost about her and I could see that she had struggled against her misfortunes with a certain amount of fortitude. I was prepared to overlook her as a possible candidate until she got talking about her hopes for the future. There it was again – that assumption, that feeling of entitlement. She told me that she'd been using dating websites as a bit of fun but I could sense that she was lying to herself. She was looking for something more serious. I didn't even need to ask which websites she was using. She told me, casually, like it wasn't important.*

*After the response to Melissa I'd started to feel a bit desperate. The press didn't get it and I was certain that the police were clueless, so I had to take action. I'd already contacted Chloe on the dating website and we'd chatted a few times so it seemed natural to suggest a meeting. She did everything just as I'd expected. Early meeting, public place but she had no idea that 'Max' wasn't going to turn up. Instead I watched her every move and waited for my opportunity.*

*The umbrella was fortuitous. I couldn't have planned things more carefully, but I didn't want to be spotted leaving the bar straight after Chloe. I'd noticed that it had started raining when I'd done a quick recce to the toilets just to see if the back door was feasible. What could have been a more perfect disguise than a huge umbrella?*

*After that it was easy. Meet her again in the club and slip her the Rohypnol. I watched her leave ten minutes after she'd taken the drug and gave it another few minutes before I'd followed her. She was heading for the taxi rank – stupid cow had even told me how she was intending to get home – so I caught up with her quite quickly.*

*She was so pleased to see me. Could I wait with her in the taxi rank? Could I take her home? She had no idea where I was leading her and when we'd crossed the bridge she'd even looked down and commented on the beautiful lights in the river.*

*I'd been glad to be rid of her after that. She was as easy as Melissa in the end. The drugs must have made her sluggish and it took very little time to leave her behind the bins and walk off with her handbag.*

*They must get it this time.*

# Chapter 23

Sam texted that Harrington's record was clean but he had been issued with a cannabis warning two years ago and a further penalty notice for disorder six months later for which he paid an £80 fine. It wasn't much but, as they turned into the street where he lived, Kate knew that they had enough to arrest him for possession if he had cannabis on him at the flat. The trick was to not allow him any time to hide his stash.

'Ring the bell for Flat One,' she instructed Hollis as they marched up the path to the front door. 'If there's nobody in, try number two.'

Hollis pressed the buzzer at the top of the row of buttons and they waited. Nothing. He leaned in and tried the next one down. This time they heard a noise inside and the door was opened by a woman who appeared to be trying to apply lipstick with one hand and hold a conversation on her mobile phone with the other.

'What?' she asked, tapping her thumb on the phone screen and lowering her hand from her ear. Kate showed her ID and the woman looked startled. 'I haven't done nowt!' she squawked.

'We need access,' Kate said. 'It's not you, it's somebody upstairs.' Hollis was already pushing past them both into the hallway as the woman opened the door wider with a shrug of disinterest.

Hollis jogged up the stairs ahead of Kate and pounded on the door of Flat 4 which was already opening by the time Kate arrived on the landing. Harrington peered around the door jamb looking baffled.

'Let us in, Josh,' Hollis advised. 'We don't want to do this out here.'

Harrington looked at Kate and then back at Hollis. 'What the fuck's—'

'Josh. We need to talk to you. Either you let us in or we arrest you,' Kate said. 'It's your choice.'

'Arrest me for what?'

Kate glanced down at the spliff nestling between his right index and middle fingers. 'Possession of cannabis, to start with.'

'Fuck off, you can't do me for a bit of skunk,' Harrington said and started to close the door. Hollis stopped him by lodging one of his huge feet next to the frame.

'We can if you've already had a warning and a PND,' Kate said with a smile. 'South Yorkshire police keep very accurate records of anybody they find with class B drugs. You're on your last strike and you've got a joint in your hand. I'd say that's possession, wouldn't you, DC Hollis?'

Hollis grinned. 'Seems fairly straightforward to me.'

'Let us in, Josh. We need to talk to you.'

Harrington's shoulders sagged as he took a last drag of his spliff. He turned and walked down the hallway towards the sitting room.

The place was exactly as Kate remembered, cramped and grubby. A small bag sat next to the ashtray and Kate couldn't quite believe their luck when Harrington grabbed it and stuck it in the pocket of his jeans before collapsing onto the sofa. He really was clueless.

Kate remained standing and Hollis strode over to one of the dining chairs under the window where he sat down without being invited and leaned forwards, forearms on his knees. 'We need to ask you some more questions about Chloe,' Hollis said. 'You weren't telling us the truth when we spoke to you last time, were you?'

Harrington mumbled something that Kate didn't quite hear. 'What?'

He frowned up at her, his face defiant. 'I said I'm not telling you anything else about Chloe. I've got to get to work so if you'll just do what you came here to do, we can all get on with our day.' His words were brave but his voice trembled slightly. He was obviously expecting a slap on the wrist and the confiscation of his drugs but he was clearly intimidated by their presence.

'It's not that easy, Josh,' Kate said. 'We need you to come down to the police station and look at some new evidence that we've uncovered. You said you hadn't seen Chloe in months. That's not true, is it?'

Silence.

'We know you saw her on the night she died. You were in the same wine bar and then you were both in X-Ray at the same time.'

'So?'

'You didn't mention this the last time we spoke. You said that you'd seen Chloe in a pub a while ago.'

'I did. She was with a bunch of her friends.'

'And last Friday?'

'What about last Friday? So I was in Madrigal's and X-Ray at the same time as Chloe. There aren't that many places to have a drink in Doncaster. I'm bound to run into her sometimes.'

Kate considered their options. She could see from the set of Harrington's shoulders that he wasn't going to co-operate. She could arrest him on suspicion of murder but she didn't want to play that hand yet – he seemed like the type to clam up if he was scared. But she knew that he wouldn't come with them voluntarily. They had to get him back to Doncaster Central and get him on record.

She looked across at Hollis and raised one eyebrow. The DC stood up and began the ritual.

'Josh Harrington, I am arresting you for possession of a class B substance—'

Harrington jumped up from the sofa. 'Wait, hang on! I've done nothing wrong!'

'The baggie of cannabis in your pocket says otherwise, Josh,' Hollis said. He hadn't given him the full caution so technically Harrington wasn't under arrest. Kate waited to see what Harrington would do next. He slumped in his seat defeated. There was no way out for him. He could either be arrested and taken to Doncaster Central, or he could submit to an interview under caution leaving Kate the option to charge him with possession later – or murder.

Kate sat next to him and sighed heavily. 'You're not giving us much choice, Josh. We need to talk to you about Chloe. We know you saw her last Friday and we know where. We have evidence. DC Hollis can arrest you for possession now and you'll end up with a criminal record. We'll take you to Doncaster Central, fingerprint you and charge you. It might only be another fine but this time it's official. If you apply for another job, you'll have to declare it.'

Harrington shook his head. 'This isn't fair.' He sounded like a small child who'd not been allowed to stay up past his bedtime.

'If you've not got anything to hide then why not just come with us? We'll do it all officially. You can have a solicitor present. Let's get this cleared up.'

'Can't afford a solicitor,' Harrington mumbled sulkily.

'Don't worry about that,' Hollis said. 'There are people available who do this all the time. We can find somebody.'

'What if I refuse to say anything? I've seen on telly where folk just say "no comment" all the time.'

'Then we charge you with possession,' Hollis said mildly.

'Got no choice then, have I?' Harrington said, standing up.

*Not really*, Kate thought. It felt dishonest in some way, like they'd tricked Harrington – which she supposed they had – but the ends justified the means and it wasn't as though they'd beaten a confession out of him. She still wasn't entirely comfortable though.

\*\*\*

It took three hours for Josh Harrington to be ready to answer their questions. The duty solicitor, a woman with the unlikely name of Sherry Pine, had spent some time in the interview room with him and she was happy that he was capable of answering their questions. Kate wasn't sure what Sherry Pine had advised but she really hoped that it was to co-operate and avoid the minor charge. If she'd managed to convince Harrington that a record for possession wasn't that big a deal, they were in trouble.

Kate stood in the observation suite with Raymond and Hollis.

'Do you fancy him for this?' Raymond asked, squinting down at the dishevelled young man on the monitor. He'd been at Chloe Welsh's post-mortem for most of the morning and seemed dispirited and downhearted. Kate sympathised. She'd attended enough post-mortems to understand the effects of watching what was once a living breathing person being cut open on a table.

'Honestly? I have no idea. You said that Kailisa confirmed the same killer as Melissa so we need to push that angle. If it's him there must be a link somewhere.'

'Could be random,' Hollis suggested. 'What if he killed Melissa first to make it look like Chloe was the second victim of some deranged serial killer?'

Kate shook her head. 'I really don't think he's that clever. And the abdominal wounds are bugging me. They mean something to the killer but I can't see what connection they might have to Harrington. I still think we should be pushing the IVF angle. I'm going back to the clinic to interview anybody who had contact with Chloe. Sam contacted them and confirmed that Chloe had made an appointment.'

Raymond opened his mouth to add to the discussion but his phone rang before he could comment further. He glanced at the screen and left the room to take the call. Less than thirty seconds later he was back and his mood had brightened.

'That was Kailisa. He's got potential DNA. Pubic hair. Caught in the hem of her blouse. Didn't show up when I was there this morning'

Raymond had already told Kate that there was no trace of semen or condom lubricant despite the evidence of rape. The similarities to Melissa Buckley's murder were too pronounced for it to be a different killer. The only difference appeared to be the fact that lividity marks on Chloe's body suggested that she'd been killed where she was found, or at least close by. She wasn't kept somewhere else like Melissa Buckley had been.

'He thinks it's from her attacker?'

'He's hopeful. Obviously there's a lot of tests to be done but even if there's nothing on the DNA database we'll have it for comparison.'

It was good news. Even if their murderer wasn't known to the police and his DNA wasn't on file, it meant that, if they had a firm suspect, they could get a DNA sample and they'd have something to compare it with. Kate couldn't help but wonder if Josh Harington would be a match.

# Chapter 24

Hollis read Josh the caution and then confirmed the identities of everybody present, his voice monotone as he went through the routine. Kate studied Sherry Pine as Hollis was speaking. She'd never met the solicitor before –hadn't even heard of her – and she was nervous about having an unknown presence in the room. The woman sitting next to Harrington was in her mid- to late thirties which suggested experience. She was dressed tidily and appropriately but not expensively and her shoes and handbag looked more M&S than D&G. *Not flashy then*, Kate thought. *Very business-like and understated.*

'You understand why you're here, Josh?' Kate began.

Harrington nodded.

'Please state your answers to our questions clearly, for the recording.'

Harrington glanced at the double tape recorder and then at his solicitor. She raised one eyebrow in a 'go ahead' gesture.

'Yes. I know why I'm here.'

'And you understand that you've not been charged with an offence but that you are being interviewed under caution?'

'Yes.'

Kate opened the folder that she'd brought into the interview room with her. The three hours that it had taken to set up the conversation had given her time to plan a strategy and she'd decided that, after their earlier antics, it would probably be best to be direct with Harrington. He would already be on guard and looking for potential traps and tricks and she didn't think that would be conducive to getting some straight answers. 'Okay. So, Josh, DC Hollis and I spoke to you on Saturday morning about the death of your ex-girlfriend Chloe Welsh. You remember the conversation?'

Harrington nodded again and then seemed to remember that he had to speak. 'Yes, I remember.'

Kate slid a piece of paper across the table, stating the evidence number of the document for the recording. 'This is a copy of DC Hollis's daybook with a record of your responses. At the time you said that you'd last seen Chloe a couple of months ago.'

'Yes.'

Kate took out the next piece of paper. It was a still from the CCTV footage from outside Madrigal's wine bar. She stated the exhibit number for the tape as she passed the photograph across the table.

'It looks like Chloe,' Harrington said.

Kate passed him the next image. 'The time stamp on the previous image was 8.07pm. This next one is from 8.17. Is that you, Josh?'

This time Harrington didn't bother to look. 'Probably,' he said, miserably.

'Please confirm,' Hollis interrupted. 'We need you to be clear.'

Harrington glanced down at the picture. 'It's me.'

Next to him Sherry Pine was starting to look uncomfortable.

'So,' Kate said. 'You just happened to be in the same wine bar as Chloe last Friday?'

'I didn't know that she'd be there. I didn't speak to her or anything.'

'And you didn't follow her when she left?'

His face contorted with what Kate knew was fake outrage. 'Course not! I'm not a bloody stalker.'

'So it's just coincidence that you left less than five minutes after Chloe and headed in the same direction?'

She passed him two stills from two hours later clearly showing Chloe leaving at 10.22 and Josh exiting the bar just over four minutes later.

This time he seemed genuinely puzzled. 'I don't remember leaving Madrigal's. Honest, I don't. I was really pissed that night. I barely remember getting there.'

Kate didn't believe him despite the tottering figure she'd seen when she'd watched the footage earlier. 'So you won't remember following Chloe to X-Ray?'

He shook his head despite the photographic evidence that Kate placed in front of him.

'You got there thirty seconds after Chloe but you weren't following her?'

'I… I don't…'

'My client has already said that he doesn't remember,' Pine interjected. 'He's answering your questions to the best of his knowledge.'

Harrington shot her a grateful look.

'So you won't remember leaving X-Ray? Or what you did afterwards?'

'No.'

'Josh, you left before Chloe did. At 1.02am to be precise.'

Harrington looked relieved as though he'd just been the butt of a silly prank.

'So I can't have been following her can I? If I left first.'

'No,' Kate conceded. 'But we spoke to your flatmate last Saturday. Jack? The one you said might remember you getting home. Funny how you knew that he was still up yet you can't remember much else. He says it was after three when you got home. That's over two hours unaccounted for. Where did you go, Josh? What did you do?'

Harrington turned to his solicitor, obviously panicking. 'I can't remember,' he said to Pine. 'I don't know where I went.'

'As my client has told you,' the solicitor said. 'He obviously left before Chloe Welsh. You have no evidence that he had any contact with her on Friday night or Saturday morning.'

'No,' Kate conceded. 'But he lied to us before when he said he hadn't seen Chloe for a couple of months. Why should I think he's telling the truth now?'

Harrington looked at Kate and then Hollis. He seemed lost. They'd backed him into a corner and he didn't seem able to think of a way out. Kate needed to capitalise on his uncertainty.

'How do you know Melissa Buckley?'

Harrington pulled back his head suddenly, he obviously hadn't been expecting the change of tack. 'Who's she?'

'You don't know?'

'I don't think so. She might have come into the shop. So many people come in nowadays I don't keep track of everybody who has my artwork.'

'So she's a client?' Kate pushed. That didn't make sense. Melissa didn't have tattoos.

'I don't know. You seem to think that I know her but I have no idea who she is.'

Kate took a photograph of Melissa from her folder. 'You don't recognise her?'

Harrington took the image from Kate, holding it carefully by the edge and studied it. 'I honestly have no idea. I can't remember ever seeing her before. Is she a friend of Chloe's?' His tone was hopeful as though he thought he might have stumbled across the correct answer to a quiz question.

This was getting them nowhere.

'Okay,' Kate said. 'Let's go back to Friday night. Why did you follow Chloe to Madrigal's? Had you seen her somewhere else and you decided to see where she was heading?'

Harrington sighed. He mumbled something to Sherry Pine which Kate didn't quite hear.

'My client would like to take a break,' Pine said.

'No,' Kate and Hollis said at the same time.

'You can have a break when you tell us the truth, Josh.' Kate tapped the pile of images on the table. 'I think you've probably followed Chloe a few times since you broke up. So what happened? Did you finally snap after you saw her on yet another date? Couldn't hack seeing her with another man?'

Harrington leaned back in his seat and closed his eyes. For a second, Kate thought she'd lost him. She fully expected the next utterance out of his mouth to be 'No comment' so she was surprised when he said, 'It wasn't like that.'

'So what was it like?' she asked, keeping her voice low, encouraging him to speak.

Another glance at his solicitor, clearly assessing whether or not he should risk getting into more trouble. Eventually Harrington focussed on Kate's face and began to speak. 'I cared about her. I couldn't stand seeing her with a different man every few weeks. It's not her. She's not like that. She's gentle and trusting and I just knew that they'd take advantage if they got the opportunity.'

Kate sensed Hollis sitting up in his seat and knew he was about to interject. She tapped his ankle gently with her foot warning him to keep his mouth shut.

'I saw her earlier this year with a funny-looking bloke in Fabrio's. I was with a couple of mates — one of them had got a voucher for half-price main courses so we all piled in. She didn't see me at first but, when she did, she smiled and gave me this look like she wanted rescuing. I wandered over and we had a bit of a chat. She was really nice to me, like she was pleased to see me and eventually the other fella left. Chloe was grateful, she said she'd met him on a dating app and she didn't really click with him. She said she'd buy me a drink sometime and then she got chatting with some of the staff. She used to work there.'

He paused and rubbed his hands over his face as if he was finding it difficult to keep his thoughts in order.

'After that I saw her with somebody else in The Lion and another man in the queue for the cinema. She never looked happy, though. I started making a point of looking for her. She'd come into town on the bus from Balby and I learnt the bus times. I didn't always see her but there were a few Fridays where I hung around the bus station and she turned up. One of them was the night I told you about — when she met some girlfriends in The Lion.'

'So you were following her quite regularly?' Kate asked.

Harrington hung his head, his face a picture of misery. 'I wasn't stalking her. I just wanted to make sure that she was okay.'

An idea was forming in Kate's mind. She wanted to believe Harrington and there was something pathetic about his confession that made her start to believe that he'd just been in the wrong place at the wrong time. But he might have seen whoever Chloe had been meeting that evening.

'So, last Friday. Talk me through what you *do* remember.'

Harrington shook his head. 'I honestly can't remember much. I had a few cans at home and I'd been, you know.' He made a gesture to indicate that he'd been smoking. 'I waited in the bus station and I saw Chloe get off the bus. She was dressed up for a night out – not flashy like, that wasn't really her thing. I followed her to Madrigal's and went inside. It all gets a bit hazy after that. There was a big crowd at the bar and it took me a while to get a drink. By then I couldn't see her and I bumped into one of my mates. I hadn't seen him for ages and he wanted to talk so we had a few drinks and a natter. I kept looking for Chloe but I didn't see her until she was about to leave. She was heading for the door so I necked the rest of my drink and went after her.'

'Was she on her own?' Kate asked.

'I don't know. She might have been with somebody but like I said, it was really busy.'

'So what makes you think she might have been with somebody?'

Harrington stared at her for a second, obviously trying to make sense of his memories. 'She was standing in a corner talking to somebody for most of the time that she was there. I couldn't see who it was, but I got the impression that whoever she was talking to was taller than her. She kept looking up and laughing.'

Kate got a sudden urge to leap across the table and grab him by the throat. Either his story was just a ploy to deflect the attention away from himself of it was their best chance yet of finding Chloe's killer.

'But you said she didn't leave with anybody?'

Harrington leaned towards her. 'I didn't see her leave with anybody but that doesn't mean that he didn't follow her. Or he might have gone to the bog and met up with her later in X-Ray. It was raining when I left, she wouldn't have wanted to hang around outside waiting for somebody so maybe she went on to the club and he met up with her again there.'

It made sense, but it was also extremely convenient. Kate wasn't convinced.

'But she left X-Ray on her own.'

Harrington shrugged. 'Maybe he did the same thing again so he wouldn't be seen with her. Told her he was going to the toilet and he'd catch her up. Or maybe the date didn't go well so she left and he caught up with her later.'

'And you don't remember seeing Chloe with anyone inside the club?'

'No. There are two floors inside and I was on the top one. The bottom floor's a bit more techno-rave. Not really my thing but Chloe always liked it down there. I don't remember seeing her in the club but like I said I was really out of it.'

'I'm not buying it, Josh. You want us to believe that Chloe was out with some mystery man who hasn't shown up on the CCTV footage yet we have clear images of you following her – which you've admitted – and there's the small matter of two hours that you can't account for.'

'I don't—' he began, but Kate continued.

'It doesn't make sense. I'm sticking with the most likely scenario that you saw Chloe out having a good time and you couldn't stand it anymore so you waited until she'd left the club and you killed her.'

'No!'

'So where were you, Josh? Where were you between leaving X-Ray at 1am and getting home at around 3am?'

Harrington stared at her, opened his mouth as though he was going to speak and then obviously changed his mind.

'You said earlier that you can't remember but you also said that you couldn't remember being in Madrigal's or X-Ray. Funny how your memory seems to have come back, but only selectively.'

Harrington gave his solicitor a pleading look. He obviously had something to say but something was holding him back. Kate decided to give him some time to think. She paused the interview and left the room with Hollis.

# Chapter 25

'What do you think?' Kate asked, slumping against the corridor wall. 'Do you believe him?'

Hollis leaned next to her. 'I don't know. It's all plausible but there's the two hours that he either can't or won't account for. If he did kill Chloe how did he get her out to the industrial estate? He could hardly take her in a taxi.'

'Unless she was still alive,' Kate said. 'And he killed her there. Kailisa thinks she was killed where she was found or somewhere close so he could have got her out there on some pretence or other. If they walked from X-Ray it'd only take about twenty minutes.'

'But you spoke to Siobhan. They were both careful when it came to meeting men. It doesn't make sense that Chloe would go somewhere like that with a stranger.'

Kate could see his point. Why would somebody as cautious as Chloe Welsh walk in the opposite direction from her flat with a man unless it was somebody that she knew or trusted? Which brought them back to Josh Harrington.

'So, what about this mystery man? You're not convinced?'

'I'm keeping an open mind,' Hollis said with a smile. It was his code for 'I haven't a bloody clue.'

Kate smiled back. 'Me too. But if Chloe was with somebody then we need to find out who. I'm going to ask Raymond for the budget to get uniforms canvassing the bar and the club – see if anybody remembers anything. And I'll get Sam to have a closer look at the CCTV footage – if this bloke did follow Chloe out of Madrigal's, he'll be on there somewhere.'

Kate's phone rang. Raymond.

'More news from the PM,' the DCI said without preamble. 'Chloe's blood tested positive for alcohol but not excessive. Maybe she'd been pacing herself all night. That's not the headline though. There was also some sort of benzodiazepine in her blood. Most likely Rohypnol.'

Kate hung up, trying to make sense of the information. Chloe *had* been cautious then. She wasn't drinking heavily or she'd put the brakes on later in the evening, but she'd had her drink spiked. That changed everything. If she was under the influence of Rohypnol her cognitive abilities would have been impaired and her judgement flawed. She might have gone anywhere with anybody.

'Bad news?' Hollis asked.

Kate gave him a brief summary of the blood work.

'Shit. That means she could have been wandering around in a right state. Anybody could have walked her over to Trafford Lane and she wouldn't have had a clue where she was going. If he said he was walking her home she'd have probably believed him.'

'And it means he could be anybody – not necessarily somebody she knew and trusted. Let's keep this to ourselves. It's not something that Harrington needs to know yet.'

She pushed off from the wall and set off back down the corridor to the interview room.

'Hang on,' Hollis said after her. 'Can I ask you something?'

She turned and saw that his face was flushed.

'What?'

He scratched his nose and looked down at his feet. 'Is there a reason why you've not let me ask Harrington anything? When I was going to jump in you stopped me. Is this about Melissa Buckley's family and the way I stuffed up?'

Kate took a deep breath. She didn't have time for this. 'I wanted to lead on this, Dan,' she said. 'And, to be honest, you seem to have lost your touch a bit lately. I know you've got a lot on your mind and it's not that I don't trust you, I'd just rather you took a back seat and observed. You'll see things that I won't if you're just listening.'

His colour deepened – Kate could tell that he wasn't convinced but she was being as honest as she could. She didn't want Hollis jumping in feet first and, normally, she would have trusted him not to, but he seemed to be so off his game that she needed to take control. If that bruised his ego then she'd have to live with the consequences. This case was more important than her relationship with her DC.

Hollis followed her back into the interview room where Harrington was still deep in conversation with his solicitor. She restarted the recording and began again.

'So? Have you changed your mind about telling us where you were?' Kate asked as she sat down. She wasn't especially hopeful but Harrington had obviously been discussing something with Pine.

'My client is willing to co-operate fully,' Pine said, leaning forwards and tucking her hair behind her ears. 'However, he is asking for confidentiality regarding the information he is about to divulge. I believe what he has to tell you will eliminate him from your enquiries as soon as you have established the veracity of his account.'

*Very formal,* Kate thought, completely unimpressed. She'd met solicitors of all shapes and sizes and was way beyond being intimidated by legal jargon. Harrington, on the other hand, looked smug as though he'd just scored a minor victory. Kate smiled, about to wipe that look from his face. 'I can't guarantee anything of the sort,' she said. 'After we receive Mr Harrington's full statement and verify what he's told us then we may be able to look upon his co-operation with some sympathy. However, that is entirely dependent on the information and its relevance to this enquiry.'

As she'd expected Harrington's face changed from complacency to panic as he took in the full implication of her words.

'But,' she continued. 'If he has information which he isn't willing to divulge it's likely that we *will* arrest him for the murder of Chloe Welsh, pending further investigation.'

Pine looked at Harrington and raised her perfectly sculpted eyebrows, suggesting that it was his call.

'Let's just get on with it,' Harrington said on a sigh. 'If I don't tell them, I'll be arrested and, if I do, I'll probably be beaten up. I think I'll take my chances with a beating.'

Intrigued Kate said, 'You think you're at risk if you tell us where you were, Josh?'

'I know I am,' Harrington said. 'It's not just where I was, it's who I was with. When I left X-Ray I wondered around for a bit. I didn't want to go home and I was feeling low after seeing Chloe again. I suppose I was coming down as well but I'd left my weed at home. The sensible thing would have been to go back to the flat, have another smoke and crash out but I'd had too much to drink to be sensible.'

Kate nodded, trying to encourage him to keep talking. This was the first time he'd shown any sign of self-awareness and she didn't want him to lose focus.

'I rang Jill. Jill Ogden, from work. You can check my call history if you want. It was probably about half one, if that. Might have been earlier. She was still up and she said I could go round to her house. She lives in one of the terraces on Dalton Street behind the market.'

'And she'll confirm this?' Kate asked.

Harrington didn't look happy about providing an alibi. 'We've been seeing each other off and on for about six months. Just casual, like.'

Kate didn't understand. It was such a simple way to put himself in the clear. And then it dawned on her. 'Jill's married?'

'Her husband works away a lot. We've been spending a bit of time together. Trouble is, if he found out, he'd give me a right pasting. He's got a vicious temper.'

Sherry Pine gave Kate a self-satisfied smile. 'I'm sure it's a simple matter to verify Mr Harrington's alibi. And after that I assume he'll be free to leave.'

Kate thought about it. She could still hold Harrington for possession but what would that achieve? If his alibi put him in the clear for Chloe's murder then they'd just be harassing him for the sake of it and she didn't want to play games.

'Can you ring her soon, though?' Harrington asked. 'Don't ring her when she gets home in case *he's* there.'

She wanted to ignore Harrington's plea just to get him into trouble for wasting so much of their time but she couldn't bring herself to be so unprofessional. She knew that Hollis would be tempted as well.

'Ten minutes,' she said, standing up. 'I need to make the call.'

Five minutes later she was back in the interview room having confirmed that Josh Harrington had indeed been with Jill Ogden from around 1.20am until nearly 3am on Saturday morning. The woman hadn't been the least bit embarrassed to admit that they'd had a drink and then had sex. Josh couldn't have killed Chloe Welsh, seen Jill and got back to his flat at around 3.15. The timing didn't fit.

'Phone,' she said as soon as she sat back down. She stretched her hand across the table and Harrington unlocked his iPhone and passed it across the table without protest. Kate tapped on his calls list and saw a number of calls to Jill Ogden – crucially, one at 1.13am on Saturday morning. She showed the phone to Hollis who terminated the interview and stopped the recording.

'What a sodding waste of time,' Kate hissed as Harrington and Pines left.

'Where does this leave us?' Hollis asked, leaning back in his chair with a heavy sigh.

'Back where we were,' she said. 'Nowhere.'

# Chapter 26

As Kate had expected, Raymond looked furious. He'd been outside the interview room waiting to pounce.

'My office, Fletcher. Now!'

She'd anticipated his anger but his flushed face and aggressive stance seemed a little over done. She knew better than to argue though and noted that he'd gone back to calling her by her surname. She was in trouble. She gave Hollis instructions to pass on to Cooper regarding the CCTV and then followed the DCI upstairs, grateful that none of her colleagues were at their desks as she slunk through the team area like a naughty schoolgirl approaching the head teacher's office.

'Sir, I—' she began as soon as she'd closed the door behind her.

'I don't want to hear it,' Raymond snapped.

Kate didn't even try to make excuses. He was right. She should have done better. But she was puzzled by the strength of her boss's wrath. She'd messed up but it hadn't harmed the investigation; it had cost them some time but it wasn't as if they'd had any other leads to follow.

'Sit!' Raymond instructed, throwing himself into his chair and pointing to the one on the opposite side of his huge desk. In her most uncharitable moments Kate speculated that the huge bulk of the desk may have been an attempt to compensate for a lack of size in other areas but now she was glad of the distance it provided from Raymond's anger.

'Sir,' she tried again. 'You're right, I know I cocked that interview up but it was a promising lead based on sound evidence.'

'I saw the end of the interview, Fletcher. He made you look like a fool,' Raymond said, his tone ominous. 'And I don't like anybody making my team look foolish. It reflects badly on me.'

Kate was puzzled. Was this about Raymond's reputation on the force then? Was he worried that his last investigation was going to make him look incompetent? That might explain his extreme reaction. She saw him look over her shoulder to where she knew he could see into the team office. He scowled, obviously unhappy with whatever he could see beyond his door.

'We've got a leak,' he said, flicking his eyes back to hers. 'Somebody's been talking to the press.' He reached down and opened one of his desk drawers, removing a couple of national red-tops and throwing them across to her.

Kate looked down at the headline.

SECOND MURDER VICTIM FOUND

She wasn't surprised. The press were always quick to jump on cases of violent death. They wouldn't have been able to keep Chloe's murder quiet for very long and it was probably time for Raymond to hold a press conference.

'I don't—'

'Read it!' Raymond snapped.

Kate followed his instructions and there it was in the second paragraph: *mutilated body.*

She read on, heart racing, as the reporter described – in graphic detail – the injuries to a body found on Town Field nearly two weeks ago and then went on to speculate that a body found on Trafford Lane industrial estate on Saturday had similar injuries. The article stopped short of using the term 'serial killer' but the insinuation was there.

'How did they get hold of this?' Kate asked.

'That's what I'd like to know. Who knows about the injuries apart from your team?'

Kate thought about it. Was Raymond suggesting the leak had come from one of their own? 'What about the pathologist's office?

They know the details as well. How do we know it's not come from there?'

'We don't, and I'll be making enquiries but, for the moment, I need to focus on damage limitation. I'm going to hold a press conference in the morning and, by then, I want to know who's blabbed. And, if it's not come directly from one of your team, then who told their girlfriend or boyfriend or husband or wife?'

Kate shook her head. 'They wouldn't. They all know the consequences of talking to the press and they know that the rules extend to family and friends.'

She was sure of her team. They all knew that any details about ongoing investigations stayed at the office. Nothing went home, not even a word or a hint. She remembered how careful she'd been when speaking to Nick about how difficult it might be to perform a caesarean section and she trusted the others to be just as careful, just as discreet.

'I just can't see it,' she said. 'They know they'd be kicked off the team, demoted, if they gave away any details of an active investigation. It wouldn't be worth it for any of us.'

'Unless there was a big sum of money involved,' Raymond suggested. 'They're only human and it takes a lot to resist a big pay-out. Especially for somebody who might be a bit strapped for cash or in debt. Anybody in your team in need of extra money?'

Hollis. He'd said something about his birth mother wanting money for a flat. But he earned plenty on his detective constable's salary. It shouldn't be that difficult for him to find a couple of grand, especially as he didn't have a family to support. Cooper was planning a wedding and that wouldn't be cheap but her partner had a decent job so they should be able to manage between them. Barratt was too straight, too much of a rule follower – he'd probably turn himself in if he ever did anything even remotely unorthodox. Which left O'Connor. Kate hadn't really got to know her DS very well. If she was honest with herself, she found him a little unpleasant and arrogant. But he got results and Raymond had a lot of faith in him. With his contacts, O'Connor would easily be able to raise a few grand if he needed money, Kate had no doubt about that.

'Not that I know of,' Kate said, reluctant to even speculate with the DCI. *If* there was an issue in her team, she wanted to be the one to deal with it and she wanted the leaker to look her in the eye and explain themselves.

'Well, find out. And fast.' Raymond swung his chair round slightly so that he wasn't directly facing her and picked up his phone. Kate knew she was being dismissed.

\*\*\*

Cooper was at her desk, focussed intently on her computer screen, when Kate left the DCI's office. Hollis was nowhere to be seen and she knew that O'Connor and Barratt were out on other jobs.

'Seen Dan?' she asked. Cooper turned to her, her eyes lacking clarity for a split second as she shifted from whatever she was doing to process Kate's question.

'Upstairs. I sent him on a coffee run. We've made a start on the CCTV. It's not easy though – there were so many people going in and out of the bar and the club that night. I'm concentrating on a period of an hour either side of Chloe's arrival and departure from Madrigal's at the minute and trying to cross-reference everybody we can even vaguely identify with the footage from X-Ray.'

'And?'

Cooper smiled. 'It looks like half of Donny was out that night and most of them hit Madrigal's between 7 and 9pm. Not quite so many at X-Ray though'

'So what are you looking for?'

'A needle in a haystack.'

'Facial recognition software no good?'

Cooper shook her head. 'I can't see that many faces, especially as it gets darker and also when it rains. I'm working from clothing and any other distinguishing features. This guy for example.'

Sam turned back to her computer and rewound the footage from the wine bar. Kate watched as people walked backwards away from the entrance in fast reverse. Eventually she slowed the video down until the frame depicted a stocky man wearing jeans and a white vest. He wouldn't have been especially unusual except for the fact that shaved into the crown of his closely cropped dark hair was a five-pointed star.

'Hard to miss,' Kate said. 'And probably easy to get an ID for. Somebody'll know somebody who knows him. Does he show up at the club?'

'Yep. At about half eleven. He leaves at 2.10.'

'No good then?'

'I've put him on the 'unlikely' list. I'm checking Madrigal's, and Dan's checking X-Ray against my list. It's not very scientific but it's the best we can do at the minute.'

'Somebody mention my name?' Hollis appeared at Kate's shoulder holding two coffees in takeaway cups with plastic tops. 'Sorry, didn't know you'd finished with Raymond or I would have brought you one,' he said to Kate, passing one of the cups to Cooper. 'We in bother for the Harrington interview?'

Kate was well aware that Dan knew that any 'bother' would be directed at Kate so she appreciated his casual use of 'we'. She was just about to tell him that he wasn't as angry about the interview as he was about the leak when she realised that she couldn't say anything. She couldn't share the information with two members of her team and not the others – it would look like she was playing favourites or perhaps that she thought that the leak had come from Barratt or O'Connor.

'I need to call a briefing,' she said, ignoring Hollis's question. 'I'm going to text Steve and Matt and get them back here.' She checked her watch. It was just after 4pm. 'I want you all in the incident room at 5.'

Hollis looked puzzled but Sam had already begun watching the CCTV footage again. Obviously she saw the next hour as an opportunity to get some more work done in the hope that she'd have something positive to present at the briefing. Kate texted O'Connor and Barratt on her way up to the canteen. She wasn't sure how she wanted to handle news of the leak but she had a feeling that caffeine might help her to decide.

\*\*\*

When Kate entered the interview room at 5pm she sensed that she didn't have to brief the others about the leak. They knew. O'Connor was waving around a newspaper, clearly furious. 'Have you seen this?' he asked. 'What the fuck's going on?'

Kate held up both hands, palms out, trying to placate him but he wasn't interested in being told to calm down.

'How are we supposed to do our job when we've got the bloody press undermining us at every turn?' There was a general shaking of heads, everybody clearly disgusted with what had happened.

'Look, the information's out there,' Kate said. She pulled out a chair and sat at the head of the table. This was going to be more difficult than she'd anticipated. The shared outrage in the room was palpable. If she mentioned that Raymond suspected that the leaker might be one of her team she might as well have thrown a grenade among her colleagues. But it had to be done.

'The pressing issue now is…'

'Where the information came from,' Barratt finished her sentence, his expression grim. He looked at each of his colleagues in turn. 'And the finger of suspicion is going to point at one of us.'

'No,' Hollis was shaking his head. 'That's not right. Nobody here would do that.'

Sam Cooper nodded her agreement but she looked like she wanted to cry. Kate understood how she must be feeling. To fall under suspicion like this was the worst thing for a police officer – especially a detective – and she really didn't want to have to tell them what her next step had to be.

'I'm sorry,' she said. 'But there is the possibility that somebody on this team spoke to the press and revealed key information, however inadvertently.' She was trying to soften the blow but Barratt was having none of it.

'Inadvertently? How stupid would somebody have to be to casually mention something like this to a journalist? If it was somebody here, then it was done deliberately and I can't believe that any of us would do that. If you think that, Kate, then you need to be able to prove it beyond doubt.'

Kate was stunned. Barratt hardly ever used her first name, despite her frequent requests that he do so. And he had never raised his voice to her. She'd expected him, of all the members of her team, to take this the hardest as he was proud of his reputation as somebody who could be trusted. Barratt knew that the others thought he was a bit anal, he'd joked about it often enough, so calling his integrity into question would really sting.

'Matt, I'm not saying—'

'Yes, you are,' he said, his usually pale face colouring as he stood up. 'And I'm not going to sit here and be accused of doing something that would compromise this investigation.' He pointed to the photographs of Melissa and Chloe that had been stuck to the whiteboard. '*They* deserve better and, honestly, *we* deserve better.'

He made a move towards the door.

'Sit down, Barratt!'

Next to her, Hollis flinched. Kate never raised her voice to her colleagues – mainly because they never did anything to merit any form of rebuke but Barratt was bordering on insubordination and she would not allow him to rip the team apart for the sake of his own pride. To her surprise he turned and stared her down.

'I said, sit down,' Kate continued. 'We need to address this leak and, to be frank, being a drama queen just makes you look guilty.'

Barratt's eyes narrowed and he looked like he was about to say something else when Cooper stepped in. 'Matt. Sit down. You're making an arse of yourself.'

Eyes still fixed on Kate, Barratt slid back into his seat.

'Right,' Kate said. 'I get that this is upsetting but I'm going to ask and I'm going to take whatever you say as the truth. Did any of you give information about Melissa Buckley's wounds to the press?'

Headshakes all round and three vehement verbal denials from the men on the team

'So where could the information have come from?'

'Pathologist's office,' Barratt suggested, his tone sulky.

'I thought about that,' Kate responded. 'But they're in the same position as us. I will be following it up with Kailisa though.'

'There's the SOCO team,' O'Connor suggested. 'I don't know what they get paid but I'll bet there's one of two who wouldn't turn down a few grand for slipping somebody a titbit of information over a pint.'

'Which would be grounds for dismissal,' Kate pointed out. 'But, again, it'll have to be investigated. Cooper, any thoughts?'

'Who has the least to lose and the most to gain?' Cooper responded cryptically.

'Oh, come on Confucius, don't talk in riddles.' Hollis's tone was light but his eyes and the set of his mouth were serious. Cooper picked up a pen with both hands and began to roll it between her palms. Kate knew how much she hated to be put on the spot like this.

'SOCOs, Kailisa's staff, us, we all have a lot to lose if we get caught talking to the press about something like this. Who saw Melissa Buckley's body and doesn't have to risk their job if they talk about it?'

'A witness,' Kate said, realisation dawning. 'Shit. Duncan Cawthorne.'

'What's to stop him accepting money from a journalist?' Cooper asked. 'He might not even realise what he's done. It's not hard to picture somebody plying him with booze and offering a sympathetic shoulder.'

She was right. Cawthorne claimed not to have got a good look at the body but he'd been cagey about why he was anywhere near it in the first place. Kate could easily imagine him saying whatever he thought might cause him the least trouble with the police.

'What do you think, Dan? You were there when I spoke to him.'

'Could be,' Hollis confirmed. 'I'll have a look at his written statement, find out exactly what he said he saw.'

'No, Matt can do it, I want you back on the CCTV footage with Sam.' She knew that Barratt would see such a task as being beneath him but Kate had to do something to let him know that his previous outburst hadn't been appreciated. 'Steve, you have a tame journalist in your address book, don't you?'

O'Connor gave her a smile in response. Kate had used O'Connor's contact on a previous case and had got the impression that there might have been more than just a professional connection between the DS and the journalist.

'See if you can get her to make some discreet enquiries and find out where the info came from. I know this case is frustrating, believe me, I feel it as much as you lot do. Raymond's going to hold a press conference in the morning, see if that'll generate anything new. Cooper, Hollis, I'll work with you two – an extra pair of eyes might help.'

Jobs allocated, Kate watched her colleagues file out of the incident room. She turned and looked at the photographs of the two murdered women and was surprised to feel her eyes tear up. The frustration was starting to get to her. It was time to try something different, and she knew that Raymond wouldn't like it.

# Chapter 27

'You want me to pay for a what?' Raymond dropped into his seat and pulled his tie loose. He'd just returned from a briefing with the Chief Super and he looked like he'd taken a verbal battering.

'A clinical psychologist,' Kate repeated. 'Kailisa thinks that the injuries to Melissa's and Chloe's bodies are ritualistic and I'm inclined to agree with him. If we can understand why this killer mutilates women in this way we might get closer to catching him.'

Raymond snorted in disgust. 'This is Doncaster not bloody LA. I never expected you to go all *Silence of the Lambs* on me, Kate.'

She'd expected this. Raymond was well known for his aversion to spending money and that aversion grew stronger if he thought the expense was for something that he was inclined to dismiss as nonsense. She knew that psychological profiling was a contentious issue and that a lot of police forces were reluctant to admit that they'd employed the services of a psychologist for fear of a public backlash, but Kate had seen results for herself on a previous investigation and she was convinced that they had nothing to lose in this case. She also knew that she might have a way to persuade her DCI.

'I know somebody who might be able to help,' she said. 'I've worked with her before, in Cumbria and she gave us some real insight.'

'Insight,' Raymond snorted. 'We don't need insight, we need a concrete lead and I don't think we'll get that from somebody telling us that we're looking for a white male in his mid to late thirties who used to torture his pet rabbits.'

Kate tried to keep a straight face. She'd expected this. While Raymond was perfectly comfortable with the technological advances that had aided modern policing she knew that he, and many others, thought psychological profiling was second only to hiring a psychic when it came to trying to find the perpetrator of a crime.

'She might do it as a favour to me,' Kate continued. 'We could keep it off the books and, that way, out of the media.'

Raymond's eyes sparked with interest. 'Free, like? No strings?'

Kate nodded. The DCI swung round in his seat and appeared to be staring out of the window but Kate knew that he was processing the potential consequences of her suggestion. She didn't tell him that she'd already put the wheels in motion, that she'd contacted her friend Anna who'd already confirmed that she'd be willing to help.

'Okay,' the DCI said, spinning his chair back round. 'I don't suppose I can stop you asking somebody, off the record, but I don't want it to direct the course of the investigation. You said yourself that it might give us some insight – that won't replace real leg work. And I don't want to read about this in next week's Gazette.'

'You won't. Cooper's got a theory about the leaker and it's not one of ours.'

'It'd better not be. Christ, I've got enough on with this press conference tomorrow without having to start an internal investigation. Do what you need to do, Kate, but if there's any shit from it, I'll make sure it sticks to you.'

Kate assured him that she'd be discreet and left Raymond's office with a big grin plastered across her face. For all his bluster, Kate knew that the DCI would defend her if his bosses questioned any decisions that she'd made – he was a dinosaur but he was fiercely loyal.

Cooper and Hollis were staring at their computer monitors when Kate went back through to the team office. Sam was running a section of CCTV footage in slow-motion, staring at it intently, while Hollis appeared to be flicking through a database of known offenders.

Leaving them to it, Kate sat at her own desk and logged on to her email on her PC. She'd already sent a message to Anna Carson about the case – not the specifics but a general outline – so her friend had been prepared. Kate uploaded a selection of case notes and images and typed a quick message. Anna was a friend from university. Kate had taken a couple of psychology units as part of her degree and she'd met Anna during a seminar on 'The Psychology of Sexual Politics'. It hadn't been the most inspiring course but Kate and Anna had been paired up to investigate attitudes to feminism in the Thatcher era and had bonded over a mutual dislike of Britain's first female prime minister.

Anna's background was very different from Kate's. Brought up in Edinburgh, the only child of two doctors, Anna had tried to downplay her middle-class roots but Kate wouldn't let her get away with any suggestion of 'Champagne socialism'. She'd played on her own working-class credentials as the daughter of a miner, to challenge and stretch her friend's political awareness. Their late-night conversations had been the start of a life-long bond. Anna had stuck to psychology and was currently working in a secure unit for violent offenders in Berkshire but she enjoyed a puzzle and was always happy to help Kate if she could.

When Kate had struggled with a serial rapist in Kendal it had been Anna who had given her the insight to view their list of suspects in a different light and now Kate was hoping that she could do the same with this case. Except that they didn't really have a viable list of suspects.

Kate quickly reviewed her message, held her breath and hit 'send' feeling a sense of finality about the keystroke. Anna might just be their last hope.

'You two got anything?' Kate asked, turning her attention to her colleagues. Hollis responded with a heavy sigh.

'Got a headache,' he said. 'It's not much fun scrolling through a never-ending parade of Doncaster's thugs and rapists. Even if one of them was on the CCTV I'm not sure I'd recognise his mug shot. Different camera angles, different hairstyles.'

'Looking for anybody in particular?'

Hollis passed her a thin sheaf of printouts, each of them a still from the footage outside Madrigal's. Kate skimmed through a gallery of half glimpsed faces and tops of heads and felt Dan's pain. She passed them back to him without comment, leaving him to continue.

'Sam, how about you?'

Cooper paused the video that was playing on her monitor but she didn't look away from the screen. 'I'm still trying to cross-match the two lots of footage. I've got three or four possible matches between Madrigal's and X-Ray and I've given Dan some of the clearer still images to see if he can identify anybody.'

'Three or four possibles?' Kate was surprised that her colleague was downplaying what could be their most significant lead so far. If she'd seen the same person entering and leaving the bar and the nightclub at around the same time as Chloe then they just might be looking at her killer.

'Hang on.' Sam closed the programme that she was running and clicked on a folder of stills. She'd paired the images so that it was easy to compare the person from Madrigal's against stills from X-Ray's camera. The four that she'd already found looked like good matches to each other. One pair was clearly the same person, shaved head and trendy rectangular glasses, he looked like Heston Bloomenthal's younger brother.

'What about facial recognition technology?' she asked. 'Now you've actually got some decent stills. Can you not run each through a programme and see if they're the same person? And can't we do the same with the database of mug shots?' She could hear the excitement in her own voice. How had Cooper not thought of this? And then she realised. Of course Cooper would have used facial recognition if it had been possible. If she hadn't used it there would be a good reason.

'I tried,' Cooper was saying. 'But facial recognition technology depends on points of comparison and the quality of the footage isn't good enough. The light's different in each one and the camera angles distort the facial features. The first pair I tried had nine common points of comparison which is really low. I put in a photograph of Dan and it showed six when compared to one of the suspects. Not great.' She turned and glared at the image that she'd frozen on the monitor as though she held it personally responsible for her lack of success.

'So all we can do is keep trawling through and see what we can spot.'

Kate wasn't willing to give in to the despondency that seemed to be infecting Hollis and Cooper. 'But you've found a few. That's something.'

'I think I've just got another one as well,' Cooper said. 'Look.'

She went back to the footage from X-Ray and showed Kate a still image of a man taking down an umbrella. His face was in shadow but she could see that he was well built and, judging by his position next to the door, he looked quite tall.

'See,' Sam fast-forwarded to 1.10. 'He's here again.' The umbrella was the same, a regular pattern of black and white, each segment contrasting with its neighbours. But, again, it was impossible to make out the features of the man beneath it.

Sam switched from the footage from the nightclub to the footage from Madrigal's. Again, the same umbrella could be seen leaving just ninety seconds after Chloe. This time the angle prevented them from seeing the person beneath except for his legs and one hand clasped around the handle.

'That could be anybody,' Kate said. 'Shame it was raining. That brolly hides his face but it looks like the same man. Better add him to your list and see if you can get a better image from when he enters the bar. That umbrella's quite distinctive. You should be able to spot it if he's carrying it. And who takes an umbrella on a night out anyway?'

Sam was still staring at the screen. 'It wasn't raining though,' she said quietly.

'What? Of course it was. You can see people putting hoods up and holding bags over their heads.'

'Not when Chloe left X-Ray.' She went back to the image of the Umbrella Man outside the nightclub. 'It had stopped by then.'

'So why put his umbrella up?'

The answer was obvious.

'He knew about the cameras,' Sam said. 'And he didn't want to be recognised.'

# Chapter 28

Nick had been amused to find Kate poring over a website selling umbrellas when he walked into her flat.

'Not your usual style,' he said kissing the nape of her neck as he peered over her shoulder. 'Not exactly easy to hide in your handbag. I'd have thought one of those automatic ones would have been better for apprehending villains. You know, push a button and whack him in the head. Those are all a bit John Steed, concealed sword-types, aren't they?'

Kate turned and grinned at him. Nick was different from her ex, Garry, in so many ways, but the one she most appreciated was that he never complained if he came over to her flat and she was working. If anything, he was usually fascinated and keen to help if he could. He didn't mind ordering pizza when he'd been promised a meal and he'd usually offer to do a run to the off licence if they ran out of wine while she was still puzzling over a problem.

'I'm thinking of suggesting them as police standard issue. At least until we're allowed guns.'

Nick smiled at her and ran a hand through his thick black hair, a gesture that made the muscles in his forearm ripple in a rather distracting manner.

'I don't suppose you've cooked anything?'

'Sorry,' Kate said knowing that he wouldn't believe her apology. 'There's a lasagne in the freezer – I made it a couple of months ago now though. If you chip off the worst bits of ice it might be okay?'

Nick was staring at her open-mouthed and she wondered what she'd said until she realised he was taking the piss.

'You cooked a whole lasagne? From scratch? And had the foresight to freeze it? My God, you'll make somebody an excellent wife one day.'

'And you'll make an excellent husband if you can learn to use the oven.'

Nick stomped off to the kitchen and she heard him rattling round in the freezer. The oven door opened and closed and then the sound she'd been listening for as Nick opened the fridge and removed two bottles of lager. A hiss and clink, repeated, as he popped off the tops and then footsteps on the hardwood floor as he returned with his offering.

'I could get used to this,' Kate said, taking a big swig of Peroni.

'Well, don't,' Nick responded. 'In case you've forgotten I come from a long line of Greek chauvinists. So tell me about your umbrella search.' He sprawled on the sofa opposite where she was sitting, his long legs dangling over one of the arms as he leaned against the other.

'I'm trying to find out if a particular umbrella is as unusual as it looks. It's huge and has alternate black and white sections.'

'Like a golf umbrella?'

'I suppose so. Is that what they're called?'

'Yep. They loan them out on golf courses when it's raining – caddies stand over you with one while you take a putt. That's why they're so big. If you can afford a caddy that is. The course I used to go to stopped loaning them out because they were always getting nicked.'

'I'm not surprised, looking at the prices,' Kate said, scrolling down yet another page of umbrellas.

'They tried branding them, having them specially made with their logo. I think a lot of the big golf courses do that. They're a bit of a status symbol among certain members of my profession. I know of one consultant who never goes anywhere without his St Andrews brolly – whatever the weather.'

His words started synapses firing in Kate's dull brain. 'Say that again.'

'Whatever the weather.'

'No,' she protested, 'the thing about the branding.'

Nick shifted position and took another swig of his lager. 'Some golf courses have their umbrellas specially made with their logo on. It was supposed to stop them from being stolen. I think you have to buy them in the club house now though.'

Kate opened the file that Sam had sent to her – the clearest image they had of Umbrella Man. On two of the white sections of the umbrella's fabric was an image. It wasn't very clear but it looked like words arranged around a shape.

'Come here,' she snapped at Nick.

He obeyed instantly with an ironic salute.

'Could this be a golf club logo?'

Nick stared at the picture, breathing gently, close to her ear. Kate shifted in her seat, unwilling to be distracted until she had an answer.

'Looks like it to me. It might not be a golf course, though. I've seen similar ones at corporate events – some companies give them out as bribes. I swear I saw one for Viagra once on one of those pop-up brollies.'

Kate reached round and swatted his leg. 'Daft bugger. Seriously though – this could be a company logo?' She was disappointed. The golf club idea had been a good one. If it had turned out to be a local club it would have given them somewhere new to look – a desperately needed new lead. If it had been handed out at a big event it could have come from anywhere. She zoomed in on the design but it blurred beyond recognition with even the slightest magnification. This needed somebody with technical finesse. Glancing round at Nick, who'd gone back to the sofa, Kate typed out a hurried email to Cooper then decided she was done for the evening.

*** 

'It's a garage,' Sam said as soon as Kate sat down at her desk the next day. Still foggy from too little sleep and too much sex, Kate struggled to connect with what Cooper was saying.

'The umbrella. It's from Benton's. The Toyota dealership in Rotherham. It's got their logo on it. They're not open yet but I'll give them a buzz in half an hour. Oh, and I can't find anybody carrying an umbrella into Madrigal's on Friday night so I'm wondering if it was already there and he picked it up.'

Which meant that the umbrella could have belonged to anybody. Still, it was the best lead they had and, if Sam was right about their mystery man not having the umbrella when he entered the bar that meant there was an image of him somewhere on the CCTV. As usual, Cooper was one step ahead.

'I've already gone back to the hour of footage before Chloe arrived at Madrigal's. There's quite a bit of activity. I should have some fairly clear images once I've sharpened them up a bit. It'll give Dan something to do today.'

Kate smiled at the thought of Hollis's face when he realised that he was going to have to spend the day looking through the same database of known criminals. It was his job now though, and she couldn't waste time starting again with one of the others. She glanced at her watch. Briefing time.

***

The team meeting was more upbeat than that of the previous afternoon. Barratt had been back through Cawthorne's statement and, when he'd not been satisfied with words on paper, he'd rung the witness to 'clarify a few points'. He'd had the definite impression that Cawthorne was being cagey but he'd not been able to get him to confess to speaking to a journalist. O'Connor, on the other hand, had had a bit more success. He'd spoken to his contact, Gail, at *The Gazette* and she'd confirmed that Duncan Cawthorne had approached one of her colleagues, thinking that the paper might pay for his information, but she couldn't give him any specifics. It looked like they'd found the source of the newspaper story but there wasn't much they could do about it.

Kate shared the image of their suspect with the rest of the team – explaining the significance of the umbrella and then allowed them some time to brainstorm – before allocating jobs. What she really wanted was for somebody to go to Madrigal's to find out who owned the umbrella but it was too early for the bar to be open. Instead she tasked Barratt with finding out when the umbrellas had been made – suggesting that he visit Benton's garage rather than simply calling.

O'Connor offered to check whether there was a connection between Ryan Buckley and Benton's garage. As a mechanic it was possible that Buckley may have worked there or may have had an acquaintance who was a member of Benton's staff.

Hollis grimaced when Kate directed him back to the CCTV images but he went back to his desk without complaint. Kate knew that, while he was in the office, there was no chance of him being accosted by Suzanne and the intensive work might offer him a distraction from his thoughts about Raymond. Which reminded her…

'The DCI's doing a press conference this morning. It'll probably be on the local news at lunch time. Have a watch if you can.'

Barratt didn't respond as he grabbed his jacket but O'Connor gave her a grin and a thumbs-up, which could have meant anything. Hollis and Cooper were already absorbed in their work.

\*\*\*

Kate had been resisting her email until she'd got back to Doncaster Central. Her return visit to the fertility clinic had yielded nothing of any significance. Beresford had confirmed Chloe's appointment and had put on a sad face when he spoke about her 'unusual situation' but there wasn't much that he could tell her. Chloe had attended a half-hour appointment with Matthias who confirmed the details but, again, couldn't add much. Neither man had seen Chloe since her visit to the clinic, and neither had an alibi for Friday night.

Even though she was desperate to know if Anna had got back to her, she reasoned that the longer she left before checking, the longer Anna would have had to formulate a response. Logging into her email, she realised that her hands weren't quite steady. Anna had done such a good job the last time they'd worked together that Kate realised she was placing a lot of her faith in her friend. That wasn't fair on her colleagues, she knew – they were all doing good solid detective work – but she felt like Anna might give her a way to cheat the game.

There it was in her inbox. Anna must have worked on it for most of the previous evening – unless the email was telling her to sod off and do her job properly. Only one way to find out. Kate clicked on the email and noticed that it had a Word attachment. She scrolled quickly through the message noting the pleasantries and the disclaimer at the bottom stating that Anna didn't want to be responsible for the direction of Kate's investigation and the notes that she'd sent were purely for guidance.

The attachment seemed to take an age to open. Another disclaimer at the top and then Anna's thoughts based on the evidence that Kate had sent. This was what she'd been waiting for.

Some of it was predictable – both victims were white which made it likely that they were looking for a white perpetrator. Anna seemed to favour the attacker being male despite the lack of semen or evidence of condom use – the nature of the violence and the bruising suggested a sustained but not necessarily frenzied attack by a physically strong individual. The control involved also suggested an age range of early thirties to early forties. Kate smiled as she remembered Raymond's comments from the previous day but she didn't bother scanning for 'rabbit torture' – she knew Anna had no time for clichés.

The remainder of the notes were disappointingly vague. Sexual issues – possible periods of impotence or sexual abuse at an early age – and a suggestion that the person in question might struggle to maintain a relationship.

And then the final paragraph.

*Given the nature of the abdominal wounds on each victim, it seems likely that the perpetrator is ritualising elements of pregnancy and birth. Furthermore, the precision of the wounds suggests skill and/*

*or practice. It is possible that the attacker is a medical practitioner
and has experience of performing surgical procedures although the
violence of the strangulation may suggest otherwise as it is inefficient
and inelegant. However, I feel that it is unlikely that the wounds
inflicted on Melissa Buckley represent the first time that he has made
this type of incision. He may have done this before – or something
similar.*

'Shit,' Kate muttered. 'I should have thought of that.' They'd
been so focussed on the ongoing investigation, especially after the
discovery of Chloe Welsh's body that it hadn't crossed Kate's mind
to see if there was a record of anything similar. She'd assumed
Melissa was the first because, if anything like it had happened
recently, she'd have heard. But what if it wasn't recent? Or what if
it wasn't local?

She logged in to the Police National Database and typed in
strangulation and abdominal wound and, keeping Anna's age
estimate in mind, limited the search to the previous ten years.
There were nine hits – all strangulation/stabbings with each one
resulting in a conviction. The PND was a fantastic resource but,
like any database it was only as good as the people who added
information to it and if Kate wasn't using the correct keywords
she could be missing similar crimes.

Frustrated, she went back to Anna's notes, her eye drawn to
the last three words *or something similar*. What if Melissa had been
the first one he'd got right? There could have been other attempts,
similar wounds perhaps, or attacks which hadn't resulted in the
death of the victim. She knew that, if she widened the parameters
of her search to include 'wounding' and 'attempted' she'd end up
with hundreds, if not thousands, of hits. How many abdominal
wounds had been recorded in the past ten years? How many
strangulations? She needed a way to narrow it down somehow or
a way to include as much description as possible.

Logging out of the database, Kate clicked on a long-neglected
icon lurking in the corner of her desktop. When she'd first been
promoted, Kate had joined an online forum where detective

inspectors could discuss the job and its issues. Ironically named *DI Blues* it had been a source of comfort for Kate when she'd moved back to South Yorkshire and needed to know others had experienced some of the same difficulties when they'd been promoted. Most of it was moaning about bosses or lower ranks but some threads had dealt with paperwork and other essential protocols and Kate had learned a lot. She hadn't logged on to moan, though. There was a sub-forum where people posted about difficult cases and sometimes asked for the thoughts of other DIs. On more than one occasion, Kate remembered, requests had been posted for any information about similar cases and at least one such appeal had yielded results.

Clicking on 'start new thread' Kate paused, considering how much information she could safely share. Eventually she decided to keep her questions brief.

*Anybody heard of women being attacked and left with abdominal wounds – possibly connected with pregnancy? Maybe strangulation involved?*

The message was anonymous – her username had no link to her real name and she'd not filled in the location box when she'd signed up to the forum but it still felt like a betrayal to go outside her immediate circle and ask for help.

She was about to ask Cooper to do some data mining as soon as she'd finished with the CCTV when Hollis pushed his seat back and clapped his hands together.

'Kate. You're going to want to see this,' he said, his face flushed with excitement.

# Chapter 29

'What've you got?' Kate asked, rushing over to Hollis's desk.

'A familiar face,' Hollis said with a grin. He'd paused the CCTV footage on a grainy image and pointed to a male figure. 'This is Madrigal's camera about fifteen minutes before Chloe arrives. Look at this man.' He tapped a key and zoomed in and then did something else and the image sharpened slightly. Kate immediately suspected some sort of software enhancement of Cooper's that wasn't technically supposed to be at their disposal. She squinted at the screen trying to see what had got Hollis so excited.

'Shit,' she said as she thought she recognised the figure on the screen. 'Is that…?'

'I think it's Tim Matthias,' Hollis announced jubilantly.

Kate leaned in closer. It certainly looked like Matthias. The angle of the camera made it hard to see his features clearly but the bald head and the bulk were obvious.

'Have we got anything clearer?'

Hollis shook his head. 'No, this is it.'

'Have you found him leaving?'

'No, but now that I know who I'm looking for I'm going through everything really slowly. I haven't seen him so far. The trouble is that, if he's put something over his head like a jacket I wouldn't necessarily spot him. I've got five possibles so far but nothing definite and I'm just about up to the time that Chloe left.'

'Show me.'

Hollis clicked on a file and opened up a series of stills from the footage. Each showed somebody with a covered head leaving the bar.

'That's not him,' Kate said immediately, pointing out one figure. 'Look at the position of his hood against the wall. He's too short.'

Rather than being disappointed, Hollis was energised by her observation and Kate shared his optimism. By ruling somebody out they were narrowing down Matthias's movements. Unfortunately, none of the other images were conclusive.

'Show me Umbrella Man again,' Kate said, drumming her fingers on Hollis's desk while he scrolled to the best image they had of their earlier suspect.

'Damn,' she muttered. The umbrella's canopy obscured too much of the man's head and upper body. It could have been anybody, including Matthias. She instructed Hollis to zoom in on the hand holding the umbrella's handle, searching for a ring, a tattoo, a scar, anything that would rule Matthias in or out but the image was grainy and she couldn't see anything to distinguish this hand from a million others.

'Keep looking,' she said. 'And if you don't see him then he must be one of the ones you've already got or he's Umbrella Man. I think we might need to talk to him again.'

'I'm checking X-Ray,' Cooper said. 'So far I haven't seen anybody who's definitely him but I'll get Dan to check because he's met him.'

Kate checked her watch. Matthias would be at work. Was it worth questioning him again? Even with the CCTV footage what had they got? He could easily say that he'd forgotten that he'd popped out for a quick drink, and Kate hadn't specifically asked him if he'd been to Madrigal's. He might also deny that the image was him – it was far from conclusive. If they did, it might alert him to their suspicions and, if he was their killer, they had nothing to charge him with yet. He could do a runner before they got something more concrete. Better to leave him alone – for now. Instead, she decided to try the bar. There might be somebody around taking deliveries or stock checking. It was worth a try and she needed to do something to take her mind off Anna's theory that their killer was much more experienced than they'd first anticipated.

\*\*\*

Madrigal's had gone through a number of incarnations since Kate had left South Yorkshire. In the early 1980s it had been converted from a small church to a flashy nightclub; she'd never been but she'd heard tales of cheap drink and loud music from some of the older teenagers on the estate in Thorpe. She'd heard that it had served a short spell as a community centre and as an independent cinema before being opened as a wine bar; famous for its Friday happy hour and cheap tapas.

The front doors with their fake ecclesiastic stained glass were firmly closed when Kate tried giving them a hefty shove. She glanced up and saw the camera that had recorded much of the footage that had been giving Hollis and Cooper such a headache for the last couple of days. An alley ran down one side of the former church and Kate followed it to the back doors that opened onto a wide yard. A lorry was just pulling away and a young man stood in the bar's courtyard with a clipboard in his hand. Dressed casually in ripped jeans and a tight-fitting, stained white t-shirt, he looked frazzled, as though the recent delivery had been as much as his nerves could take.

'Hello,' Kate said giving him a redundant wave considering he was less than ten yards away.

He glanced up, dark eyes peering out from beneath a long blonde fringe, which he pushed back to get a clearer view of whoever had interrupted him. 'You're not supposed to be back here,' he said. 'It's private property.'

Kate took out her ID. 'Can we talk inside?' she asked, nodding towards the open door.

'Just a minute.' He made a point of finishing whatever he was checking on his list before finally leading the way inside the club.

Kate had been in dozens of pubs and bars and clubs while they were closed and she found them all, without exception, utterly depressing. It used to be the smell; stale cigarette smoke mixed with spilled drinks, but after the smoking ban the odour had changed to sweat and loss of hope. Madrigal's was no different. Pale sunlight filtered through more stained glass, highlighting scuffs on the wooden floor and spills on the table tops. Obviously the cleaners hadn't been yet, unless that was why the man with the clipboard looked so fed up. Maybe it was his job and he just couldn't face it.

He gestured towards a table set in a gloomy alcove. 'Have a seat. Want a drink? Coffee? Tea?' Kate declined, not trusting the kitchen to be any cleaner than the rest of the place. Social niceties observed, the man sat opposite her, folding his long legs beneath the table being careful not to touch hers. He introduced himself as Ed Carpenter: manager, head barman and 'general dogsbody'.

'So what's this about? Is it to do with the CCTV footage that we sent you?'

'Just following up a couple of things,' Kate said, deliberately vague. 'Were you working on Friday night?'

'I work every night,' Carpenter said, his voice heavy with resentment. 'My uncle owns the place and he wanted somebody from the family keeping an eye on it. I got the short straw.'

'And your uncle is?'

The man looked at her as if he was assessing her suitability to be trusted with sensitive information. 'Tony Benton,' he said, finally.

'Of Benton's garage?'

'The one and only,' the sarcasm distorted Carpenter's face as he sneeringly gave an account of his uncle's ownership of Madrigal's and how he'd installed his nephew as manager on not much more than minimum wage.

Kate tried to follow his account but she was already thinking about Barratt and his trip to Benton's garage. It looked like it might be pointless now that she had a possible link to the umbrella. Kate took out her phone and scrolled to a picture of Chloe that her friend Siobhan had supplied.

'Do you recognise her?'

Carpenter looked carefully at the picture before shaking his head. 'No, sorry. We get a lot of people through here and I'd say about twenty per cent are regulars that I'd recognise. She's not one of them.'

'How about him?' Kate flicked to the still image of Tim Matthias.

Again, Carpenter shook his head. 'I'm guessing that's from our camera but I don't know him.'

'I think you might recognise this though.' Kate showed him the picture of the umbrella causing Carpenter to scowl at her.

'I don't recognise whoever's holding it, but that umbrella's mine. I kept it out the back in case it's raining when we get a delivery and it wasn't there when I went to look for it last Saturday. If you find out who he is, tell him I want it back.'

'When did you last see it?'

He thought for a few seconds. 'Earlier in the week. Must've been Wednesday because I used it when we had a soft drinks delivery and that usually comes on a Wednesday morning. It wasn't there on Saturday when I was tidying up in the back.'

'Can I have a look where you kept it?'

Carpenter shrugged as though it was no business of his if Kate wanted to waste her time and led the way behind the bar. He pointed to a corner next to a door.

'It was there, leaning against the wall.'

Kate studied the layout of the bar area. The corner where the umbrella had been kept would be just about visible to customers but any bar staff would have their backs to it while they were serving drinks.

'Where does this door go?'

Carpenter opened it, allowing Kate to step through into a dark corridor. There was another door immediately opposite with GENTS stencilled across the top panel. She tried to imagine the sequence of events. Could Chloe's killer have spotted the umbrella and realised that it could provide him with cover from the camera as he left? It would have been fairly easy for him to head for the toilet and stick his hand round the door to the bar area. He could then hide his identity as he left Madrigal's and entered X-Ray.

It wasn't much, but it was another piece of the puzzle.

# Chapter 30

'Tim Matthias,' Kate said, pointing to the picture displayed on the whiteboard. 'He works as a counsellor at the fertility clinic and had contact with Melissa Buckley and Chloe Welsh. By his own admission he only has an alibi for part of the Saturday when Melissa was murdered. This picture is from Madrigal's fifteen minutes before Chloe Welsh entered the bar.'

She looked around at the team who were studying the image intently. 'We have him arriving but nothing showing him leaving. Sam and Dan have found three people who might be him but we can't be sure. Then there's this.'

She moved on to the pictures of the man with the umbrella.

'He leaves Madrigal's soon after Chloe, arrives at X-Ray soon after Chloe, and leaves again soon after Chloe.'

She showed three stills in turn, highlighting each instance of him being recorded on camera. 'Notice that the umbrella is up when he leaves the club even though it wasn't raining by that time on Saturday morning. Which makes me wonder if he was trying to disguise himself.'

'Anything showing Matthias at X-Ray?' Barratt asked.

Sam shook her head. 'Nothing.'

'So,' Kate continued. 'Either one of our three unidentified figures is Matthias or he's the man carrying the umbrella. It would have been easy for him to steal it from behind the bar and then dump it once he was out of range of any cameras. Which is where you come in.'

She raised her head so that she was addressing the group of uniformed officers who'd gathered at the back of the room. 'DS O'Connor is going to coordinate a search of the area around X-Ray in the hope that the umbrella's in a skip or has been dumped in somebody's front garden.'

O'Connor turned and grinned at the group.

'DC Cooper and DC Barratt have an appointment today,' Kate said with a wink at Sam. She'd already briefed Cooper but hadn't had chance to catch up with Barratt and she was keen to see his reaction to her proposal. 'Sam, Matt, I've arranged for you to visit the fertility clinic for a psychological assessment. You'll be posing as a couple – I'll leave the details to you – but you'll have a counselling session with Matthias.'

'What?' Barratt spluttered. 'I'm not... I mean she's...' He looked at Cooper expecting her to help him out but she was grinning at his shocked expression.

'Come on, Matt, I'm not happy about being your wife or girlfriend or whatever but Matthias has met Dan already and Kate's a bit old for...'

She blushed deeply as she realised what she'd said. 'Oh, shit,' she said, turning back to Kate. 'I didn't mean... you're not that...'

'It's fine,' Kate reassured her with a smile. 'You're right, as long as you were going to say that I'm a bit old for having any more kids. Anything else and you'll be back in uniform by Monday.'

She was glad of the light relief; it broke the tension and she needed her colleagues open and receptive to what she had to say next. After a brief outline of her previous experience with Anna Carson she explained that she'd contacted the psychologist who'd given her some insight into their killer.

'He's done it before?' Hollis asked. 'Wouldn't we have heard? It's pretty unusual.'

Kate took a sip of her coffee trying to decide how to respond. She didn't want to suggest that she'd dropped the ball and not searched for other similar crimes but she also wanted to be clear that she trusted Anna's assessment. 'He might not have done *this* before, but he may have done something similar. I checked the

PND but I don't seem to have been very imaginative with my choice of key words so I drew a blank there.'

Cooper raised a hand like a child in primary school desperate to give a correct answer.

'Hang on, Sam,' Kate said. 'Let me finish. I've been in touch with DIs from other forces around the country to see if our cases ring any bells with them and I got a possible lead.'

She couldn't tell them how excited she'd been that morning when the icon for DI Blues on her desktop had a red asterisk next to it. She'd read the response and, even though the similarities to Melissa and Chloe were superficial, something about it felt right.

'There was a case in Haltwhistle, in Northumberland, four years ago. A woman was attacked on her way home from a night out. The attacker strangled her into unconsciousness and, when she was discovered, she had a cut across her abdomen.'

'Shit,' O'Connor said. 'That's a bit close. What happened to the woman?'

This was the part that Kate had been dreading telling them. 'She survived. Made a full recovery. Sadly, her baby didn't.'

'He cut the baby out of her?' Hollis's face was contorted with disgust. 'What kind of sick bastard...?'

Kate held her hand up, palm out as though holding up traffic and the buzz of conversation around the room stilled. 'She was only a few weeks pregnant at the time. She lost the baby a couple of days after the attack. My source said that her doctors suggested the stress of the attack may have caused a miscarriage.'

'And the attacker wasn't caught?' Cooper asked.

Kate shook her head. 'According to the woman's statement she can't remember the attack. Nothing at all.'

'What about the father of the baby?' Barratt wanted to know. 'Was he questioned?'

'I don't have all the facts yet but I've requested contact details for this woman. I'm hoping to interview her later today. Fancy a road trip, Dan? Right. Same time tomorrow morning unless I tell you different.'

'I can't believe you did that to Matt,' Hollis said with a smirk as soon as the incident room had emptied. 'He'll be imagining all sorts. I bet he thinks he's got to give a sample.'

'He'll be fine. He's a big boy. Sam'll look after him, she's good at thinking on her feet.'

'And are we really driving up to Northumberland? That's your old stomping ground, isn't it?'

'I lived in Cumbria,' Kate corrected him. 'Northumberland's the next county over. Did you not take geography at school?'

'I get a bit confused about the frozen wastes of the north. Isn't it just hills and sheep up there?'

Kate was suddenly reminded of the view from the back door of her house in Kendal.

'Mostly,' she agreed.

***

'Not seen any sheep yet,' Hollis said as they turned onto the A69 at Newcastle. 'It's all a bit built up.'

Kate had accessed the case notes from four years ago and got an address and phone number for Sarah Armstrong. She'd briefly considered phoning her but her gut was telling her that she needed to have this conversation face to face, so she'd booked a pool car and they'd set off up the A1 just after 9am. As soon as they'd stopped at the services at Wetherby for coffee, Kate knew that she'd made the right decision in bringing Hollis. He seemed to have shrugged off some of his despondency from the past couple of weeks and was much more like his old self. She'd asked about Suzanne and had been relieved when Dan had told her that he hadn't heard from her since her revelation about his possible paternity.

'Just wait,' she told him. 'You're in the land of big skies now. That'll cheer you up.'

And, just as she'd promised, the landscape opened up as soon as they'd passed the billowing chimney of the chipboard plant at

Hexham. Towns gave way to fields which rose up from the narrow thread of road like the panels of a patchwork blanket, stitched together by drystone walls.

Kate checked the address she'd been given against the satnav. 'Ten minutes,' she said. 'It's just this side of the town.'

They turned off the main road onto a street of dark stone terraced houses, which looked like they might have been built from the remains of the famous Roman wall that lay just a couple of miles to the north.

'Just here,' Kate said, pointing to a gap in the cars parked along either side of the road. She checked her watch. According to the most recent information she'd been able to find, Sarah Armstrong worked part-time as a teaching assistant at the local primary school. A quick phone call had established that it was her day off but she'd be in work the next day. As long as Sarah hadn't planned a shopping trip to the Metro Centre or a coffee morning with friends, Kate thought they had a good chance of catching her at home.

Gravel crunched underfoot as Kate followed Hollis up the short path to the front door of a middle terrace. It was neatly kept, the window surrounds newly painted and the uPVC door spotlessly white. Hollis rang the bell and a blurred figure appeared behind the upper glass panel of the door.

'Yes? Can I help you?' The woman standing on the doorstep wasn't quite what Kate had been expecting. She knew from the case notes that Sarah Armstrong was in her early thirties but this woman looked twice that age.

'We're looking for Sarah Armstrong,' Hollis said, holding out his ID. 'South Yorkshire Police.'

'Can I ask why?' The woman folded her arms across an ample bosom making her look like a bouncer at an old people's home.

'We need to speak to her about an incident that she was involved in a few years ago.'

The crossed arms tightened, cardigan-covered shoulders moved higher.

'Look,' Kate said, from behind the DC. 'We've come a long way and we'd really like to speak to Sarah, if she's here. If not then can you tell us where to find her? It's concerning a case in Doncaster which may have a link to what happened to her four years ago. I think she might be able to help us.'

Before the woman could reply a voice sang out from further down the hallway.

'Who is it, Mam?'

Kate saw jeans-clad legs approaching the front door topped by a baggy, pale yellow T-shirt. When the woman peered over the shoulder of the self-appointed gatekeeper, Kate could barely contain a gasp of surprise. The owner of the voice was the spitting image of Melissa Buckley.

# Chapter 31

Barratt was humming as he pulled into the car park of the fertility clinic.

'What's that tune?' Cooper asked, unable to place the vaguely familiar rhythm.

'It's the theme from *The Addams Family*. Don't you think this place looks a bit like their house?' He dropped his voice to a hoarse whisper. 'Who knows what horrors lurk inside?'

Sam stared out of the car window. Barratt had a point – the building looked much more like a gothic mansion than a clinic. She hadn't been keen on this assignment despite the way she'd teased her colleague in the briefing; it was way beyond her comfort zone even though it wasn't strictly under cover. They'd worked out their story on the short drive over. Matt was a car salesman and she worked in the library. They'd been married for three years and had been trying to conceive naturally for two of those. Month after month of failure had compelled them to take the first steps towards IVF. Money wasn't an issue.

'Come on then,' Barratt said, opening the car door. 'Let's get this over with.'

Sam followed him up the steps and into the reception area trying to take in the details of her surroundings but her eye was drawn to the state-of-the-art computer system on the receptionist's desk. Barratt caught her eye and shook his head almost imperceptibly. The message was clear: now was not the time to get into a discussion about technology. She allowed Barratt to explain who they were and why they were here to the receptionist who responded with a smile to everything that Barratt said and then directed them to wait in a soft seating area in the bay window.

'I feel like we're on display,' Barratt whispered, nodding to the clear panes, unadorned by curtains or blinds. 'Not exactly private.'

'And nothing to be ashamed of, either,' Sam responded. Matt was obviously getting into his role as reluctant husband. They'd decided that she'd be the one most keen on IVF while Barratt was to play the long-suffering husband who was just humouring 'the little woman'.

'Mr and Mrs Barratt?' a voice called from behind Sam. She turned to see a tall, well-built man in an immaculate navy-blue suit, which made Barratt's look like he'd bought it second-hand from eBay. A lavender tie and white shirt completed the look, which wouldn't have been out of place at a summer wedding. He reached out to shake Barratt's hand and Sam watched as the arm of his jacket strained across the muscles of his upper arm. When he took her own hand his grip was firm, warm and dry. She smiled up at him trying to assess whether his baldness was natural or due to shaving. The latter, she knew, was a favourite trick of the forensically-aware killer.

'Come through,' Matthias said, holding the door open to allow Barratt to lead the way. 'Up the stairs then second on the right.'

Mathias's office looked more like a domestic sitting room than a treatment room. Two large sofas flanked one corner with a low coffee table between them. The only sign that this was a work space was a desk pushed up against the wall, opposite the window. Here, again, was a top-of-the range PC and, next to it, a small selection of medical text books.

'Please, sit,' Matthias instructed and Sam settled next to Barratt on one of the sofas. Matt took her hand and, as they'd planned, she pulled away from him and shifted position slightly so that she could lean forwards towards Matthias. She knew that the psychologist couldn't have missed her actions or their message. This was not a happy marriage.

'So, you want to explore whether IVF is the right option for you?'

'We do,' Sam said firmly. 'I've always wanted children and, well, no matter how hard we try, it's not working.'

'So why IVF? Have you tried artificial insemination? I'm sorry but I don't have your notes yet.'

They'd prepared for this. Barratt cleared his throat. 'I er… my sperm have very low motility. I had tests through my GP and they showed that AI was unlikely to be effective. We were told that, if we were prepared to pay, we could go straight to IVF.'

Another understanding nod from Matthias. Sam could feel the sofa cushion vibrating as Barratt's right leg twitched up and down next to her. Either he'd decided to add a nervous twitch or he felt really uncomfortable talking about sperm in front of her. She filed the information away so that she could tease him later.

'Tell me about yourselves,' Matthias said. 'What's brought you to this point?'

For the next forty minutes they told their story: happy marriage, good jobs but Sam felt that something was missing. Barratt agreed with her but allowed some reluctance to add a slight edge to his account. They wanted to make it seem like he was just going along with her to shift the focus – and potentially Matthias's sympathy – onto Sam. Barratt made it clear that Sam came from a wealthy family who were willing to pay for the procedure and, again, added a dash of resentment suggesting that he didn't want handouts from his in-laws.

Sam noticed that Matthias didn't make notes, instead he just listened, only asking questions for further clarification of factual details. She'd been expecting to be asked how she felt about it all but there was no attempt to gauge the emotional state of either herself or Barratt, instead Matthias seemed to focus his attention on the stability of their relationship; he'd obviously picked up on the tension between the two of them.

Finally, he seemed satisfied and urged them to make another appointment where they could 'really explore the emotional impact of their decision'. They all stood up and, after another handshake, he directed them back to reception where they could book another appointment.

Sam could barely hide her disappointment as she and Barratt descended the stairs. She'd expected something overt from

Matthias, some specific interest in the friction between husband and wife, but he seemed to have almost ignored the obvious signals that she'd been giving. They booked an appointment for the following week and Sam handed over her credit card – she'd offered to make the payment and claim it back later as it backed up their story that her family were paying for the treatment.

Just as they'd slammed the car doors and Barratt started the engine a tap on the window made Sam jump. Matthias was standing next to the car, a mix of embarrassment and determination on his face. Sam wound down her window.

'I'm really sorry, Mrs Barratt,' Matthias began. 'There's been a problem with your credit card. Would you mind coming back inside?'

She made irritated noises and protested that there shouldn't be a problem but, intrigued, she followed the psychologist back up the steps and into the foyer of the building. The receptionist wasn't at her desk and Sam wondered if Matthias had sent her off on an errand so that she wouldn't witness this conversation.

'It's not your card,' he explained. 'The payment was fine. I just got the impression that you didn't want to open up in front of your husband. I see a lot of couples who think that they want counselling together but, quite often, one or the other would rather not share their feelings with their partner. I offer one-to-one counselling, away from the clinic, and I just thought you might be interested. If I'm mistaken, feel free to ignore my intrusion but, if I'm not…' He handed her a business card. 'Here's my personal number. We can set up an appointment at your convenience.'

Sam simply nodded, not trusting herself to speak, and pocketed the business card. She waited until they were on Thorne Road before finally turning to Barratt with a huge grin.

'Got him!' she crowed.

# Chapter 32

Sarah Armstrong smiled at Kate and Hollis as she settled into an overstuffed armchair but her eyes were wary.

'What's this about?' she asked. They'd already established that she lived here with her mother who had been persuaded to go into town on a probably pointless errand. Kate suspected that Sarah had wanted her mother out of the way if she was going to have to relive her ordeal. In Kate's experience it was much easier to get victims of crime to speak out if they weren't surrounded by family members.

'It's about the attack that you reported four years ago,' Kate said. She needed to get straight to the point and there was no sense in sugar-coating the reason for the visit. 'We think the attacker might be active in South Yorkshire and we'd like you to help us. I know it's painful for you to remember what happened but I was hoping that something might have come back to you since you made your statement. Something that might help us to catch this man.'

The young woman's face paled and she suddenly looked much younger than thirty-one as she thrust her hands in the pockets of jeans and pulled her legs up onto the seat of the chair. 'I told the local police everything I can remember,' she said. 'I really don't want to talk about it again.'

Kate nodded, completely understanding the woman's reluctance to relive the horrific event, but they needed the information. 'I'm sorry, Sarah, I truly am. If there were any other way I'd not be here, but somebody has killed two women in Doncaster in the last two weeks and I think it may be the same man who attacked you.'

Her pallor took on a slightly greenish hue and Kate wondered if Sarah was about to be sick. 'He's killed two women?' Her voice was little more than a whisper, her dark eyes round with horror.

'Two that we know about,' Kate said. 'The injuries were similar to the ones that you suffered. It took us a while to make the link but there's a real possibility that this killer is your attacker. The first victim bore a striking resemblance to you.'

She turned to Hollis who took out his phone and scrolled to a photograph of Melissa Buckley. Sarah barely glanced at it, her eyes drawn quickly back to Kate.

'Was she pregnant?'

Kate shook her head. 'No. She was having IVF to try to get pregnant. The other victim wasn't pregnant either. Do you think that's important?'

The other woman shrugged and lowered her eyes. 'It seemed important when he attacked me. You know I lost a baby?'

'I know,' Kate said. 'And I'm terribly sorry. If it is the same person then he's escalated his behaviour. I don't want any more women to die.' Kate was choosing her words carefully and moderating the tone of her voice despite the frustration she felt at Sarah's reluctance to talk. She could see that the woman was fragile but her experience could provide vital information.

She pressed on. 'You said that your pregnancy seemed important when you were attacked. Did he say something to give you that impression?'

Another shrug.

'Okay,' Kate said, holding back a sigh of frustration. 'Let's try going back to what happened. You were attacked outside a pub in Haltwhistle?'

Sarah nodded.

'And your attacker dragged you down an alley behind the railway station?'

No response. The woman's eyes had become fixed on a point on the wall above Hollis's head as though she were willing herself not to remember, not to relive what had happened to her.

'He strangled you until you were unconscious and when you came round you were in hospital in Hexham. You can't remember anything about him. This was all in your statement Sarah. Is it correct?'

'Yes.' The response was strong, definite, but Sarah still couldn't look at Kate.

Kate decided to change tack.

'The baby? Was it your boyfriend's?'

'I... er... I didn't have a boyfriend. I'd had a one-night stand and got pregnant. Stupid really. You'd think I was old enough to know better.' Sarah smiled but the movement was almost mechanical and the emotion didn't reach her eyes. Something wasn't right here. Kate glanced across at Hollis. He was frowning at Sarah, his head slightly tilted to one side – obviously he'd sensed it as well.

'Dan, could you make us some tea?' Kate suggested. It was a strategy that they sometimes used when an interview subject seemed to have more to say but was showing reluctance. One detective could sometimes be a lot less intimidating than two and she thought it might work with Sarah Armstrong. Kate knew that Hollis would take his time and she trusted him not to interrupt at a crucial moment. She noticed that he left the sitting room door ajar as he left. He'd got the message.

'Sarah,' Kate tried again, leaning forwards to convey a sense of confidentiality. 'I'm getting the feeling that there's more to this than you're telling me. Your original statement is very vague and I'd like to flesh it out. Can we try to fill in some gaps?'

A single tear spilled down from Sarah's right eye and she brushed it away distractedly, still refusing to look at Kate.

'Shall we start with the baby?'

'I had a one-night stand,' Sarah repeated. 'I honestly did. And I got pregnant.'

'And you don't think the father is the man who attacked you? To get rid of the baby?'

Sarah shook her head vehemently. 'There's no way he could have known that I was pregnant.'

'But somebody did. You weren't that far along so you would have barely been showing. Do you think your attacker just happened to notice?'

'I *think* he was going to rape me!' Sarah spat. 'And when he saw that I was expecting he cut me instead. That's what I *think* but I was unconscious. How would I know?'

Kate knew from the report that Sarah hadn't been raped, yet she had been undressed from the waist down so the attacker may have noticed her swollen belly. Maybe the woman was right and he'd been intending to rape her but the pregnancy had put him off for some reason. It still didn't quite add up though – the report Kate had read suggested that Sarah had only been a few weeks pregnant. Would a random attacker have spotted her condition? And if not, then why would he have cut her in such a specific way?

'Sarah. I think you know who attacked you and you're too frightened to tell me,' Kate said, praying that her instinct was right. To suggest this to the young woman was a huge gamble but, if Kate was right, it might be the shock that Sarah needed to get her talking.

Silence.

'Sarah? Talk to me. If you know who this man is, then you can help me to stop him. He's killed two women and he might kill more. Please, help me.'

More silence.

'Chloe Welsh was going to be a child psychologist. She loved kids and wanted to help them. Melissa Buckley's husband loved her and wanted a family with her.' Kate hated doing this but she had to get through to Sarah somehow. 'Two lives cut short, Sarah. Don't let him do it to anybody else.'

Sarah shook her head. 'It's not my fault.'

'I know. You're scared. But we can protect you if that's what you're worried about.'

'No you can't,' Sarah sneered. 'Who am I? Just a stupid woman from a grotty town. He's educated, he's clever. Nobody would ever believe me.'

'Is that what he told you?'

Sarah nodded miserably.

'Come on, Sarah,' Kate reached out and placed a hand on the other woman's knee. 'Talk to me. Tell me what really happened.'

# Chapter 33

Hollis placed three mugs of tea on the side table next to Sarah's chair and positioned himself on one corner of the sofa, unobtrusive but present. Kate had finally persuaded Sarah to talk and the young woman had agreed to have Hollis present to make notes. She looked terrified. Whatever her attacker had threatened her with, it had worked. He'd bought her silence for four years and it had taken all of Kate's powers of persuasion to break down the barricade that Sarah had erected in her own mind.

'Let's start from the beginning,' Kate said 'How...?'

'No.' Sarah interrupted. 'I need to tell this my way. I don't want to answer lots of questions, I want you to listen.' It was as if, having made her mind up to talk, Sarah had tapped some inner reserves of strength, leaving Kate and Hollis no choice but to listen.

'I used to go out in Carlisle,' Sarah began. 'I could get the train in with my friends then we'd share a taxi back or crash on somebody's floor. Usually on a Friday or a Saturday. We'd get hammered, you know, stupid really but it always seemed like fun at the time.'

She was talking like somebody twice her age and Kate sensed that the attack had distanced her from the carefree days of her early twenties.

'There was one club we went to a lot on West Walls. I can't remember what it was called – it seemed to change its name every other week but the drinks were cheap early on and the music was usually good. That's where I met him. I was at the bar trying to get drinks for me and my friends but the barman wasn't taking any notice. This figure appeared behind me, leaned over and got his attention straight away. He even paid for the drinks.

'It was good at first. He was charming. Older than me though – that's why I didn't tell anybody I was seeing him. To be honest I thought he might be married because he didn't want to meet my family or friends, but he always just laughed when I said that. Anyway, we'd been seeing each other for about three months and we had a big row. I can't really remember what it was about – something to do with me pressuring him to meet my mum I think – and he stormed off. I ended up getting drunk and I went home with this art student that I met. Stupid really but it was in the heat of the moment. I ended up pregnant and I wasn't sure whose it was. I so badly wanted it to be *his* even though we'd not seen each other for a few weeks. In the end I texted him and we met up. I told him that I was sorry for pressurising him about meeting my family and then I told him that I was pregnant and that it was his. It could have been. I was on and off the pill at the time.'

Kate glanced over at Hollis who was scribbling in his notebook. He had to have noticed what she had. So far Sarah hadn't named the mystery man. They needed a name.

'He was shocked,' Sarah continued. 'I could tell from his face that he wasn't expecting it but then he started calling me all sorts of names and accusing me of going off with somebody else. I denied it, obviously, and told him that the baby was his. I was still convinced that it could have been. Until he dropped a bombshell on me. He couldn't have kids. He had a condition that meant that he didn't, you know… ejaculate. I felt so stupid. I'd not noticed. We used condoms, he insisted, and I'd just not noticed.'

She looked to Kate for corroboration but Kate simply raised her eyebrows, urging her to continue.

'So that was that, I thought. He dumped me. I decided not to keep the baby and started looking into arranging a termination. And then… and then I was attacked.'

'And it was him?' Kate asked.

Sarah nodded.

'You're sure?'

'I looked into his eyes as he strangled me and I was so sad that his would be the last face that I ever saw. Yes, I'm sure.' Sarah turned to Hollis. 'I hope you got all that because I don't want to have to repeat it.'

Hollis gave her a sympathetic smile. 'I got it all.'

Kate took a deep breath. 'We need a name. Sarah,' she said on the exhale. 'If we're going to arrest him, we need a name.'

Sarah shook her head. 'I can't. If he finds out that I spoke to you he'll kill me.'

'How would he find out? Is he local? Do you still see him?'

'No. I couldn't live here if there was any chance I'd bump into him. But he'll know. He's clever.'

Kate thought for a few seconds. 'How about I give you a name and you nod or shake your head? Could we try that?'

Sarah shrugged noncommittally. Kate wasn't convinced that she'd get the truth but it was worth a try.

'Was his name Tim?'

The other woman shook her head. Kate felt sick. She'd been so sure that this trip was going to lead them to Matthias and now it felt like wasted time.

'What about Mike?' Hollis asked.

Another headshake.

'Max?'

Kate realised what Hollis was doing. Siobhan had told them that Chloe was meeting a Mike or a Max. If he'd been using an alias he might have used the same one with Sarah. The young woman had started to cry, silently, tears running down both cheeks and dropping off her chin like the start of a heavy storm. Slowly, so slowly, Sarah turned to Kate and nodded.

'Was Max his real name?' Kate asked. 'Did you ever hear anybody call him it? Or did you see any bills in his name?'

Sarah was starting to curl up into herself on the armchair, arms folded across her chest against the barrage of questions.

'Sarah,' Kate continued, lowering her voice and speaking slowly. 'Where did Max live? Did you go to his house?'

'He had a flat on Portland Square in Carlisle. It was one of the big corner buildings but I can't remember the number. It was Flat 5.'

Inspiration suddenly struck. Kate grabbed for her phone and opened her email account. Cooper had sent her some of the stills from the CCTV footage. One of them was the clearest shot they had of Matthias.

'Sarah, is this Max?'

The other woman glanced at the screen and then back at Kate. Her eyes were wide with shock. She inclined her head, only once and only slightly.

'Thank you,' Kate breathed. 'Thank you. Sarah, I know this has been really hard for you but you might have given us what we need to get this man locked up for a very long time.'

'It'll never be long enough,' Sarah muttered. 'I know he'll find me. But if I'd told the truth those two women would still be alive so I probably deserve it… I won't testify though. You'll have to get him for these other two because I don't want to have to see him again. If he gets away with it, he'll come after me. You don't know what he's like.'

The sound of the front door opening prevented Kate from offering any reassurances. And, really, what could she say? If Sarah had identified her attacker four years ago there was a very strong possibility that Melissa Buckley and Chloe Welsh would still be alive. If she wasn't prepared to face Matthias in court, then her evidence only served to confirm what Kate and her team already suspected. It was nowhere near concrete enough for the CPS without Sarah herself.

Sarah's mother took in the scene in her sitting room, dropped her bag of shopping and rushed over to her daughter.

'What have you done to her?' She glared accusingly at Hollis who was stuffing his notebook back into the inside pocket of his jacket.

'Sarah's been very helpful,' Kate said, standing up. 'She may have given us an important lead.'

She looked at Sarah, make-up smudged across her face, dark tear stains on her t-shirt, and forced a smile. 'We'll be in touch,' she said, heading for the door.

\*\*\*

'Shit,' Hollis said as he closed the driver's door of the car.

'Couldn't put it better myself,' Kate responded. 'Looks like we've got reasonable grounds to bring Matthias in. Trouble is I'm not sure we can get him for the murders. It's all circumstantial at the moment. And if we question him about Sarah, it's her word against his. Especially after all this time. And she's said that she won't testify.'

Hollis started the engine.

'You do think it's him though?'

'It's him. I realise now why he seemed familiar when we met him. It was his accent. It's a bit watered down but you can still hear the Cumbrian vowels. That's what I was picking up on.'

Kate's phone vibrated in her pocket. An email from Cooper. She read it quickly.

'Back to Donny,' she said to Hollis. 'Cooper might have something concrete.'

She was about to slip her phone back into her pocket when it rang in her hand. She sighed when she saw Raymond's name on the screen. She hadn't wanted him to find out about her trip to Haltwhistle until she was back in Doncaster and really didn't fancy explaining everything to him over the phone.

'Kate. Where are you?'

'Northumberland,' she admitted.

'What the hell are you doing all the way up there?' From Hollis's expression, Kate could tell that he could hear Raymond shouting at her. 'No, don't tell me. That can wait. You need to get back here now. We've got another body. O'Connor's at the scene with Kailisa. I've sent Barratt over there as well.'

'Same injuries?' Kate asked.

'Sounds like it,' Raymond said. 'A bit older this time. O'Connor thinks it's a sex worker, based on the way she was dressed. Oh, and we've got an ID and she's got a record. Suzanne Doherty? Ring any bells?'

Kate glanced at Hollis. His knuckles were white, hands gripped like claws around the steering wheel. He'd heard every word.

# Chapter 34

Kate stared down at the body on the table. She'd never met Suzanne Doherty but, even in death, the woman looked brash and brassy. Studying the face Kate searched for any similarities to Hollis in the hooked nose and strangely startled-looking blue eyes. Finding nothing she shifted focus, trying to concentrate on what Kailisa was saying rather than on the memory of Dan slamming the car door and marching away from her at Scotch Corner services.

He'd driven from Haltwhistle in silence and Kate couldn't think of a way to speak to him that wouldn't sound trite or clichéd. When he'd eventually pulled in she'd tried to say something but he'd cut her off by storming away.

Ten minutes later he'd texted her. *Go back without me. I'll sort myself out.*

She'd texted back – pleading with him to come back to the car but when he didn't respond she went in to find him. She didn't have to look far – he was in the queue at M&S with a bottle of whisky in his hand.

Rather than make a scene, Kate had walked over to him, placed a hand on his shoulder and said quietly. 'Get a taxi to the nearest railway station, Dan. Find me when you're ready to talk.'

Hollis had turned to her and nodded. That had been forty-eight hours ago and still no word.

'…appears to be in her early to mid-fifties.' The intercom crackled into life. Kailisa had started.

The woman's clothes had already been removed and the pathologist was working a high-powered magnifying lens along the body looking for trace evidence. He paused two or three times, leaning in, tweezers in hand to remove items that Kate couldn't see. Each was placed in a plastic evidence bag, held by Kailisa's ever-present, ever-vigilant assistant.

Kate listened as Suzanne's general health and any identifying marks were described in minute detail and then Kailisa reached the abdominal wound. A long pause as the pathologist tilted the lens left and right, up and down. He seemed unhappy about something. Kate pressed the intercom button next to her seat.

'Problem?'

Kailisa looked up to where she was sitting then back down at the body on the table. 'Come down please, DI Fletcher.' It was more an instruction than a request and Kate rushed to comply.

'What is it?' she asked, tying the strings at the back of her gown and leaning in close to the body.

'This abdominal wound is not the same as the other two.' He pointed to the edges of the massive cut. 'See here? The blade used was wider and not as sharp. There are hesitation marks on the right-hand side. My examination so far is superficial but I'd suggest that whoever made this cut was either inexperienced or in a hurry. There is also a section of the wound which is much deeper suggesting a stabbing. I'd suggest that the woman was still alive when this occurred as there is clear reaction from the tissue. Her assailant may have blood on his clothes. I think the longer wound is meant to disguise the fact that she was stabbed.'

Kate studied the marks that Kailisa had pointed out trying to make sense of what she'd been told. What did it mean? She could clearly see the small red scratches around one side of the wound but, to her inexpert eye, the bigger cut looked the same as those inflicted on Melissa and Chloe – she couldn't see the stab wound at all.

Kailisa's attention had moved to the dead woman's neck. Kailisa tilted her head to one side and then the other holding a ruler against the bruises while his assistant took photographs. Kate watched him as he called up the digital images on a computer. He flicked backwards and forwards between these new photographs and two other sets.

'Here,' he said.

Kate moved closer, leaning in to see what he'd spotted.

'The distance between the thumb and finger marks on this woman is different from the other two. See?' He pointed at a set of figures running down one side of the screen which made no sense at all to Kate.

'Whoever strangled this woman had smaller hands than the killer of the previous two.'

'It's not the same killer?'

'It is not the same killer,' Kailisa confirmed.

Kate stared at the computer screen trying to work out the implications of the pathologist's findings. Two killers? Were they working together? Or was Suzanne Doherty's murder the work of a copycat? She silently cursed Duncan Cawthorne for his stupidity in speaking to the press. By sharing details of Melissa's murder he'd opened up Kate's pool of suspects to anybody with the means and opportunity to kill Suzanne Doherty.

She turned back to Kailisa, who had turned back to the body again.

'Has she been raped?' she asked.

Kailisa sighed, obviously irritated that she wanted him to check but he moved down the body and parted the legs.

Kate turned away.

'No evidence of recent sexual activity,' Kailisa said, 'I'll take swabs to confirm but, judging by the condition of the vulvar tissue, I'd say that she wasn't raped.'

'And do you have any thoughts about time of death?'

Another sigh. 'Judging by the lack of rigor mortis and the skin slippage on the hands I'd estimate that she's been dead for at least seventy-two hours, possibly longer. Of course, analysis of any insect activity, stomach contents and some tissue samples *may* be able to narrow that down.'

Kate's pulse raced as she thought back over the two days leading up to this woman's death. She'd been thinking about motive and, if sexual assault was ruled out there wasn't much else.

The woman's handbag had been found with the body in deep undergrowth around Town Fields and her purse was inside and intact. In addition there had been no ritualistic positioning of the body; it actually looked like whoever killed her had tried to hide what he'd done, judging by the crime-scene photographs that she'd seen. She could only draw one conclusion; whoever had done this had simply wanted Suzanne Doherty dead. And she knew of two people who might share that sentiment.

*Mockery. That's how they'd decided to play it. Another dead woman so it has to be me who killed her. How can they even think that? I'd heard the news reports, listening avidly for clues that the police won't have spotted. She's a common whore for Christ's sake! As if I'd have anything to do with a woman like that. But I'd heard a whisper that she was the third – that I was officially a serial killer. Couldn't they see the difference? The radio report says that this woman might have been dead for a few days, hidden in undergrowth. Hidden! How could that possibly be connected with me?*

*The wounds are 'similar'. Impossible. I've had the training. I've been taught how to cut flesh with precision and confidence. I've seen inside a human being, held their life in my hands in a very literal sense, and seen how frail the body really is. If I'd stuck with surgery I would have been one of the greats; none of my fellow students had the empathy or the understanding to feel the raw power of the human spirit made flesh. Weaklings.*

*And they thought I'd been the weak one for choosing a different route. For electing to study the mind rather than the body. If they'd only realised that it was my own mind that I wanted to understand, my own impulses that I wanted to either contain or indulge.*

*So now I have to repeat my message. And go on repeating it until they understand. Until they all understand.*

# Chapter 35

'So we're not going to arrest him?' Sam Cooper looked at Kate in utter disgust.

'Not yet,' Kate tried to reassure her. 'We don't have the evidence. Everything we've got is circumstantial and could be explained. We can't even prove that the image on the CCTV *is* Matthias. I could bring him in and question him under caution but I don't think it would get us anywhere. If we had to let him go afterwards he might just take off.'

Cooper shook her head in frustration. 'What about the phone number he gave me? I know it's not the same as the one that's on Melissa Buckley's phone but it shows that he's offering his services outside office hours. Melissa's car was found near his house. He was in the same bar as Chloe on the night she was murdered.'

'He might not want his employers to know that he was moonlighting – that might be why he gave you the number with no witnesses present. And Melissa's car could have been parked there for any number of reasons.'

The room was heavy with tension. O'Connor's team had finally located the missing umbrella in an alley two streets away from X-Ray and it had been sent away for fingerprint analysis. If Matthias's prints were on it and on the database then it would add to the evidence against him and point to him following Chloe out of the club in the early hours of Saturday morning. They still had the hair that Kailisa had discovered on Chloe's body – a DNA match with Matthias would be difficult for him to explain but Kate would have bet a large amount of money that he'd say it was consensual sex. Of course, the lack of semen and lubricant supported Sarah's claim that Matthias had some sort of reproductive 'issue' but it would be very difficult to argue that the *lack* of evidence pointed to Matthias. They needed something more concrete. They couldn't search his home unless he was arrested and they couldn't arrest him on such thin evidence – the CPS would throw the case out straight away.

'What about the latest victim?' Barratt asked. 'Anything on her?'

This was the one question that Kate wanted to avoid. She hated keeping information from the others but she wasn't sure whether it was wise to give them the opportunity to speculate about a second killer just yet. Not until she'd had a chance to confront Dan and Raymond. She was dreading the former discussion and couldn't even contemplate the latter but she owed it to her colleagues to treat them with respect rather than launching in with accusations.

The problem was the timeline. Hollis could easily have killed his mother within the timeframe that Kailisa had offered, unless he had a strong alibi and, if Suzanne Doherty had been killed in the evening two days prior to her being found, then it was likely that Kate's DCI would also have had the opportunity. Raymond was looking less likely though. He'd shown no reaction to Suzanne's name or to the crime-scene photographs. She knew in her gut that the killer could be anybody, that it might have been a random attack made to look like the others, but she knew of at least one person with a strong motive for wanting Suzanne Doherty dead. Possibly two. There was no way she could ignore Hollis's link to the victim. He'd admitted that the woman had been hounding him. What if he'd confronted her and things had got out of hand? What if Suzanne had approached Raymond and he'd lashed out? Were either of them capable of this? Kate truly didn't want to believe it was either of her colleagues but her training was forcing her to consider the unthinkable.

She focussed on Barratt's enquiry. 'Still waiting on lab results,' Kate fudged. 'Nothing conclusive from the initial examination. Similar wounds, found on Town Fields, time of death sometime on Tuesday night but that's tentative at the moment.'

'Similar wounds?' Barratt persisted. 'Not identical then?'

Kate could see that she wasn't going to be able to avoid the inevitable barrage of questions from Barratt. She loved his tenacity and the way he wanted to interrogate any situation but she'd been hoping that he'd accept what she said at face value. That he hadn't said a lot about his character – and the fact that she'd tried to be vague said a lot about her own. Time to come clean.

'Kailisa's not convinced that it's the same killer,' she said. 'The wounds on Suzanne Doherty's body are similar but far from identical. The abdominal cut looks hesitant and may have been an attempt to cover up a stabbing. Also she wasn't posed.'

'So he got careless? He was interrupted? There are a lot of reasons why the wounds might not be the same,' Barratt said, his colour rising. Kate knew that none of them wanted to even contemplate the idea of a copycat. If nothing else, it could cast doubt over Matthias's guilt in the first two murders and they needed a cast-iron case. Any chance that he might get off and all their hard work would have been for nothing.

'We wait for the lab results,' Kate said evenly. 'If, and it's a big if at the moment, this most recent murder was committed by a different perpetrator then the whole thing is a complete mess. The details of Melissa Buckley's murder were all over the press – anybody could have copied them.'

'So now what?' Cooper asked. 'We're fairly certain that Matthias killed Melissa and Chloe but we can't touch him?"

'We keep digging,' Kate said. 'He attacked Sarah Armstrong four years ago. How likely is it that he's waited all this time to do it again? Sam, get into the PND, use your magic and find us some more cases where he might be the attacker. Look for similar wounds, rape, lack of semen, strangulation. Any combination. There must be something there. Matt, with Cooper. I think two heads'll be better than one on this. Look at Stoke-on-Trent as that's where he claims to have been before Doncaster. And check Cumbria and Northumberland.'

Barratt nodded and jotted something in his notebook.

'Steve, get back out to Town Fields, ask around about this Suzanne Doherty. Who was she last seen with? What was she doing there? The usual stuff. Raymond seems to think she was a prostitute, follow that up. Did she have a pimp? Had she crossed anybody?'

Kate looked around her team. It felt odd giving out jobs when Hollis wasn't there but she'd texted and told him to stay away for a few days. He couldn't be involved now anyway. As soon as her superiors found out that Suzanne was Dan's biological mother, he'd be removed from the case. Better that she remove him quietly rather than having the others know all the details.

'Where's Dan?' Barratt asked. 'He on a special mission or just not got out of bed yet?'

Cooper smiled and O'Connor sniggered. They'd obviously all noticed the deterioration in their colleague's appearance and mood.

'He's taken some personal time.'

'In the middle of a murder investigation? Who did he have to sleep with to get that?' O'Connor shook his head in disbelief.

'I know it's unusual but I signed him off. You'll just have to trust me on this one. He doesn't need to be here at the moment – for his own good.' She wanted to add *and for the good of the investigation* but she couldn't give too much away or open herself up to too many questions.

Kate's colleagues exchanged quizzical looks but seemed to be satisfied with her non-explanation. She knew that they trusted her but so did Hollis and she needed to have his back at the moment. She could keep him away from the worst of the rumour and speculation by keeping him away from work. He'd been a mess for a few weeks just because his mother was back in his life so Kate couldn't even imagine what her death had done to his mental state. Part of her wanted to add *if he didn't kill her* to that thought but she couldn't allow herself to be so disloyal. Not without evidence. When the woman's link to the DC became public he was going to need her support. She wondered if the same would be true for Raymond.

Having allocated jobs to the team, Kate finally had to face the task that she'd been putting off for as long as possible. It was time to talk to her DCI. In private.

# Chapter 36

Raymond was staring at a file on his huge desk when Kate knocked on the door of his office. She studied him through the glass looking for anything that might suggest that he was Hollis's father but, apart from their height, they seemed to share no physical characteristics. Where Dan was blond, Raymond's hair, what was left of it, was still black. Where Raymond was still stocky despite his recent weight loss, Hollis was slim verging on skinny. There was nothing in their faces either. Raymond's bulbous nose and full lips were almost the polar opposite of Dan's aquiline, sharp nose and thin mouth.

'Fletcher? To what do I owe the pleasure?' Raymond said as he beckoned her into his office. His tone was genial but his expression severe – he clearly wasn't expecting good news.

'It's about Suzanne Doherty,' Kate said, slipping into the chair opposite Raymond's own – a chair which was at least a couple of inches lower than the DCI's.

'Have you got a lead?'

Kate shook her head. 'Not yet. You'll have read Kailisa's preliminary report?'

'Different killer? I think that's crap,' Raymond said flicking the thought away with one of his huge hands as though he was wafting away an especially noxious fart. 'It's too much of a coincidence.'

'Can't argue with the science,' Kate said. 'But I hope he's wrong. The thing is, this murder isn't like the other two in a few ways and it's got me thinking.'

Raymond curled his top lip in a sneer which seemed to suggest that he wasn't going to like what Kate had to say.

'Suzanne Doherty was very different from the first two. Age, economic background, physical appearance, no evidence of sexual assault, everything really. And the body wasn't posed like the others – if anything, the killer tried to hide her.'

'So?'

'I just can't see the link between this murder and the first two. It looks to me like somebody used the previous killer's signature to cover up the murder of Suzanne Doherty.'

The sneer had been replaced by a sceptical stare. 'But who'd want to get rid of some old prostitute and make it look like something else? God knows, enough working girls get killed every year but it's usually psychos who take their games too far or they're fulfilling their twisted fantasies.'

'Which is precisely my point,' Kate said. 'The likelihood of two men having the same fantasy is too tiny to even calculate. Melissa and Chloe were killed by somebody who had a ritual and it meant something specific to him. Whoever killed Suzanne can't have had the same fantasy. It's just not possible. How many men are there out there who want to perform pseudo-caesarean operations on their victims? And even if there were two – what are the chances that they'd both end up in Doncaster?'

Raymond leaned back in his seat, rested his elbows on his desk and propped his head up on his fists, staring at her.

'Sir. Suzanne Doherty was killed because of who she is. Either a client got carried away and cut her to make it look like she was another victim of our first killer, or she was targeted specifically. I'm really sorry to do this but I know of two people who might want her dead.'

Raymond didn't change position, waiting her out, forcing her to continue even though she didn't want to have to say what was on her mind.

'You knew her, sir. And so did Dan Hollis.'

Raymond's eyes widened, the disbelief and outrage convulsing his features. 'You…' he couldn't seem to find the words to get his next sentence started. 'You…? You think I murdered this woman?

Christ, Fletcher, I've heard some good ones in my time but this tops the lot. What's my motive?'

'To keep her quiet,' Kate was aware that she was mumbling. She could feel the weight of her boss's wrath bearing down on her but, now that she'd started on this course, there was no turning back.

'About what?'

'About the affair that you had with her when she was seventeen.'

'Affair!' The word tore from Raymond's mouth and sat between them like an unexploded bomb waiting for somebody to cut the wrong wire.

'Suzanne Doherty is Dan Hollis's biological mother,' Kate began, the words tumbling out in a rush. 'He was adopted when he was seven. She says that his father is somebody who works here. Somebody high up in the force. She's not been specific but Dan says that she's dropped a couple of huge hints that it's you. And he says you were out in the car park with her a couple of weeks ago.'

Raymond's eyes had shifted from Kate's own and were focussed on the window in the wall next to his desk. He seemed lost in a memory.

'Suzanne Doherty?' he mumbled. 'Suzy?'

Kate kept quiet.

'Was she known as Suzy? On the street?'

'I don't know, sir. Not that I've heard.'

He nodded as though that was confirmation enough. 'It's probably not *her* then.'

'Her?' Kate prompted. To her surprise, Raymond, stood up, crossed the room and closed the blind on the window in the door of his office.

'This goes no further, Kate,' he said, sitting back down. He seemed smaller, somehow, as if what he was about to confess had shrunk him, made him a lesser man.

'I knew a young working girl called Suzy over thirty years ago. She always called herself Suzy Q, after that song?'

Kate had no idea which song he was referring to.

'I arrested her twice. Both times she offered to have sex with me if I'd let her off. I refused obviously. I was just a young copper on the beat. Idealistic, you know? Wanted to do a good job. But I liked her. I saw her around quite a bit and we'd sometimes talk. Long winter nights can get a bit lonely when you're walking the streets – we both felt it – so we'd often have a bit of a natter. Then, one night, she told me that she was pregnant. She didn't know who the father was, I suppose it could have been anybody. She was only sixteen and a real looker – probably had men queueing round the block for her. She asked me for money so that she could go away and "get rid of it" but I said no.'

It was easy to imagine. A young girl finding a bit of comfort and safety with a policeman and the man being flattered by the attention of a nice-looking girl. She probably expected him to be easy to manipulate.

'So you didn't give her any money?'

Raymond lowered his head. 'I couldn't. It wouldn't have been right. She called me a few choice names and that was that. I saw her a few times after but she just ignored me. I think she made a point of making sure I'd see her getting in a car with a client. Just so I'd know that I'd left her no choice but to carry on working. A couple of months later she'd disappeared. I suppose screwing pregnant girls is a bit niche for most men. I did hear that she'd had the kid but that was all. I started working towards my promotion and never saw her again. I'm not the father of her child because I never slept with her. And I haven't seen her for over thirty years.'

Kate believed him. Not because he was her boss, or because he told his story in an especially convincing way but because he looked genuinely sorrowful that the girl that he'd known had ended up murdered in a dingy park. Suzanne had obviously meant something to him at a time when he was vulnerable, but Kate believed him when he said that he'd behaved honourably.

'So the baby was probably Hollis, eh?' The sorrow in his eyes deepened as he contemplated the position that the young DC was in. 'And he's the other person that you think might have killed her?'

She didn't want to admit it but she'd seen the state that Dan had been in. He'd seemed broken by Suzanne's revelations, lost and confused. The confident, likeable man that she'd known had transformed into somebody that she'd hardly recognised. The only improvement had come on their trip to Haltwhistle – according to Kailisa this could have been the day after Suzanne Doherty had been murdered. The timing didn't look good.

'It's a possibility and, as much as I want to, I can't ignore it,' Kate said. 'I need to talk to him, to see what he has to say.'

'I'm assuming that he's off the investigation?' Raymond's eyes had hardened and he was suddenly all business again.

'I signed off on personal leave for him,' Kate admitted. She didn't see any point in telling the DCI about Hollis's behaviour at Scotch Corner or the fact that she'd left him at the motorway services with a bottle of whisky and an instruction to catch a train. She felt embarrassed when she thought about how callous that might seem to somebody who didn't understand her relationship with Dan. Even Nick had raised an eyebrow but Kate knew that he wouldn't comment on a work-related matter unless invited.

'Where is he? Do you know?'

'At home I assume,' Kate said, but she had no way to be sure. 'He's got a flat somewhere out Bentley way. HR will have his address.'

'Let me know when you get it. It might be a good idea if I come with you. It looks like there's a few things that I need to straighten out.'

Kate stood up to leave.

'And Fletcher?'

She turned back to her boss.

'You've got a lot of gall coming in here and accusing me of murder. By rights, I ought to tear a strip off you and kick you back down to uniform. But it must've taken a lot of guts as well. This is not up for discussion with your team. If you still feel that you need an alibi I'll provide one – if I've got one. Until then this goes no further.'

Kate's hand trembled on the door handle as she let herself out of Raymond's office. She'd expected him to be angrier, to be outraged, but his frankness had been much more convincing than a shouted denial. She just hoped that Hollis would be able to keep his emotions in check when she and the DCI spoke to him later.

# Chapter 37

'Matt, come and look at this.' Cooper summoned her colleague over to her desk and pointed at her computer screen hoping he'd confirm what she was seeing.

'Where's this?' Barratt asked, leaning over her to get a closer look.

'The car park on Town Fields. Where the sports facilities are. I pulled their CCTV footage after the third body was found. I've been looking through it, going back to the earliest estimate of time of death for Suzanne Doherty. This is from late Tuesday evening.'

Barratt tutted and shook his head. 'Naughty. You're supposed to be scouring the PND.'

'I needed a break,' Sam said. 'Inputting key words gets a bit boring after an hour or so.'

Barratt stepped back, the shock on his face obviously fake. 'No! Sam Cooper bored with data mining. I don't believe it.'

'Sod off,' Sam said through a grin. It had taken her a long time to accept teasing from her colleagues. She'd been convinced that they thought she was some sort of robot who used artificial intelligence to solve problems but she'd gradually come to accept that, if she wanted to be part of the team, she'd have to put up with some ribbing. Now, she could give as good as she got and the banter made her feel more human, connected. 'Is it her?'

She leaned forward and tapped the screen, causing ripples to distort the plasma and set the image fluttering.

'Who?' Barratt asked.

'Suzanne Doherty?'

He looked again. Sam needed confirmation because the only images she'd seen of the woman were from the crime scene. She'd got a good description: height, hair colour et cetera but the grainy black-and-white footage wasn't clear enough for her to be certain. She knew Barratt would only be using the same information that she had but, if he confirmed her hunch, then she had something a bit more concrete to present to Kate at the next briefing.

'Could be,' Barratt was saying. 'The height and build look right and the clothes match the ones she was wearing when she was found.'

*Trust Barratt,* Sam thought, *every detail memorised.* He probably even knew what shoe size the dead woman wore.

'That's what I thought,' she said. 'So who's that with her?'

The frame Sam had chosen to pause on showed a woman and a man. The woman, probably Suzanne Doherty, was leaning in, possibly having difficulty hearing what the man was saying to her.

'Dunno,' Barratt admitted. 'But it's not Matthias. Much too small.'

The man in question was about three or four inches taller than the woman and of slight build. Balding and clean shaven, he was wearing a waterproof jacket and pale trousers and looked to be in his late sixties.

'Maybe just a random punter?'

'That's what I thought,' Sam said. 'But watch.'

She hit a key on her keyboard and the footage began to play.

The woman backed away from the man, shaking her head and raising her hands as though warding him off, even though he remained where he was. She turned to walk away but then stopped and turned back. More conversation and then the man reached into his inside jacket pocket and took out what looked like an envelope.

'See. Punter,' Barratt said.

'No. Keep watching.'

The woman took the envelope, seemed to peer inside checking the contents and then stuffed it into her handbag. The man seemed to be talking to her again but she shook her head, turned and walked out of the view of the camera.

The man watched her for a few seconds then crossed the car park and got into a dark-coloured hatchback. Another few seconds passed and then the car moved out of shot.

'So, he's meeting her somewhere else. She didn't want to get in the car with him.'

'That doesn't make sense,' Sam said. She'd watched the transaction a few times and hadn't been able to make it fit any reasonable scenario connected with Suzanne's profession. 'How much does a prostitute charge?'

Barratt's face flushed. 'How should I—'

'Oh, come on, Matt. I'm not asking if you've ever paid. What's a hand job or a blow job go for these days. A tenner? Twenty?'

'Maybe twenty,' Barratt mumbled reluctantly. 'Probably about fifty for sex. You'd probably pay more at a brothel but a quickie in the car would be cheaper.'

'That envelope looked like it contained more than fifty quid. She flicks through it like there's a substantial wodge of cash in there. So why would this man be giving her a lot of money? And why wasn't it recorded among her possessions? She only had thirty quid in her purse.'

Barratt looked back at the screen as though the answer might be hiding somewhere in the pixels. 'He arranged for her to go somewhere with him for something a bit more dodgy than vanilla sex and took the cash back when he'd finished?'

'That's what I thought,' Sam said. 'But she doesn't get in the car.'

'So she meets him somewhere? Maybe he has a fantasy about picking up a hitchhiker or he wants her to pretend that she's missed the last bus or something.'

Sam sat back, shocked. 'That's oddly specific, Matt,' she said with a grin. 'Something you'd like to share?'

Barratt just laughed and shook his head.

'So then what?' Sam persisted. 'He meets her somewhere else. She gets in his car and he does his thing – whatever it is.' She could see than Barratt hadn't found any flaws in her theory so far. 'And then he strangles her and cuts her, dumps the body and drives off.'

'She wasn't raped,' Barratt said.

Sam had been expecting this. It was the one sticking point in the timeline she'd been forming. 'I know. Maybe his thing isn't sex. Maybe his thing is murder.'

She could see that Barratt was mulling this over.

'And he tries to make it look like a murder he read about in his local paper? Maybe he thinks it's the only way he's likely to get away with it.'

'Hence the difference in the wounds,' Sam said.

'Can you see the car reg in the footage?' Barratt pulled up a chair and squeezed next to Sam so that he could see her monitor without having to lean. She resisted the urge to move her own seat a few inches away, allowing him the proximity despite her discomfort.

'It's blurry. I'm running it through some image-enhancing software. So far all I've got is this.' She tapped an icon in the toolbar and the programme displayed a close-up of the number plate. The first two letters were clearly YM and the numbers looked like sixty-two but the rest of the front of the car had been in shadow and, even with enhancement the letters were still vague.

'Is that an F?' Barratt suggested. 'Or maybe a P?'

It could have been either. Sam grabbed a pad of paper and scrawled the first two letters and the numbers on it. She then added the possible P or F.

'Hang on,' Barratt said, standing up. He took two paces back from Sam's desk, tilted his head and squinted at the screen. 'I get YM62 PPT or FPT.' He paused and tilted his head the other way. 'Or PFT. The last letter must be a T because it can't be an I.'

Sam scribbled down Barratt's suggestions and logged on to the PNC database.

'Okay,' she said. 'PPT comes up as a white Astra.' She typed in the next suggestion. FPT is a red Skoda Fabia. PFT doesn't exist.'

She crossed out each possible registration number as she checked the database. None of them could be the car in the CCTV footage unless the number plates were stolen – a possibility that she didn't want to contemplate.

'FFT?' Barratt suggested.

Sam typed in the three letters and got a hit.

'Navy Golf. Could be.' She scrolled down to the details of the registered keeper of the vehicle and suddenly felt nauseous when she saw the name. 'Matt, look.' She ran her finger underneath the relevant line of information.

'Shit in a bucket,' Barratt hissed. 'It can't be…'

Sam looked back at the screen, willing the name to change to something else. Anything else.

# Chapter 38

They pulled up outside a three-storey town house on a side road just off the main high street through Bentley. Bright white doors and window frames stood out starkly against red brick that glowed faintly in the mid-morning sun. The curtains to the windows on the first and second floors were drawn and there was no sign of life, but Hollis's Sportage was parked in a bay in the designated parking set back from the street and marked 'PRIVATE'.

'Not quite what I imagined when you said Hollis had a flat. I'd got something a lot more pokey in mind,' Raymond said, gazing up at the herringbone pattern in the Edwardian brickwork.

'You've seen Dan,' Kate responded. 'How could you have thought he'd live in a shithole? He probably owns this place.'

'I've not really had much to do with the lad, to be honest,' Raymond admitted. 'He seems a decent enough detective but he's always struck me as overly concerned about his looks.'

Kate smiled and looked the DCI up and down. 'A few months ago I'd have taken that at face value,' she said. 'But look at the state of you. Slimmer, good haircut, nice suit.'

Raymond scowled and Kate worried that she might have overstepped. 'Fair point,' the DCI conceded. 'I was a bit of a scruff. If I hear you repeating that, though, you're fired.'

Kate was once again struck by the mixed emotions that accompanied her interaction with Raymond. She'd always found him a bit intimidating and a bit old-fashioned but he'd been a fair and decent boss. She'd have been loath to admit it to her colleagues but she knew that she was going to miss him despite his curmudgeonly ways and his tendency towards negativity. She was already starting to dread what would happen when he was gone. She'd had enough adjustment settling back into life in Doncaster; she didn't feel ready for the challenges of breaking in a new boss as well.

Raymond strode up the short concrete path to the door and pressed the top doorbell. He stepped back and looked up again at the windows and Kate half expected him to shout, 'Come on, we know you're in there', but he just stared seemingly lost in his thoughts.

A minute passed with no answer so Raymond tried again. Kate took her phone out of her pocket and sent Hollis a quick text: *Better answer the door. It's me and Raymond. Need to talk to you.*

A few seconds after sending the text Kate heard footsteps and the door opened.

If Hollis had looked bad at work he looked terrible now. His blond hair was sticking up at odd angles as though it had been gelled and styled in the dark and his eyes were shadowed, the whites bloodshot. The smell of stale alcohol seemed to be seeping from his pores.

'Come to arrest me for murdering my mother?' he asked with a sardonic smirk. 'Come on then.' He held out his arms, wrists together.

'Don't be daft, lad,' Raymond said. 'Let us in.'

Hollis slumped against the wall of the hallway, allowing Kate and Raymond to push past him. 'Upstairs,' he said. 'The door on the left.'

Kate led the way, following his directions into a spacious sitting room splashed with bars of light from large windows in two walls. A beige sofa dominated the room as it angled across the dark brown carpet, the perfect position to lie down and watch the huge flat-screen television which hung on the chimneybreast. Shelving lined a deep alcove in one corner and Kate saw that one shelf held a mini stereo system and speakers, the others were lined with books – mostly fantasy and horror.

The only things that seemed out of place were an empty wine bottle on the coffee table and two crushed lager cans that lay abandoned in the deep pile carpet next to the sofa. Hollis had obviously had a heavy night.

'Coffee?' he asked, hovering in the doorway like a nervous parent meeting his child's fiancée for the first time.

'Black,' Raymond said at the same time as Kate shook her head. The DCI flopped down on the sofa but Kate couldn't settle; this felt like such an invasion of Dan's privacy but there was no other way for them to have this conversation. Kate wanted him to be somewhere that he felt safe because what they had to say was likely to unsettle him even further.

Leaving Raymond in the sitting room, Kate followed Hollis down a short hallway to the kitchen where she wasn't at all surprised to see him fussing over a high-end bean-to-cup coffee machine.

'Can I change my mind?' she asked as the bitter smooth aroma of espresso assaulted her senses. 'Does that thing do cappuccino?'

'It should do the ironing and vacuuming the amount I paid for it,' Hollis joked. He turned to her with a ghost of his usual grin and Kate's feeling of self-loathing deepened. This was her colleague, her friend, a man who'd risked his own life to help save her son. How could she have ever thought him capable of murder? But she had to consider the possibility that it might have been an accident, a moment of panic and poor judgement.

She watched as Hollis reached up effortlessly to a high cupboard and removed a stainless steel jug. Like everything else in his flat, Kate could see, the coffee was going to be made to perfection.

'What's he doing here?' Hollis asked, lowering his voice. 'Come to turn my leave into an official suspension?'

'No. It's not official,' she said, trying to reassure him. 'You need to stay away from work until this is sorted out but the official line is that you've been given some personal leave. You can't be anywhere near this investigation.'

Hollis nodded bleakly. 'I know. I thought I'd probably be a suspect. Have you established time of death yet? Hopefully I'll have an alibi.' His words, so similar to Raymond's made Kate feel even more disloyal. How could she be discussing the need for alibis with her DC and DCI?

'And what about him?' Hollis pointed his thumb in the direction of the sitting room. 'Is he on leave as well? He's got as much of a motive as me.'

'I'm not sure that's true,' Kate said. 'You need to listen to what he has to say. I'm not sure you're going to like it, but the two of you need to have this conversation.'

Hollis turned back to the coffee machine and fussed with the milk steamer, his silence saying more than if he'd spoken. Kate could tell that he didn't want to hear what Raymond had to say and she couldn't blame him. Suzanne had really got inside his head with the notion that the DCI might be his father and Kate felt that Dan needed to hear the truth from Raymond.

'Here,' Hollis said, passing her a mug of coffee piled high with milk froth. 'I've not drawn a pattern in the foam – thought that might be a bit much. Better start practising my barista skills in case I'm going to be out of the job.'

If he was joking it wasn't very funny but Kate tried to give him a smile as he grabbed a mug of coffee in each hand and pushed past her into the hallway.

\*\*\*

The two men sat at opposite ends of the sofa, empty coffee mugs on the table, silence heavy in the room. Raymond had explained his relationship with Suzanne Doherty carefully and concisely. He'd been honest about how and where he met her but, to Kate, it was obvious that nothing about his mother's past came as much of a surprise to Hollis. She'd thought that Dan might ask questions, try to clarify details but he'd accepted the story and then told one of his own. It was painful for Kate to imagine him at seven years old, dragged from his mother by a police officer and driven away in a police car. It was only when talking about his adoption that he seemed more grounded, settled, and Kate could see that it had been the defining experience of his life. As Dan himself admitted, he could have ended up anywhere, doing anything, none of it good, if he'd been left with his birth mother.

'So I'm not suspended?' Dan eventually asked.

'No. But you're on extended leave until we find out who killed Suzanne. You couldn't be involved anyway. She's family.'

'But I'm under suspicion?'

'By your own admission she'd been trying to blackmail you. She'd disrupted your life and had placed a lot of stress on your mental health,' Raymond said.

'All good reasons to want her dead,' Hollis admitted. 'But I didn't do it.'

Raymond nodded gravely and Kate took his response as an admission of belief in his colleague. 'I'm sorry,' he said. 'If there was another way—'

He was interrupted by Kate's phone beeping to let her know that she'd got a text message. Cooper asking that Kate ring her ASAP. She stepped out into the hall without explaining. Raymond and Hollis would understand that it was work-related.

'Sam? What have you got?'

Cooper's voice on the other end of the phone was higher and breathier than normal as she quickly explained what they'd found on the CCTV footage.

'So find him,' Kate said. 'We need to know who this mystery punter is.'

'That's the problem,' Cooper responded. 'We traced the car reg. We know who he is.'

'And?'

'The car's registered to a Joseph Hollis from Chesterfield. Kate, he's Dan's dad.'

# Chapter 39

'What a complete and utter shitting mess!' Raymond was shouting as Kate tried to concentrate on parking the pool car. 'Not only do we have a prime suspect for two murders who you won't touch but we've now got another suspect who's related to your bloody DC.'

Kate pulled on the handbrake and concentrated on keeping her temper. Raymond had fumed all the way back from Bentley and somehow seemed to be blaming all this on her. The problem was that, on some level, he was right. If she'd told somebody about Hollis being blackmailed, warned them to look out for Suzanne Doherty then the situation might not have escalated. And she should have been much harder on Sarah Armstrong. The woman could be the key to the murders of Melissa and Chloe but she didn't want to get involved. *Well, tough*, Kate thought. She *was* involved and Kate might need her help if she was going to put Matthias away.

'Now what?' Kate asked Raymond.

'Now you bring Hollis's dad in and you question him. And, if he killed this woman, you make sure that he's charged.'

'What about Matthias?'

'You keep digging until you find something to pin on him. If we arrest him we can get his prints and ask for DNA and we can access his house, see what a search might turn up.'

He undid his seatbelt and left her sitting in the car, slamming the door after him. For the first time in years, Kate felt at a loss. She'd let people down who were relying on her and she didn't know what to do to get things back on track. She thought about ringing Nick. Just pouring everything out and letting him soothe her until she was ready to face the rest of her team. But that wasn't a possibility. She couldn't allow herself to rely on him to prop up her self-esteem – that wasn't how their relationship worked and she didn't want it to go down that road. She'd learned everything she ever needed to know about linking her self-image to a man when she was married to Garry and she certainly wasn't going to allow herself to fall back into that trap.

Sighing heavily, she eased herself out of the car and trudged up the steps to the back entrance to the police station.

\*\*\*

'Right,' Kate began, when the remaining members of her team were gathered in the incident room. 'As you've heard we're looking for Dan Hollis's father in connection with the murder of Suzanne Doherty. If possible, the familial link goes no further than this room until we know what Joseph Hollis's involvement is in this case. I've notified Derbyshire and they've sent somebody round to his house to arrest him. He'll be brought over here for questioning later today.'

'His involvement looks pretty obvious to me,' Barratt muttered.

'And that's why it goes no further,' Kate snapped. 'Dan's our friend and colleague. Of course we can't protect a family member if they've killed somebody but, for now, it's still an *if*. And the only way we can protect Dan is to be discreet and sensitive.'

Barratt looked up at her, obviously with more to say and Kate wondered whether she should just get rid of him. Send him out on a job until he'd calmed down. But then she noticed that Sam Cooper couldn't meet her eyes and even O'Connor was looking a bit shifty. They needed to know the whole story.

'Okay. I think you've worked out that there's more to this than I've been telling you. To be honest, it's not my story to tell and Dan won't thank me for this but I think I owe it to you to be up front. Suzanne Doherty was Dan Hollis's birth mother.'

'What?' Cooper spluttered. 'She was Dan's mum. How long had he known? Is that why he's been such a mess lately?'

Kate held her hands out deflecting the barrage of questions that she knew she was facing by revealing Dan's secret. 'He's always known. She's made contact with him again recently and she's been threatening to tell me, and anybody else who'll listen, exactly who she is. Dan didn't want the embarrassment but he didn't know what to do. She's totally messed up his head and she's been telling him all sorts about who his dad might be. Including one allegation that's proven to be false.'

'Not being funny,' O'Connor said, his sardonic smirk contrasting with his words. 'But how do we know that Hollis didn't do away with her? If she was blackmailing him.'

Kate glared at the DS and Cooper turned round and did the same. 'This is Dan we're talking about,' she said, her face reddening with fury. 'He's one of us. How could you even think that?'

O'Connor wasn't going to budge. 'I can think that because I'm a copper and it's my job. Just like it's yours, Cooper. He had a motive. It needs to be considered regardless of who he is.'

Cooper turned back to Kate. 'Is that why he's not here? Is he a suspect?'

'He's on leave until the investigation into Suzanne's death is completed,' Kate said. 'Raymond and I interviewed him this morning and he's given a preliminary statement.' This wasn't quite true but Hollis had denied murdering his mother and there was no evidence to suggest otherwise.

'Does he know about his dad? His adoptive dad, I mean, and the footage?' Barratt wanted to know.

Kate shook her head. 'I couldn't tell him. It would have gone against protocol.'

Cooper looked mutinous. 'But he needs to know. If he was a mess before then Christ knows what this'll do to him. You have to tell him.'

'And I will,' Kate said. 'As soon as the arrest is made I'll ring Dan myself.' She'd already promised herself that Hollis would hear the news of his father's arrest from her. There wasn't much she could do for him at the moment but her sense of loyalty and decency wouldn't let him hear it from anybody else.

'I know this has been a shock but we can't let ourselves get distracted. We've got a suspect for Suzanne Doherty and we need to get on with the other two murders.' She glanced at the photographs of Melissa and Chloe stuck to the whiteboard at the front of the room. 'We know it's Matthias. Sarah Armstrong corroborates our suspicions but we haven't got enough to arrest him. Sam, you were scouring the PND, what have you got?'

'Two possibles,' Cooper said, all business again after her outburst. 'Both from Staffordshire Police.'

'How possible?'

'One's an attempted strangulation with some kicking to the abdomen. The woman claims that she didn't know her attacker but that he threatened her with something that looked like a scalpel. The other is a rape and strangulation – no evidence of semen or lubricant. The assumption was that an object was used but the victim contests this.'

Nothing exactly like either Sarah, Melissa or Chloe but Kate could see the similarities in both cases. She knew that she'd never have managed to dig them up on her own but Cooper's knack with data might have paid off yet again.

'We need to speak to both women and see if the picture of Matthias jogs either of their memories.'

She waited for somebody to volunteer but the lack of enthusiasm was obvious.

'Something wrong?'

Barratt shook his head, O'Connor looked away and Cooper blushed. They'd obviously got more to say. 'We've been talking about Sarah Armstrong,' Barratt admitted. 'She knew her attacker and won't testify against him. If either of these women can identify Matthias there's still no guarantee that either of them will be prepared to make a statement. He's obviously got a way of manipulating and terrifying his victims. We need something more concrete.'

Kate struggled against a sudden flare of irritation. 'Do you think I don't know that? Any one of these cases might give us cause to apply for a warrant to Matthias's house. If we can get access we might turn up some forensic evidence to tie him to Melissa or Chloe's murders. There might be something on his PC, his phone, who knows?'

Even as she spoke, Kate could hear how desperate she sounded. They were right. Even with fingerprints from the umbrella from Madrigal's and DNA from Chloe's body their chances of a successful prosecution were 50/50 at best. Sarah Armstrong's testimony would only ensure that he was charged with *her* attack and, after such a long time, and bearing in mind Sarah's reluctance to talk, even if she did speak out, a good lawyer might accuse her of some sort of malicious intent. 'Okay,' she said. 'You've obviously been cooking something up between you. Care to share it with me?'

Cooper flashed Barratt a wary look which told Kate that whatever they had planned she wasn't going to like it. Just as Barratt was about to speak Kate's phone rang. An unknown number. She held up one finger to hush the DC and hit *accept* on the phone's screen.

'Fletcher.'

'DI Neale, Derbyshire Police.'

It was the call that she'd been waiting for about Hollis's father.

'Have you got him?' she asked. A pause on the other end of the line told her that the news wasn't good.

'Sorry. No. I went round to the house myself an hour ago. Hollis isn't there and his wife's missing as well. I've checked both their places of work and no sign of them. One of the neighbours told my DS that he thinks they might have gone away on holiday as he saw Hollis packing a suitcase into his car the day before yesterday. That's it. I'm sorry.'

Kate hung up, mind racing. What the hell was going on?

# Chapter 40

'So, what's your plan?' Kate asked, trying to switch focus back to Cooper and Barratt. She'd think about Joseph Hollis when she'd finished with her team and, hopefully, found a way to move forward with Matthias.

'We think that Melissa Buckley had an off-the-books appointment with him on the day she went missing,' Barratt began. 'Her car wasn't far from his house and her body was left pretty close as well.'

'Which suggests it might not have been him,' O'Connor argued. 'Who'd dump a body on their own doorstep?'

'He might have been panicking. He might not have known about her car. There are any number of reasons,' Barratt responded with a scowl. 'He might just be *that* arrogant.'

Kate sensed his animosity towards the DS and made a mental note to have a chat with them both. It wasn't the first time they'd butted heads and it certainly wasn't conducive to a productive relationship.

'Anyway,' Barratt continued. 'Matthias gave Sam a personal number and offered her an out-of-hours appointment. If we can get Sam into his house and monitor their conversation she might see something or get him to slip up.'

'Or he might strangle and rape her before we can get to him,' O'Connor added.

Barratt shook his head. 'Not if we're careful. If we give Sam a script, maybe run it past Kate's psychologist friend first to check for potential triggers. And we'll be listening. If he makes a move somebody can be there in seconds if there's a surveillance team in position.'

Kate thought about it. They needed access to Matthias's house. If somebody could get in even to form a general impression it might help. There were always ways to get access to other rooms – ask for a drink, use the bathroom – but it was seriously risky. And expensive.

'I don't think so,' she said. Cooper's face fell but Kate was sure there was some relief mixed in with the disappointment. 'It's too risky and I can't see Raymond signing off on an expensive surveillance operation.'

'Hang on,' Barratt said. 'If Sam knows exactly what to say and her every word is being monitored, where's the harm? We could do it low budget; a van with a couple of undercover officers – dress them up in high-vis and set up a few cones around a manhole. I'll sit in the van and listen. I just think it's our best chance to engage with him. You said yourself that any evidence we've got could be explained away by a good defence lawyer. The only thing that might get us a warrant is if that woman in Northumberland changes her mind but I can't see her doing that after four years. What have we got to lose?'

'Cooper,' Kate said. 'That's what we've got to lose.'

'But if I'm willing to give it a go?' Cooper said. 'Surely it's worth a try. Especially if I have a script.'

Kate tried not to imagine what could happen. What if Matthias realised that Sam had a concealed mic? What if he attacked her and they couldn't get there quickly enough? Kate knew from first-hand experience what it felt like to be at the mercy of a violent attacker, the adrenaline fighting with the feelings of hopelessness, and she wouldn't wish that on any of her colleagues. But Sam Cooper had experience. She'd been instrumental in helping apprehend one of the cleverest killers that Kate had ever encountered, and she'd probably saved Kate's life on a dark canal bank earlier in the year.

'I still think it's risky,' she said.

'So we minimise the risk,' Cooper responded. 'I'm not stupid. I'm capable of recognising potential danger and getting myself out of the house if I need to.'

'Unless he's got his hands round your throat,' O'Connor chipped in.

A tense silence blanketed the incident room. Every instinct Kate possessed told her that this was a bad idea, but they had nothing else. If Matthias wasn't stopped he'd kill again, Kate had no doubt about that at all.

'I'll run it past the DCI,' Kate said, eventually. 'If he says yes then you can set up an appointment and we'll work out the logistics. But safety is paramount, Sam. If we go ahead with this, we need to make sure that we look after you.'

Cooper and Barratt looked at each other again.

'What?' Kate snapped. 'What am I missing?'

'She's already got an appointment for Saturday,' Barratt admitted. 'We thought we might as well set it up in case you gave us the go-ahead. Nothing to stop her cancelling, though.'

At least Cooper had the good grace to look embarrassed as Kate glared at her. 'I think you'd better be prepared to make that cancellation,' she said. 'Steve, we need a bit of light relief. How are you doing with your interviews with our local working girls?'

'Not great. Nobody remembers seeing Suzanne Doherty in the window we've been given for time of death. Maybe when the doc narrows it down I can jog some memories. To be honest a lot of the girls are a bit reluctant to talk. You remember I said that there seems to be a bit of a power struggle going on? One of them suggested that there's a new face around, possibly a pimp, and whoever he is he's angling for a bit of poaching. Two girls admitted that they'd been approached by another woman about better pay and safety but they weren't interested. Too scared, probably.'

Kate was only half listening. O'Connor liked to show off his extensive knowledge of the seedier side of the area but, mostly, she found it quite dull. She wasn't especially interested in the pissing contests of the local pimps unless it directly related to a case – and she couldn't see a connection here. She was already planning her remaining tasks for the day. And number one was to speak to Dan Hollis about his father.

\*\*\*

Hollis answered on the fifth ring and he sounded almost disappointed that it was Kate. She asked about his day but they'd never really done polite small talk and he was obviously suspicious.

'Can we get on with whatever it is?' he asked, half question, half demand.

Kate had tried to work out the best way to approach the issue of Hollis's father and had decided that, out of respect for her friend and colleague, she needed to be direct. 'Dan, have you heard from your dad?'

'No. Why?' His response sounded natural, genuine. And curious.

'I've got some news and I wanted you to hear it from me.' Kate outlined what Barratt and Cooper had found out from the CCTV footage and explained that Hollis senior had since disappeared. 'We need to find him, Dan. He may have seen or heard something that'll help us to find out who killed Suzanne.'

As Kate had expected, Dan saw straight through her clumsy explanation. 'You need to question him, you mean. He might be the last person who saw her alive and he had a reason to want her dead. I don't know where he is but, if I did, I honestly don't know if I'd tell you. You don't know him Kate. There's no way he's a murderer.'

Most people said that when faced with the crimes of their loved ones. *'He couldn't have done it.' 'She's not like that.'* But eight times out of ten he or she was guilty and the family were left devastated. Kate hoped for Dan's sake that his father was one of the two out of ten.

'Dan, I know you need to believe in him but if there's anything you can tell me that might help then you know it's the right thing to do.'

Silence at the other end of the line.

'Dan? You know you can't help him by staying quiet. If you know of anywhere they might have gone…'

'They?'

'Your mum's missing as well.'

'So, how do you know they've not just gone away for a few days?'

'Come on, Dan, look at the timing.'

He sighed heavily like a gale blowing through the phone's earpiece. 'I don't know where they might be but I'll have a think and let you know.'

He sounded despondent, broken, and Kate wondered what, if anything, she would be able to do to help put him back together when this was over. She just hoped that they could find a way through and that he'd return to being the talented police officer that she knew.

Hollis hung up and Kate put her phone away. Time to talk to Raymond about Barratt and Cooper's idea.

# Chapter 41

Kate watched as a high-vis-clad detective sergeant placed a rectangle of cones around an open service hatch in the pavement. The day was fine and sunny – the bright yellow of his jacket almost painful to look at even through the tinted rear window of the van. The inside of the Transit was kitted out with electronic equipment and felt claustrophobic in the growing heat. The stuffiness wasn't helped by the close proximity of Barratt and a techie called Irving. Kate had never met him before but Barratt claimed to know him from training college and they'd greeted each other like old friends as they'd piled into the back of the van like teenage festival goers eager for their first joint.

Irving had been keen to explain the key elements of the surveillance equipment as soon as Kate appeared, talking her through the switches and speakers like a parent showing off their favourite child. His tousled red hair and sandy beard added to the nutty professor persona and Kate found herself warming to him despite his over use of the word 'cool'.

Cooper had been fitted with a microphone taped between her breasts and mostly hidden by her bra. It was wired to a tiny battery pack that fitted discretely in the waistband of her jeans. Kate had supervised the fitting much to the embarrassment of both herself and Sam and the hilarity of Barratt and O'Connor.

Raymond had lurked in the background, scowling and muttering. He wasn't happy with the idea of sending Cooper off like prey but, like Kate, he was completely out of ideas. He'd agreed to a low-budget operation but he'd also insisted on checking each element himself to ensure the safety of his officers.

Kate had spent the previous evening with Sam and her partner, Abbie, briefing the former and reassuring the latter. They'd produced a script and Anna had obligingly checked it over, after promises of alcohol from Kate and a tentative plan to meet up before the end of the summer. It was fairly straightforward. Sam was to play the disgruntled wife, desperate for a child while her 'husband' didn't seem to share her enthusiasm. They'd given her a bit more backstory and painted Barratt very much as the villain in Sam's eyes.

With Abbie playing Matthias, Kate had directed Sam through the script, preparing her for questions and suggestions that a therapist might offer. She made sure that she steered Sam clear of anything that Anna had suggested might provoke Matthias, particularly any suggestion that Sam blamed her 'husband' for his inability to provide her with a child. Kate had looked up *anejaculation* on the internet, after various searches based on Sarah Armstrong's explanation of Matthias's condition. It fit exactly with Kailisa's assessment of the rapes of Melissa and Chloe – the lack of semen or lubricant – if the killer couldn't ejaculate there was no chance that his DNA would be found and no need for a condom.

Now, hunched in the back of a van that was increasingly feeling like an oven on low temperature, Kate worried that all their preparations might not have been enough. And, if that was the case and Matthias attacked Cooper, she prayed that the two men pretending to be inspecting the gas pipes were up to the task of protecting her.

'She's just approaching the house,' Barratt whispered. The van's side mirror had been fitted with a rear-facing camera and Kate watched as Sam strolled down the street, appearing to check the numbers on doors and gates as she passed. They'd spent a long time deciding what Cooper should wear and finally settled on skinny jeans and a pale green blouse which was slightly more feminine than her usual style. She couldn't wear anything too revealing as she needed to hide the microphone with its wires and battery, so the blouse was perfect. The other problem was Sam's hair. Her short, blonde pixie cut exposed her ears, which meant that she couldn't wear an earpiece. She'd be able to communicate with Kate's team but they wouldn't be able to give her advice or instruction. To overcome this problem they'd devised a code. Kate would ring Sam's mobile and cut off after two rings if there was any hint of danger in anything that Matthias said to her.

Sam stopped in front of Matthias's wrought-iron front gate and checked the number against a piece of paper she'd taken out of her back pocket. Seemingly satisfied that she was in the right place, she pushed open the gate and approached the front door.

Kate slipped on a pair of Bluetooth headphones, tucking them deeply into her ears with trembling fingers. She couldn't risk missing a single word of Cooper's conversation with Matthias. Watching footage from the mirror camera, Kate saw the door of Matthias's house open and heard Cooper apologise for being a bit early. Matthias reassured her that it wasn't a problem and invited her inside. The door closed behind them and Kate tilted her head back, closing her eyes to allow her to focus more clearly on the audio.

'So,' Matthias's voice was deep and clear. 'As I explained on the phone, these sessions have nothing to do with the clinic. I'm seeing you as a private patient. I'll write up any notes I make and send you a copy if you wish, although a lot of my clients prefer to collect them at each subsequent session rather than risk their husbands opening them.' His tone was reassuring, his vocabulary formal and professional.

'That's fine. I'll do that then,' Kate heard Cooper say. 'I mean I'll collect them.'

Kate smiled. They'd agreed that Sam should seem a bit unsure of herself, a little unfocussed, until she spoke about her desire to have children.

'Good. Well, have a seat and we'll make a start.' Kate heard hollow footsteps and assumed that the room they'd entered had wood flooring.

'Right,' Matthias began, 'Can I ask what made you decide to have counselling without your husband?'

'I think... I don't think he really understands how important it is for me to have children.'

'And how important is it? To you I mean?'

'It's all I think about,' Sam dropped her voice as though she were ashamed of the admission. 'Ever since we got married we've been trying but every month it just got harder to accept that it wasn't working. I got depressed but I couldn't take the medication the doctor gave me because I thought it might mess up my fertility, and Matt seemed oblivious to it all. He'd happily do his part – what man wouldn't – but that was as far as it went with him. The idea to try IVF was all me. I don't think he's bothered.' Kate heard the slight catch in Sam's voice as she spoke about her disappointment with her husband and her fears for their future. A nudge reminded her where she was and she opened her eyes to see Barratt grinning at her.

'She's really good,' he said. 'Could have been on stage.'

Kate smiled back. Barratt was right. The woman on the other end of the microphone wasn't anything like the Sam Cooper that she knew.

'So your husband took some persuasion to attend the clinic?' Matthias was asking. Sam must have confirmed this because Matthias carried on. 'And how did that make you feel?'

Barratt rolled his eyes.

'If I'm honest,' Sam said, 'it made me angry. Why should it all be up to me? Why do I have to make all the decisions and arrangements? He's the man so why can't he take some responsibility?'

The uncertainty in Sam's tone had gone and she sounded genuinely aggrieved. Kate listened for another fifteen minutes as Cooper described her disappointment with her fictitious husband, prompted by occasional comments from Matthias. There was nothing to suggest that Matthias had anything other than a professional interest and his contributions were all entirely appropriate for his role. Checking her watch Kate shook her head at Barratt. They'd been listening for half an hour and everything sounded like a meeting between a client and a therapist. This wasn't going to work. She hoped that Sam had an opportunity to implement the next part of the plan. She needed to either get rid of Matthias for a couple of minutes or get herself access to the rest of the house by asking to use the toilet.

'To be honest, I think it's his fault,' Sam was saying.

'In what way?'

Kate held her breath. This wasn't in the script.

'I'm worried that he's infertile – that's why he's been resistant to all this.'

'Shit,' she said. 'This isn't part of the plan.'

Barratt glanced across at her, worry etched into the lines of his face. 'She's smart,' he said. 'I'm sure she knows what she's doing.'

Kate wasn't convinced and scrabbled in her pocket for her phone.

'No,' Barratt said. 'Give her a minute. She'll probably ignore you anyway if you ring to warn her.'

He was right. Kate had to trust that Cooper knew what she was doing.

'Do you have any evidence of this?' Matthias asked.

'No. He won't tell me any details of the tests that he's had. I know he told you that his sperm had low motility but I'm not sure what to believe any more. I thought if I could get him to counselling we might get past it but, after we left the clinic, he was even more resistant. He keeps saying that if it's meant to happen it'll happen naturally.'

'So, what if it turns out that he can't father children?'

Silence stretched the seconds into a minute as Kate cupped her hands round the headphones, listening for the slightest indication that Cooper was in trouble.

'I'll divorce him,' Cooper said finally. 'I don't want to be with him if he can't give me what I want.'

'That's a bit drastic,' Matthias said. 'There are other options. Don't you love your husband?'

'I do,' Kate could hear the fake reluctance in Cooper's voice. 'But I want a family. And I know we could adopt or use a donor but it's not the same. I want a real partnership with a man and if *he* can't give me what I want without having to get somebody else involved then what's the point in staying with him?'

'Would you see your husband as less of a man if he's infertile? If he can't give you children?'

That was enough. Kate scrolled to Cooper's name on her phone and tapped, hard. Two rings and she'd hung up. Cooper was still speaking.

'It's not that he's less of a man, it's just that he wouldn't be the man I thought I'd married. If I'd known he wasn't able to have kids I wouldn't have married him. I think most women would feel the same. It might be different if they found out later but none of my friends would knowingly get into a relationship with a man who couldn't give them kids.'

Kate rang Cooper's number again. She was completely off script now and improvising dangerously.

'Well, that's an interesting perspective,' Matthias said. Kate could hear the tightness in his voice. Sam had rattled him. 'Perhaps we should discuss it at our next session?'

'I'd like that,' Cooper said. Kate heard rustling and then footsteps. Obviously the session was over. She opened her eyes and watched the monitor, waiting for Matthias's door to open. More sounds from the microphone and then Matthias's voice, clear and angry. 'You're all the same aren't you? Fucking bitches! Take, take, take and the minute you get what you want, you're done.'

There was no response from Cooper. Kate pressed the headphones more tightly to her ears. Was that Cooper trying to speak? There was a retching sound, then a thud.

# Chapter 42

Hollis checked the satnav for the fifth time in less than twenty minutes. He thought he'd be able to remember the way even after all these years but he'd only been a teenager the last time he'd been here; he'd never had to drive these narrow, drystone wall-bordered lanes. The left turn that he was supposed to have taken was barely a farm track and hadn't looked at all familiar so he'd continued slowly, looking for a more likely access road. Two minutes later he felt his stomach flip as he went up and over a railway bridge and there it was. Dentdale. Location of happy childhood holidays.

He swung left and eased the car down a steep hill into the valley proper, imagining the signal bars on his mobile phone blinking out with each foot of descent. He'd loved this place. Most of his friends had been taken abroad for their holidays and he'd listened to accounts of their drunken exploits in Lanzarote and Tenerife with only the slightest niggle of jealousy. Yes, he'd have liked the opportunity to experiment with alcohol and he envied them the swimming pools and beaches but, in this tiny corner of the Dales, he'd had something more important. He'd had peace.

Dan's mum and dad had first brought him here when he was eight. Three months after he'd gone to live with them they'd asked him if he'd like a holiday and he'd responded in the negative. He really didn't have much idea what they meant but his real mum had often told him that she'd been on holiday when he'd been left with a foster family for a few weeks so he hadn't imagined that it could be anything good. And then they'd arrived in Dentdale and his understanding of the word holiday had changed completely.

For the next eight years he'd spent at least one week every year walking in the hills, fishing in the streams and generally enjoying the freedom and security of a family break. He'd had his first legal drink in the White Lion when he was sixteen – a half of lager with a meal – and he'd lost his virginity in a caravan to a girl from Lancaster whose name he couldn't recall but he still remembered her red hair and the freckles on her shoulders.

When Fletcher had phoned to tell him about his dad, Dan's thoughts had immediately been drawn to the Dales. His parents had bought a caravan of their own six months ago and kept it pitched on a new, small site nestled next to an old Victorian viaduct in one of the valley's tiny hamlets. Aware of the lack of phone signal in the valley, Dan had decided to drive across to see if his hunch was correct but, as he turned into the gateway of Scale Gill Farm, he wasn't sure which would bring him the most relief – if his dad's car was there or if it wasn't.

Following signs around the farmyard, avoiding ewes protectively guarding lambs that would be taken from them in a couple of months, Dan swung into the camping field. Three large tents with fluorescent yellow guy ropes were lined up against a drystone wall, their flysheets flapping in the gentle breeze. Two of the three were zipped up, their owners obviously absent and the entrance to the third was guarded by a pair of border terriers lazing in the sun on a fleece blanket. Beyond the tent area, a dozen or so caravans were arranged in an arc around the top end of the field. Next to the furthest one, the one highest up the hill, was a dark blue Golf.

He'd found them.

A corner of the field had been allocated for 'visitor parking' so Hollis dumped his Sportage and set off towards his parents' caravan on foot. The sun warmed his back as he walked and lapwings swooped and dived around him, their strange call reminding him of childhood video games. The caravan wasn't new but it looked like it was in good condition. The outside looked like it had been recently washed and the awning was tightly stretched across a curved pole and tidily pegged down. He peered around the nylon door. Two chairs were set up at either end of a small table that had been laid with two plates and two sets of cutlery. The door of the van was open and he could hear voices within. Dan checked his watch. Lunch time.

'Anybody home?' he said, raising his voice slightly.

A figure appeared in the doorway of the caravan holding a glass and a tea towel.

'Dan?' His father looked at least ten years older than when he'd last seen him and his eyes skidded across Dan's face as though he couldn't look his son in the eye. 'I didn't expect them to send you.'

'Didn't expect who to send me?'

'The police. I wouldn't have thought you were allowed to arrest members of your family.'

Dan smiled, trying to reassure the older man. 'I'm not here to arrest you, Dad. I need to talk to you. Can I come in?'

Joe looked over his shoulder. 'It's a bit cramped in here to be honest. Stay there. Mum's making lunch, do you fancy a sandwich?'

Dan wasn't really hungry but it seemed impolite to refuse so he asked for cheese and pickle and settled on one of the seats in the awning while his dad disappeared back inside the caravan.

He reappeared a couple of minutes later with a third folding chair that he positioned at the awning's entrance. 'Not much room here either,' he mumbled before sitting down. He seemed distracted and a little disorientated.

'You okay, Dad?' Hollis asked.

His father smiled sadly. 'It's just that I've been expecting somebody to come for me. You can't hide anything these days and I knew as soon as I heard that she was dead that somebody would make the connection. Didn't expect it to be you, though.'

His father still couldn't look at him and, for the first time, Hollis felt a flicker of doubt. 'What did you do, Dad?'

'What did who do?' Maggie was standing in the doorway holding a plate in each hand. Where Joe looked tired and haggard, Dan's mum looked exactly like she always did. She even had an apron tied around her waist like she did when she was cooking at home. Her shrewd dark eyes flicked from her husband to her son and back again and Dan wondered exactly how much his dad had told her.

She stepped carefully down into the awning and placed the plates on the table. Hollis noticed that his sandwich was cut into quarters just like she used to do when he was a child. He couldn't help but smile at the nod to his place in the family.

'I'll ask again and I expect an answer. What did who do?' She crossed her arms and scowled at the two men, making Dan feel like a naughty teenager who'd just been caught out in a lie.

'It's something I did,' Joe admitted.

'It's about that woman, isn't it? Suzanne? I told you he'd find out.'

'You don't know the half of it,' Joe said, his voice thick with misery.

Maggie sat down next to him and placed a hand gently on his shoulder. 'I don't know what you've done, love,' she said. 'But whatever it is I'm sure you thought it was for the best.'

Dan felt tears prickling behind his eyes. He'd taken it for granted that his parents loved each other but he'd never seen such stark proof.

'I've been stupid,' Joe admitted.

Dan took a bite out of his sandwich. 'Start at the beginning, Dad. There must be a way to sort this out.'

Joe nodded, staring miserably at his own sandwich. 'I found out where your... where Suzanne had been staying from her sister and I arranged to meet her,' he began. 'We talked and I told her to leave you alone but she just laughed at me and called me a stupid old man. And then she went all sly like and said she'd leave you alone if I gave her some money. I just laughed at her but she was serious.'

'She asked me for two grand to back off.'

'She asked me for the same amount,' Joe admitted. 'Of course I said I didn't have it, so she said that she'd make your life a misery. Came out with all sorts of foul stuff, she did. In the end I decided to pay her off. She swore that she'd leave you alone if I gave her the cash and I believed her.'

Joe picked up his sandwich and looked at it as if he had no idea what he was supposed to do with it. 'So I arranged to meet her again – with the money.' He glanced at Maggie. 'I'm sorry love, I know I told you it was only a couple of hundred but I had to give her what she asked for. I couldn't have her hurting Dan any more than she already had.'

Maggie's lips set in a thin line that Dan recognised from his childhood as her stern face, but she nodded for her husband to continue.

'So I met her again in a car park and gave her the cash. She counted it and just walked away. Didn't even thank me.'

'What did you do then?' Dan asked, unable to conceal the tremor in his voice.

'I drove home. What else could I do? I knew I'd have to explain where the money had gone to your mum, but all I could think about was getting as far away from that woman as I could. I thought I'd done the right thing.'

'So you didn't see her after that?'

Joe shook his head. 'I heard on the news that her body had been found but I didn't kill her, Dan. She was alive when I pulled out of the car park.'

Hollis tried to think about what he'd just heard. What were the implications for his father? How could he even begin to prove that Joe wasn't a murderer? 'What about when you got home? Was mum there?'

'I was at bingo,' Maggie said. 'It was a Tuesday.'

Of course it was. Joe would have planned that so he wouldn't have to explain his absence to his wife.

'Dad. The police have you on CCTV giving an envelope to Suzanne. They think you were the last person to see her alive and you've got a good reason for wanting her dead.'

Joe smiled sadly. 'Why do you think I'm here, son? As soon as I heard it on the news I knew they'd come for me eventually and I don't have an alibi. I just wanted a few days with your mum before they lock me up.'

'You're not going to be locked up,' Hollis promised. 'We'll find a way to prove that you didn't kill Suzanne. There has to be something.'

# Chapter 43

Kate leapt out of the van gesticulating wildly at the undercover officers who had been taking pretend measurements around the access shaft in the pavement.

'He's got Cooper. Go! Get in there now!' Kate yelled running towards Matthias's front door. She saw one of the yellow clad figures bend and grab a battering ram from his tool box before sprinting across the road. She arrived at the door breathless as the officer took a swing at the door. The frame around the lock started to give and he swung again.

'Police!' Kate yelled. 'Step away from the door.'

With a splintering creak the wood gave and Kate leapt forwards into the tiled hallway. Cooper was slumped on the floor, her back against the wall, eyes closed.

Barely aware of the figures pushing past her Kate squatted next to her colleague and felt for a pulse in her bruised neck. Nothing. She steadied herself, took a breath and tried again slightly higher up. There it was, weak but regular.

'We've got you, Sam,' she said easing the younger woman onto the floor and folding her jacket behind her head. 'Help's on its way.'

\*\*\*

Cooper smiled weakly as Kate entered the hospital ward. She was sitting up in bed and looked much better than when Kate had last seen her – unconscious and being loaded into an ambulance. She was still pale and the bruises on her throat stood out like dark clouds against a light sky but her eyes were bright and alert. If the bruises had been covered up she'd look like a teenager with a really bad hangover.

'Brought you something,' Kate said. She held out the slim package that Nick had helped her to select. She knew that Cooper wasn't much of a reader but she did like comedy shows. Kate had bought a tablet computer and downloaded episodes of most of her favourites. She'd included some stand-up shows and a couple of series of dramas that she thought Sam might like. It was a small gesture and did nothing to assuage Kate's deep sense of guilt. First Dan and now Cooper. She wasn't being much of a leader to her team. She needed to be stronger; to do better.

'There's headphones in there so you don't inflict your appalling taste on anybody else. And the pin is your birthday – you might want to change that.'

Sam's smile widened into a full grin.

'This is amazing thanks. You really didn't—' Something over Kate's shoulder caught Sam's attention and she stopped midsentence, smile fading.

'I was wondering when *you'd* show up.'

Kate turned to see Abbie leaning against the door jamb, arms folded across her chest, face furious. She was dressed in a jeans and a baggy jumper, despite the promise of heat in the air outside and, as she spoke, she tucked her hands into the opposite sleeves, wrapping her arms around herself as though for protection. Her face, however, wasn't fearful, she was furious.

'You had a plan you said. She'd be safe, you said. What a pile of shit.'

'Abbie…' Sam started to say something but her partner shook her head sending her dark red curls into a tsunami of disapproval.

'Don't you bloody defend her. Don't you dare.'

'Abbie. It wasn't Kate's fault. The plan was solid. I've told you I've only got myself to blame.'

Even though that was true Kate couldn't help but feel responsible and she knew that Raymond held her accountable. He'd asked for a debrief but, until she'd spoken to Cooper, she didn't have any answers.

'We need to talk about what happened,' Kate said, pulling up a battered plastic chair and perching next to the bed. 'I need to know what you were thinking, provoking him like that.'

Abbie entered the room properly and took the chair next to the head of the bed watching the interaction between the other two women.

Sam shook her head and Kate could see that she was close to tears. 'Did you get him?' she asked. 'Please tell me you got him.'

'He's in custody,' Kate said. 'He'll be charged with the assault on you and we're going to question him about Melissa and Chloe. Steve and Matt are leading the search on his house. They're over there at the moment.'

Abbie's scowl softened.

'What about the fact that Sam was wearing a wire? Isn't that entrapment?' she asked.

'What wire?' Kate asked. 'The paramedics didn't mention anything and they'd have seen it when they brought her in.'

'You mean you…?'

'I found out about Sam's plan to try to get Matthias to confess so we followed her to his house. Somebody heard yelling so we broke the door down. That sound about right, Sam?'

Cooper blushed and nodded. She wouldn't like the deception but if Matthias suspected that he was being monitored he was bound to try to use it in his favour.

'So, come on. Why did you provoke him after being told explicitly not to?'

Sam ran a hand over her head, reaching round to scratch the back of her neck.

'The plan wouldn't have worked. I couldn't ask to use his bathroom because there was a downstairs loo just off the hallway. I had no reason to prowl around upstairs and he'd have seen me pass the living room door anyway.'

'You couldn't get rid of him?'

Sam shook her head. 'It was like he'd thought of everything. He'd even left a jug of water and a glass next to the chair that he told me to use. There was nowhere for me to go so I did the only other thing I could think of and wound him up. I didn't think he'd gone for it, though. I remember him walking me into the hallway and then he just turned and grabbed my neck. Everything's a blank after that.'

Kate wasn't surprised. Cooper had been deeply unconscious when the door had been broken down so she hadn't been aware of the yelling and the scuffle in the alleyway behind Matthias's house as Barratt and Irving had arrested him. He'd run out of his back door and through neighbouring gardens but Barratt had realised that he could possibly escape that way and he'd left Kate to go in the front, taking Irving round to the rear of the houses.

'So now what?' Cooper asked.

'Now we see what Matthias has to say. Kailisa's put a rush on the hair from Chloe's body and we should have DNA in the next twenty-four hours. We've got decent prints from the umbrella from Madrigal's. Three sets. We're trying to match them against Matthias's.'

Kate's phone beeped. A text from Barratt. They'd found something in Matthias's house. She showed the screen to Sam and Abbie.

'We'll get him,' she promised as she stood up to leave.

# Chapter 44

Kate stared at the man sitting across the table from her feeling nothing but utter loathing. It had taken Tim Matthias six hours to crack. She'd seen teenage shoplifters hold out longer. The evidence that Barratt and O'Connor had found in his house was damning. A scalpel set from his parents wishing him luck in his future career, two unregistered mobile phones one of which corresponded to the number on Melissa's account and, most conclusively, Chloe's handbag.

Kate had taunted Matthias about not being good enough to be a proper doctor and he'd completely lost it. He'd launched himself across the table, calling her names and screaming that she knew nothing about him. After his solicitor had coaxed him back to his seat the tirade had begun – his disgust with women, all women and their pathetic biological needs. He'd confessed to murdering Melissa and Chloe stating that they'd both 'deserved it' and that he had every right to save other men from their entrapment. Kate had expected a challenge, a battle of wits but the pathetic figure in front of her wasn't worth wasting any more of her time. She instructed Barratt to charge him and left the interview room. O'Connor was waiting outside leaning against a wall looking pleased with himself.

'I've got a present for you in interview three,' he said with a sardonic grin.

'What is it?'

'More like *who is it?*'

Kate sighed. 'I'm really not in the mood, Steve. Just tell me.'

'Come and have a look.' He led her to the observation room where a screen showed a frightened-looking teenager huddled in a chair in an interview room. The boy was jiggling one of his legs up and down and biting the nails of one hand. He looked sweaty and greasy, his dark hair plastered to an acne-spotted forehead.

'Who's this?'

'His name's Carlton Towers. He works for Jakey Green.'

Kate looked at him blankly. The names meant nothing to her, but she wasn't surprised. O'Connor loved to show off his knowledge of Doncaster's gangsters and pimps even if nobody was ever really impressed.

'And? The lad's name sounds like a block of flats.'

O'Connor shook his head as if he couldn't quite believe he was having to explain this to her.

'Green runs a lot of the girls around Town Fields. You remember me telling you that there was some unrest? Somebody new muscling in?'

Kate nodded, not quite sure where this was going.

'Towers works for Green. We picked him up yesterday afternoon when he tried to steal a car. Routine stuff really except that he had an envelope in his pocket with nearly two grand in twenties stashed inside and something that looked suspiciously like a bloody fingerprint on the front. There was blood on his trainers as well.'

Kate waited. There was obviously more to come but O'Connor seemed determined to tell her in his own way.

'We took samples of the blood and it matches Suzanne Doherty's blood group – she's B negative, which is unusual apparently. Too soon for DNA but Scrote Face in there doesn't need to know that. Raymond got Kailisa to fast-track it while you were interviewing Matthias.'

'So he killed her?'

'Tried to deny it at first. Said he'd stumbled across the body and just took the money. When I told him that the blood spatter pattern didn't match his story he started backtracking.'

'You got blood spatter profiling as well?'

'Course not. But he didn't know that.'

Kate couldn't help but smile.

'Turns out Jakey's had him keeping an eye out for whoever's been trying to poach his girls. He'd seen Suzanne Doherty talking to a few of them over the last couple of weeks so Towers has been following her.'

Kate had seen the CCTV footage of Hollis's father in the car park.

'And he saw Hollis's dad give her the cash?'

'Bingo. Decided that he'd like a cut of it so he grabs her when she's heading across Town Fields. There's a struggle, he strangles her, stabs her, then panics. He remembered the girls talking about a murder where the woman's abdomen was cut open so he tries to do the same to make it look like it's the same killer. Stupid little shit makes a balls up of it and runs away with the two grand.'

'And he's confessed to this?'

'Oh, yes. He's scared that he'll get blamed for the other two murders.'

'Why would he think that?' Kate asked with a laugh.

'Not a clue,' O'Connor said grinning back at her.

*** 

As soon as O'Connor left the observation room Kate took out her phone. She had two calls to make. The first was to Hollis with the news about Carlton Towers. It went straight to voicemail so she left a message for him to call her back as soon as possible. She outlined what O'Connor had found out and told him to tell his father. The second was to Nick who answered on the first ring.

'Hey you,' he said, his deep voice as soothing as a warm bath.

'Hey yourself,' Kate responded. 'You'd better pick up a decent bottle of wine after work. You've got a date at my place. And I'm cooking.'

**THE END**

# Acknowledgements

Thanks to all the Bloodhound team for their continued faith in my writing. Thanks once again to Clare for the edit. As always, I'm tremendously grateful to the other Bloodhound authors for their encouragement and – sometimes – downright oddness.

A massive thank you to everybody who bought and read the first two books in the series – your support is greatly appreciated.

I'd also like to acknowledge all the online bloggers who do an incredible job in helping to promote authors.

Finally, thanks to Viv – the coffee's always fantastic!